THE CARNIVAL MURDERS

IRINA SHAPIRO

Paperback ISBN: 978-1-83700-315-0

Cover design: Debbie Clement
Cover images: Arcangel, Shutterstock

Published by Storm Publishing.

For further information, visit:
www.stormpublishing.co

Also by Irina Shapiro

The Invite

A Tate and Bell Mystery

The Highgate Cemetery Murder

Murder at Traitors' Gate

Murder at the Foundling Hospital

Murder at the Orpheus Theatre

Murder on Platform Four

Murder on the Prince Regent

Murder on Devil's Ridge

Wonderland Series

The Passage

Wonderland

Sins of Omission

The Queen's Gambit

Comes the Dawn

The Hands of Time

The Hands of Time

A Leap of Faith

A World Apart

A Game of Shadows

Shattered Moments

The Ties that Bind

The Summer Solstice

The Winter Solstice

The Christmas Gift

Echoes from the Past

The Lovers

The Forgotten

The Unforgiven

The Forsaken

The Unseen

The Condemned

The Betrayed

The Broken

The Lost

PROLOGUE

Billy Sykes strolled down the street, his rattle in his hand and his truncheon at his side. Pride was one of the seven deadly sins, but was it wrong to feel just a little bit proud? His father and grandfather had been nightsoil men, and Billy couldn't think of a more demeaning occupation. To spend one's life shoveling shit was a fate worse than death as far as he was concerned, but here he was, a constable with the Metropolitan Police Service, a man of consequence at eighteen. Billy adored his uniform, with its shiny buttons, cane-reinforced top hat, and black-and-white duty band. He represented law, order, and justice, and if he worked hard and proved his worth, he might move up the ranks and make inspector one day.

Oh, to be on the murder squad, Billy thought dreamily as he sauntered along. That would be the thing, and all the shop girls who turned up their noses at him now would long to step out with him on their afternoons off. He'd have his pick, but he knew exactly who he'd ask to join him for a cup of tea at that new tearoom that had opened up in Vauxhall Bridge Road. Lizzie Camp—

Billy stopped, his daydream rudely interrupted as he peered into the alleyway between the Rose and Thorn and the haberdashery shop next door. A young woman lay on the ground. Her skirts were bunched up to reveal shapely calves, and her petticoats frothed about her knees. Her boots were unlaced, as if she'd put them on in a hurry, and, once Billy had skirted the stack of empty crates beside her to see the woman more clearly, he saw she wasn't wearing a bonnet. Her fair hair was spread about her head and a few glossy locks covered her pale face. Despite her disheveled appearance, Billy didn't think she was a streetwalker. Her gown was too modest for a lady of the evening, and a thin gold band glinted on her ring finger.

What was she doing lying on the ground next to a rubbish bucket full of rotting vegetables? Was she drunk? Surely not. It was barely nine in the morning, but she was next to a tavern, so perhaps she'd been there since last night, sleeping off the drink. The alley smelled strongly of hops, but it was difficult to tell if the odor was coming from the woman or the public house's back door.

"Ma'am," Billy called as he approached the woman, his hand on his truncheon in case she should wake and go for him. "Ma'am, do you require assistance?"

Whatever had happened to her, she clearly hadn't been robbed. Billy congratulated himself on this astute observation and squatted next to the woman. Perhaps she had become ill, ambled into the alley, and fainted dead away. Constables didn't carry smelling salts, but Billy hoped he might be able to revive her or at least get her some help. He reached out and gently pushed the hair out of the girl's face.

A strangled scream caught in his throat, and he yanked his hand away as if he'd been burned. He hadn't been on the job long, but he didn't need to spend years walking the beat to know that the girl was dead and that someone had violated her corpse. He sprang to his feet and ran out of the alley, his hand trembling violently as he clanked his rattle for all he was worth.

CHAPTER 1

Wednesday, July 20, 1859

Sebastian Bell pulled out his pocket watch and consulted the time. He had been due to meet his fiancée at nine o'clock, but Gemma appeared to be running late, so he decided to take a short walk and see something of the neighborhood. He'd been to Pimlico a number of times, but never with a view to settling down in the area, and he wanted to take in the street as a possible tenant rather than as a police inspector.

Sebastian and Gemma had spent some considerable time discussing where they would like to settle once they were married and had narrowed it down to a few neighborhoods, including Pimlico. It was a respectable area—although Millbank Prison was a few streets away and the gas works weren't far—that was inhabited mostly by mid-level professionals and civil servants, so Sebastian and Gemma would fit right in with their neighbors. The rent was reasonable and, if they were still content once the lease was up, they could either renew or look to settle in Pimlico permanently and purchase a house of their own. They had seen two other prospective rentals that would become available in August, but thought they should view a few more properties before making a final decision. The wedding wasn't until September, so they could afford to be choosy and pick a house they both liked. If the description in the advertisement was accurate, then the house they planned to see today might be their first home together.

As Sebastian approached the building again, he saw Gemma alight from a cab and quickened his step, eager to greet her. After months of seeing her in nothing but mourning black, it gladdened his heart every time to see her wear color. Gemma was dressed in a gown of pale green-and-burgundy striped satin and wore a matching green bonnet with mauve flowers made of stiffened silk. She clutched a beaded velvet reticule, a gift from Anne Ramsey, bestowed on her during one of Anne's more lucid moments.

"I'm sorry I'm late, my dear," Gemma said as soon as Sebastian was within speaking distance.

He smiled, reached for her hand, and brought it to his lips. "You've nothing to apologize for. It is I who was early."

She sighed heavily. "Mrs. Ramsey had a difficult morning, and it took longer than I expected to get her settled. Have you had a chance to explore?"

"I quite like the area," Sebastian replied. "And the building is fairly new."

It wasn't until he and Gemma had started to look for a house that he'd realized just how much he longed to leave the boarding house where he currently lodged. The Quinces weren't bad, as far as landlords went, but it had been nearly four years since he'd moved in and he was more than ready for a home of his own. And the thought of finally sharing his life with Gemma filled him with such joy, he wished they could move up the wedding and marry as soon as possible. But she had given Colin Ramsey her word that she would remain until the end of August, by which time Colin would have found a new nurse to care for his rapidly declining mother. Sebastian held Colin and Anne Ramsey in great regard, and, much as he would have liked to, he couldn't allow himself to ignore their needs and pressure Gemma to break her promise. He would wait patiently until September and not put any undue stress on her to hurry things along.

Sebastian had just lifted his hand to the door knocker when he heard the unmistakable clanking of a police rattle. A few moments later, a flustered and very young constable came towards them, his cheeks stained pink with the effort of running and his eyes wild with what could only be fear.

"Constable, what's amiss?" Sebastian asked. "I'm Inspector Bell of Scotland Yard," he hurried to add when the young man looked like he might race past him.

The young man skidded to a stop and sucked in several deep breaths. "A body, sir. Just there." He pointed in the direction of Vauxhall Bridge Road. Sebastian assumed the constable was on his way to Cottage Street, where the nearest station was located. The station was part of B Division and patrolled Westminster. "Constable Sykes, sir," the young man added when he realized he'd failed to identify himself.

"Do you have reason to suspect foul play, Constable?" Gemma asked. The constable stared at her, his eyes widening in incomprehension. "I'm a nurse," she said when he looked to Sebastian for guidance.

"I think she's been murdered," Constable Sykes said. He was addressing Sebastian, but his gaze slid to Gemma. "And she was..." The constable's cheeks turned beet red. "Tampered with. That is to say..." His voice trailed off as he tried to articulate what he wanted to tell them without causing offense. "The young woman deserves justice, sir. She is not a harlot. Begging your pardon, ma'am," he quickly added for Gemma's benefit.

"Show us," she exclaimed.

Sebastian would have liked nothing better than to commend the constable on his diligence and direct him to the Cottage Street station. He hadn't had a day off in a fortnight, and he very much wanted to see the house and spend a few hours with Gemma. But she was already moving in the direction Constable Sykes had come from, and the young man, eager to pass on the responsibility to a senior officer, gestured to Sebastian to follow.

Together, Sebastian and Gemma trailed the constable to a public house on the corner. The Rose and Thorn was a wattle-and-daub Tudor building that had seen better days. The white paint had yellowed, and the dark wood posts had shifted over time, so no two beams ran parallel. The second floor extended over the pavement, and a flaking black sign with a red rose and a thorny stem creaked in the breeze. The mullioned windows that would normally reflect the morning light were in shadow, and the black-painted door was firmly shut.

Constable Sykes trotted past the front door and turned into an alley that ran between the pub and the adjacent building. He stopped before he reached the end, clearly reluctant to get too close to the body. A number of things the constable had failed to recognize became immediately apparent—the woman was pregnant, she had been dead for some time but must have been dumped in the alley a few hours before if no one had spotted her until now, and there was no blood or any obvious signs of violence. Sebastian was about to say as much to Gemma, but when he turned to her she was staring at the deceased in horror, her face ashen and her hands trembling as she clutched her reticule to her middle.

CHAPTER 2

"Gemma," Sebastian called out to her, but she barely heard him.

She handed him her reticule and crouched next to the woman. It was obvious she was dead, and had been for some time, but, even though Gemma understood the odds, she pressed her hand to the woman's swollen abdomen, just below the corset. All she felt was firm flesh. There was no ripple of life or a feeble kick to let her know that the child was still alive. And she had known it wouldn't be. The baby would have died not long after the mother, minutes after the woman's heart had stopped pumping life-giving blood. What alarmed Gemma though wasn't the loss of life, although it was heartbreaking when a young life was cut short—it was what she had spotted beneath the woman's fair locks. She reached out and pushed the hair back to reveal a seam across the woman's forehead, the skin held together with neat black stitches.

"I told you she'd been interfered with," the constable said, his tone somewhere between horror and pride at having spotted the stiches.

Gemma ignored him and quickly undid the buttons on the woman's bodice. She pulled the fabric apart and yanked down the chemise to reveal her shoulders. Two neatly stitched seams ran from the woman's collarbones downward in a V shape. Gemma couldn't see inside the loosely laced corset and didn't want to expose the poor woman in an alley, but she was sure the victim's abdomen had been bisected right down the middle and that the incision ended at her pubic bone. She heard a gasp behind her and then the sound of retching as the inexperienced bobby surrendered his breakfast to the slimy cobblestones.

"I'm sorry, sir," Constable Sykes choked out as soon as he could speak, but Sebastian didn't reply. He stood next to Gemma, his grim gaze fixed on the body.

Gemma did not need to explain the significance of what she had discovered. Sebastian had seen similar seams before and knew that someone had autopsied this woman and then disposed of her corpse in a back alley, as if she were rubbish. It didn't bear thinking about, but the question uppermost in Sebastian's mind would not be why the body had been left by the Rose and Thorn, but whether the woman had been murdered. Gruesome as this discovery was, if the deceased had died of natural causes there was no case to pursue; but the only way to find out would be to perform a second postmortem to determine the cause of death.

"Gemma, are you all right?" Sebastian asked, his tone more insistent this time.

She adjusted the woman's bodice and got to her feet. "I'm absolutely fine. Let's get her to Colin."

"Not yet." He handed Gemma her reticule, then squatted next to the body and deftly did up the buttons on the bodice, before arranging the woman's hair to hide the ugly stitches. "Constable Sykes, fetch the publican," Sebastian instructed once he'd straightened up. "And be discreet about it."

"Yes, sir," the constable muttered, and wiped his mouth with the back of his hand. The gesture did little to make him look more presentable, since some bile had splashed onto his tunic and shoes, but that was all he could do at the moment.

Constable Sykes walked around the side of the building, leaving Sebastian and Gemma alone with the corpse.

"We need to try to identify her before we take the body away," Sebastian explained. "Someone left her here, so they must have thought her body would be seen to."

"Seen to?" Gemma echoed.

"Perhaps they thought her family would be notified."

"Do you really believe that whoever did this was driven by consideration for the deceased?"

Sebastian looked thoughtful when he replied. "She is fully dressed, which makes me think that they wanted her to look presentable when she was found. And she's still wearing her jewelry."

Now that she thought about it, he made a good point. Why would someone go to the trouble of putting a corset and petticoats on a corpse? They could have just pulled on her chemise and left her half naked, but they had even put on her boots, even though they hadn't bothered to lace them up. And the fact that the deceased still wore her jewelry spoke volumes and helped to narrow the timeframe of the disposal. Even if whoever had left the woman's body in the alley hadn't been interested in profiting from her death, if she had lain in the alley longer than a few hours her remains would have been picked clean. The clothes and shoes, which were intact and of good quality, would fetch a tidy sum at any rag-and-bone shop, and the jewelry would sell for a few quid.

Sebastian glanced towards the mouth of the alley. "It's also possible that this was the first dark passageway they came across, and perhaps they didn't have enough time to relieve her of her valuables."

"It doesn't take long to slip off a ring and grab the boots," Gemma observed.

"No, it doesn't," he agreed. "Unless every second counts."

"She can't be more than eighteen," Gemma said with a sad sigh. "And the child... She was very near her time."

She regretted the words as soon as they were out of her mouth. Sebastian's wife had been murdered when she was seven months pregnant, along with their son, and, given Sebastian's haunted expression, the memory of Louisa's body had to be swimming before his eyes. The similarity between the two fair-haired young women could not have been lost on him as he valiantly tried to remain objective.

"I'm sorry. That was thoughtless," Gemma murmured, but he shook his head.

"It's not that," he replied, having clearly understood what she was apologizing for.

"Then what is it?"

But Sebastian didn't get the chance to respond. A burly man of middle years exploded into the alley, Constable Sykes trailing him with obvious reluctance. The man was red in the face, his breath came in ragged gasps, and his gaze reflected his terror. He pushed past Sebastian and fell to his knees next to the woman's body.

"Did you know her?" Sebastian asked, but the man did not reply.

A heart-wrenching sob tore from his chest as he gathered the young woman into his arms, and he wept unashamedly, his shoulders heaving with the violence of his grief.

"Tamzin," he moaned. "Oh, my sweet girl."

It was obvious Sebastian was desperate to speak to the man, but he gently took Gemma by the arm, and together they retreated to the mouth of the alley to give the man a few minutes with the deceased. While Gemma wiped away her own tears, Sebastian flagged down a passing wagon and asked the driver if he would be willing to detour to Blackfriars. The man was about to refuse, but the promise of easy money appeared to sway him, and he nodded and cocked his head towards the empty wagon bed.

Once the publican's grief finally subsided and he let go of the body, Sebastian took him aside for a quiet word, and, after an introduction and a few moments' discussion, Sebastian and Constable Sykes loaded the body onto the waiting wagon. The publican hurried inside and returned with a length of sacking, which he carefully tucked around the body and made sure to cover the face.

"Constable, you are to go with Miss Tate and help Mr. Ramsey bring the body into the cellar," Sebastian instructed the young man. Then he handed Gemma onto the bench. "Gemma, I will meet you at Colin's as soon as I'm able."

She would have liked to remain and learn more about the victim, but it was hardly fair to ask Constable Sykes to deliver the body on his own, and she would need to explain the circumstances of the case to Colin before he started on the postmortem. She smiled down at Sebastian and squeezed his fingers, and then the wagon was on the move, their intention to see the house quite forgotten in view of the morning's events.

CHAPTER 3

The publican stepped behind the bar and poured himself a large brandy. He stood with his back to the taproom and tossed back the drink, then poured another and drained it. When he turned around, tears ran down his ruddy cheeks, and his hand shook as he set the glass on the counter. A dark-haired woman, who looked puffy and tired for so early in the day, gaped at Sebastian, then turned to her employer.

"What is it? What's happened, Mr. Macklemore?" she cried.

The publican shook his head, clearly unable to formulate the words, then stalked towards a door in the corner and slammed it shut behind him. Sebastian understood only too well what the man had to be feeling, but he couldn't leave him to his grief. He needed answers, and he needed them now, but he could afford to allow the bereaved a minute to compose himself.

He was just about to question the barmaid when two men carrying a heavy cask came through the door that led to the cellar. They set it behind the bar.

"Do you need anything else, Mum?" the younger man asked. "It's only that we need to get going."

"Go on with you," the barmaid said. "I can manage."

The older man, presumably the barmaid's husband, smiled and tipped his cap, and then the two men left without another word.

"I need help with the casks," the woman explained. "Mr. Macklemore has a bad back, so my men give me a hand before they go to work."

"That's kind of them," Sebastian said. He showed the woman his warrant card and asked for her name.

"Tessa. Tessa Garrett. What's this all about, Inspector?" she asked. She still looked exhausted, but now her gaze was alert, and she looked around the taproom as if searching for a familiar face and finding none.

"Were you here last night, Mrs. Garrett?" Sebastian asked the barmaid.

"Yes, I was."

"How late did you stay?"

"My shift ends at eleven, and then I have to tidy the taproom and take out the piss buckets, so I rarely finish before midnight," she replied.

"Do you live on the premises?"

"No. I live in Douglas Street. What's happened?" she asked again.

"What time did you arrive this morning?" Sebastian asked, ignoring her question.

"Nine. Mr. Macklemore doesn't see the point of opening too early."

"Which way did you go in?"

"By the front door." Tessa's hazel eyes were wide with incomprehension, but then her gaze slid towards the door the publican had just walked through, and her brow furrowed with worry.

"Is it Alice?" she whispered. "Has something happened to Alice?"

"No," Sebastian said.

He knew that the deceased woman's name was Tamzin, but he had yet to establish her relationship to the publican and determine whether a crime had been committed. He nodded his thanks and went into Macklemore's office, then shut the door behind him.

The man sat behind a narrow desk, his head in his hands, but he looked up sharply, a scowl of outrage on his face, when Sebastian entered.

"What do you want?" he demanded.

"I would like to ask you a few questions," Sebastian said quietly, and settled in a guest chair.

"Where is she? Where's Tamzin?" the publican cried. "I should have never let you take her, but you forced my hand. Are you not ashamed to take advantage of a man's grief?"

"I'm sorry," Sebastian said, and wholeheartedly meant it.

The only thing worse than losing a loved one was to know that they would undergo a postmortem, their body butchered and then sewn back together like a rag doll. Mourning rituals afforded the bereaved a sense of decorum and wrapped their pain into a socially acceptable parcel. They knew exactly what needed to be done and how to go about their days; but when the deceased was a victim of a crime, decorum—and the numbness it afforded—were stripped away, leaving the mourner to their bewilderment and pain, which were sure to be tainted by scandal and vicious gossip.

"Don't you want to know what happened to Tamzin?" Sebastian asked softly. "Surely she deserves that much."

Macklemore nodded miserably. "I do," he said, his voice low and gravelly. "And when I find out who did that to her, I will tear the blackguard limb from limb before her grave."

Sebastian did not react to the man's promise. It was natural to crave retribution, and just as natural to back down when it came to administering justice. Few men followed through on such threats, and fewer still carried out the deeds in public. True vengeance happened under the cover of darkness, and, if the vigilante knew what they were about, no one ever learned of the crime or discovered the corpse.

"May I know your full name?" he asked the publican.

"Hume Macklemore," the man replied gruffly.

"And the deceased?"

"My daughter Tamzin. Tamzin Norris. And… my grandchild," Macklemore added brokenly.

"When was the last time you saw Tamzin?"

"Last Sunday. She came to church with me and her sister, Alice."

"And Tamzin's husband?" Sebastian asked carefully.

Whenever a woman turned up dead under suspicious circumstances, the husband was always a suspect, since the man the victim had lived with had more reason than most to give in to his rage. Given what had been done to the poor woman, it was highly unlikely that the autopsy had been carried out by her husband, but anything was possible and, if the man wasn't a surgeon himself, he may have sold the body to someone who was willing to pay for a fresh corpse and would erase all evidence of a crime in the course of the dissection.

"Jonah works at the prison. He's a guard," Macklemore said.

"Mr. Macklemore, can you think of anyone who might have wanted to harm Tamzin?"

It was the most delicate way to phrase the questions Sebastian really wanted to ask. Despite his duty to the deceased, he couldn't bring himself to point out to her father that she had been dead for days and that someone had clearly made free with her corpse before dumping it in the alley.

Hume Macklemore shook his head. "Tamzin was a good girl. A dutiful daughter, and a devoted wife. She never said a cross word to anyone."

"Did Tamzin live here at the tavern?" Sebastian asked.

"No, she lived with her husband, as a decent woman should. They were happy," Hume added after a brief pause. "Jonah loved her. Had done since he was hardly more than a boy."

"Do either you or Jonah have any enemies?"

"Who'd do this to Tamzin? No, we don't," Hume snarled. He was clearly done answering Sebastian's questions.

"May I speak to Alice?"

"You may not. She doesn't know anything, and I will not have her interrogated about her sister's death." He fixed Sebastian with a tearful glare. "I need to bury my girl. There's nothing more you can learn from her remains."

Sebastian wasn't sure if the publican had noticed the ugly seam beneath Tamzin's hair. Perhaps he hadn't, or he hadn't understood what it meant. He didn't think he should explain. The man was suffering enough already, and Sebastian felt it his duty to comply with his request.

"I will see to it that Tamzin's body is returned. You have my word."

Hume nodded. "See that you do. Now, please, leave me alone."

Sebastian got to his feet and saw himself out. The taproom was empty, and Tessa Garrett had nothing more to offer him. He would have liked to confer with Colin, but his friend would require time to carry out the postmortem, and Sebastian was too close to Millbank Prison not to question Tamzin's husband. He left the Rose and Thorn and turned his steps towards the prison. While he walked, endless questions raced through his mind, but he didn't have the answer to a single one, at least not yet.

Had Tamzin been murdered, or had she died a natural death? Why had her body been dissected, and who had carried out the postmortem? Why had they dumped the corpse near the tavern? Was it a message for Hume Macklemore, or had Tamzin's remains been left for her father as an act of kindness? It didn't seem very kind to dump a corpse in an alley, but it was vastly preferable to never knowing what had become of one's child and never being able to decently bury them and mark their final resting place.

Why had Hume Macklemore insisted on burying his daughter when it was her husband's right to see to his wife's and child's remains? And why did Sebastian feel a duty to the poor soul? He could have sent Constable Sykes to the Cottage Street station and turned the case over to them instead of taking possession of the body and sending it to Colin. But Sebastian knew why. Cottage Street was no match for Scotland Yard, and a less experienced detective might bungle the investigation. And Sebastian wanted—no, needed—to find out what had happened to Tamzin Norris.

Besides, Gemma would never forgive him if he handed over the case. Sebastian had seen the stricken look on her face and knew that she wouldn't rest until she got justice for Tamzin and her baby. And as much as Gemma exasperated and worried him at times, he loved her boundless compassion and understood her desperate need to right a wrong. It helped her to make sense of the world and explain away the senseless slaughter she'd witnessed as a nurse in Crimea. To save one life, to solve one mystery and bring someone peace, allowed Gemma to retain her faith and know that she'd made a difference in the world. And that was a good enough reason for him.

CHAPTER 4

Millbank Prison was a massive, fortress-like structure that resembled a six-petaled daisy. There was a central hexagonal courtyard dominated by a chapel, and six three-story radial wings. At the center of each wing was an enclosed courtyard with its own watchtower, and the entire complex was surrounded by a high outer wall that was punctuated by nearly two dozen more watchtowers and several gates. Due to its proximity to the river, the prison was cold and damp, and susceptible to frequent outbreaks of disease. Millbank housed hundreds of prisoners and employed dozens of men. Currently, the prison was primarily used to detain convicts bound for Australia, so inmate turnover was extremely high, due to deportation and illness. The prison was the first of its kind and considered vastly efficient by some misguided politicians, but the awkward structure also meant that it took a long time to locate a particular individual.

Sebastian tried several different gates before he was directed to the section of the prison where Jonah Norris worked. He showed his warrant card to the guard and waited patiently while the man squinted at it in the shadowy gloom of the anteroom.

"I need to speak to Jonah Norris. Is he on duty today?" Sebastian asked.

"I don't know." The man looked thoroughly bored, and Sebastian could smell the alcohol on his rank breath. He'd probably only just dried out from last night. "Let me find someone to check," the guard said when Sebastian glowered at him and he finally realized that obstructing an investigation could cost him his job. "Wait here," he added, and stalked off.

It took nearly half an hour for the man to return, and, when Jonah Norris finally made an appearance a few minutes later, he looked terrified. He was a tall, wiry youth of about twenty-five. His dark hair was clipped close to the skull, and his eyes were so dark that in the poor light of the waiting room they resembled black holes.

"Is there somewhere private we can talk, Mr. Norris?" Sebastian asked once he'd displayed his warrant card and replaced it in his pocket.

Norris nodded and led Sebastian to a small, windowless room. There was nothing but a scuffed bench, and Norris sank onto it as if his legs had buckled.

"Is there something you wish to tell me?" Sebastian asked once he'd shut the door and taken a seat at the opposite end of the bench.

"My Tamzin is dead," Norris moaned. "I feel it in my bones."

"Perhaps you feel it in your bones because you were the one to kill her," Sebastian replied.

Norris's head jerked up. He looked horrified, and Sebastian regretted his bluntness when the man's eyes filled with tears. Norris could be putting on an act—he wouldn't be the first to try to deceive the police—but if he was innocent of his wife's death he deserved Sebastian's sympathy.

"I didn't kill anyone," Jonah cried desperately. "What happened to my Tamzin?"

"I don't know," Sebastian said. "And I'm sincerely sorry for your loss."

"Then how do you know she's dead?" Jonah mewled. For just a moment, there was a spark of hope in the young man's eyes, but it went out as soon as Sebastian began to answer.

"Tamzin's body was discovered this morning, in the alley by the Rose and Thorn."

"Oh, God," Jonah cried. "Do Hume and Alice know?"

"Yes, Mr. Macklemore knows. He identified the body. I expect he has told Alice."

Jonah buried his face in his hands, and although he made no sound his shoulders heaved, and Sebastian could tell he was crying . But he couldn't afford to give Jonah time to grieve. If he was to discover what had happened to Tamzin he needed information. The more time passed, the colder the trail would get, and the man or men responsible for her death would get away.

"Mr. Norris, when was the last time you saw your wife?"

Jonah raised his head and looked at Sebastian, his dark eyes gleaming like wet pebbles. "Last Monday morning," he muttered. "We breakfasted together, and Tamzin said she'd make a chop for my supper on Tuesday. It's my favorite," he said, his voice breaking.

"What happened afterwards?" Sebastian asked.

Jonah's initial horror had distilled into shock and he stared at Sebastian dazedly, as if he had difficulty understanding the question.

"I went to work, as usual," he said at last. "I work a double shift on Mondays, so I came home just after noon on Tuesday. Tamzin wasn't there."

"What did you do then?"

Jonah stared into space as he tried to recall his movements. "I made tea, had a slice of bread and butter, and went to sleep. When I woke, the house was dark. Tamzin had not come back."

"Did you look for her?" Sebastian asked.

"I went next door. June Lasker and Tamzin are friendly. Were friendly," he amended numbly. "And I'm mates with her husband."

"And what did Mrs. Lasker tell you?"

"She said Tamzin went out around six on Monday evening. She saw her through the window."

"Where did she go?"

"Mrs. Lasker didn't know, but Tamzin sometimes went to the Rose and Thorn when I was working the night shift. She didn't like to be alone. She'd have supper with Alice and Hume, and sometimes she'd spend the night in her old bedroom."

"Did you go to the Rose and Thorn when Tamzin didn't come back?"

Jonah shook his head. "Alice came looking for Tamzin on Wednesday morning. She said she hadn't seen her sister since Sunday. So I told her Tamzin was out. I didn't want to worry her. I thought Tamzin would come back," he said, and his voice caught.

"Did you not think to report her absence to the police?" Sebastian asked.

"No."

"Had Tamzin gone off before?"

The young man nodded. "Once, a few months ago."

"Why did she leave?"

"We had a row, and she was upset," Jonah said.

"Where did she go?"

"She went to stay with her friend Ruth Winn for a few days. Ruth is widowed and always glad of the company."

"And did you check with Mrs. Winn if Tamzin had come to her?" Sebastian asked.

"Yes, yesterday. Ruth hadn't seen Tamzin since early last week."

Sebastian bristled with impatience. "Mr. Norris, did you and your wife have an argument before you left for work on Monday?"

Jonah stared at the floor and nodded.

"What about?"

"Tamzin went to see her father and Alice on Sunday, and didn't come home until suppertime. She said she thought I'd want to sleep in, since I'd worked through the night on Saturday, but I only wanted to spend time with her. She was always running to the tavern. I suppose I was jealous."

"And did you make up?"

"Yes. We were fine. Tamzin was fine," Jonah cried.

"Was she happy about the baby?"

Jonah seemed to have forgotten about the child, but now his eyes filled with tears again. "Oh, God, the baby," he moaned. "Is it…?"

"Deceased. I'm sorry," Sebastian said softly.

"Tamzin was a bit scared, on account of the birth and all, but she wanted a family. She looked forward to having a little one. We both did."

"Mr. Norris, can you think of anyone who'd wish to harm Tamzin?"

"No, I can't." Jonah sucked in a shuddering breath and asked the question that must have been uppermost in his mind while they talked. "How?" he choked out. "How did Tamzin die?"

"I don't know yet, but I will find out."

"Did she look like she had suffered?" Jonah asked.

His gaze begged Sebastian to say that she hadn't, but he really didn't know. He hadn't noticed any wounds or bloodstains on Tamzin's clothes, but that didn't mean she hadn't met with a bad end.

"No, she didn't," Sebastian said. "She looked to be at peace."

Jonah's shoulders slumped, and he nodded. "Well, there's that, at least. Where is she? Is she at the Rose and Thorn?" He was already getting to his feet, ready to go to the tavern.

"She is not. I sent the body to a surgeon of my acquaintance."

"I don't want her body butchered." Jonah's hands bunched into fists as he rounded on Sebastian.

Sebastian immediately sprang to his feet, not wishing to be caught at a disadvantage if Jonah decided to attack. "Do you not want me to investigate her death?" he demanded of the angry young man.

"I do," Jonah said, and instantly backed down. "But I don't want her mutilated. She doesn't deserve that."

Sebastian chose not to tell Jonah that Tamzin had been mutilated already. The poor man was hurting badly enough. "I cannot discover what happened to her if I don't know how she died," he explained patiently. "I promised Mr. Macklemore that I will return the body to him. Unless you would prefer to bury Tamzin yourself, I intend to keep my word."

"It doesn't matter who buries her. She's gone, and nothing will ever be the same," Jonah exclaimed. "Nothing."

"Mr. Norris, I need your home address, as well as the addresses for June Lasker and Ruth Winn."

Sebastian jotted down the addresses and returned his notebook and pencil to the inner pocket of his coat. Jonah sat down heavily. All the fight had gone out of him, and he looked like what he was, a man who'd just lost everything.

There was nothing more Sebastian needed to ask him at present, so he left Jonah to his sorrow and traversed the maze of corridors until he finally found the exit. He felt an overwhelming sense of relief once he left the confines of the soul-crushing dungeon and stepped outside into the summer sunshine. As he walked along the perimeter of the outer wall, he thought that there was no worse fate than the loss of one's liberty, not even death.

CHAPTER 5

When Gemma returned to the Ramsey house, Colin was out, so she unlocked the cellar from within and directed Constable Sykes and the wagon driver to bring the body inside. They set it on the dissecting table and were out the door before she could thank them properly. Which was just fine because she was in no mood for idle chatter. Gemma locked the door, pulled a sheet over Tamzin's remains, and headed upstairs to check on Mrs. Ramsey.

In the past, they'd had to keep Anne's room locked, since she had been prone to wandering and had even gone out in the middle of winter once in nothing but her nightdress, but she had shown little interest in going outside since the terrifying fall down the cellar steps that had left her with broken bones and an even more fractured spirit. The bones had knitted, but, although Anne was ready to resume light physical activity, she always put up a fight when Gemma tried to get her out of bed. The pain and confusion caused by the fall had triggered rapid cognitive decline, and Anne was even more lost to them than before, her moments of lucidity coming less frequently and lasting mere seconds. Most days, she refused to get dressed and lay propped up against the pillows in her frilly nightdress. She either slept or spent hours muttering under her breath, the words making little sense and upsetting Colin, who was desperate for a glimpse of the mother he had loved.

"Good morning, Mrs. Ramsey," Gemma said cheerily. "It's a fine day. Perhaps I can help you get dressed, and we can sit in the garden until it's time for luncheon."

"I don't like cucumber sandwiches," Anne replied.

"I'm sure Mabel will make us something nice."

"Cucumbers are wet," the older woman said with disgust.

"So is soup, but you like soup," Gemma reminded her.

"Cream of asparagus," Anne said dreamily.

"We can ask Mabel to make it. Perhaps we can have it for supper, or for luncheon tomorrow."

Anne stared at Gemma balefully. "Who's this Mabel you keep mentioning?"

"You remember Mabel," Gemma replied as she took out Anne's favorite day gown. "She's your maidservant."

"I don't know any Mabel," Anne said sulkily, then her face brightened. "Can she make raspberry ice? I simply adore raspberry ice."

"I will ask Colin to get some ice, and Mabel can make us some. I'm quite partial to it myself."

"Colin," Anne whispered reverently. There was a brief moment of awareness, and then the spark went out of her eyes. "I'm tired. I'd like to sleep now."

Reasoning with Anne rarely worked and usually resulted in her becoming agitated, so Gemma nodded and returned the gown to the wardrobe. "I will bring you luncheon after your nap."

Anne didn't respond. She shut her eyes, and her head lolled to the side, her mouth going slack as she sank into unconsciousness. Gemma patted Anne's hand, then left her to rest and locked the door. The precaution was for the older woman's safety, but Gemma felt like a jailer every time she turned the key in the lock and left Anne trapped in both her mental and physical prisons.

Downstairs, Gemma found herself quite alone. Mabel didn't serve lunch until one o'clock and was busy in the kitchen, and Gemma now recalled that Colin had planned to attend a lecture at the Royal College of Surgeons. She had several hours to herself, and, presented with an opportunity not to be missed, she made a beeline for the cellar.

True to his word, Colin had permitted Gemma to attend several postmortems over the past few weeks. He talked as he worked, explaining the workings of the human body and bringing her attention to various points of interest. He had even allowed her to close up a body and watched closely as she stitched the lifeless skin. Gemma valued Colin's tutelage, but she longed to do more, and would have liked the chance to come to her own conclusions before he overrode her theories and gave his own summation. Gemma couldn't autopsy Tamzin's corpse without Colin's permission—that would be a breach of etiquette that might ruin their friendship forever—but she could examine the body and see what she could learn. She would be curious to see if her assumptions aligned with Colin's and if there might be something he had missed. He was a skilled surgeon but, as a man, he was at times at a disadvantage when it came to understanding female bodies.

Gemma pulled back the sheet and looked at Tamzin's chalky face. She thought the young woman had been dead for at least two days but couldn't be sure. While nursing in Crimea, Gemma had seen plenty of bodies, but the soldiers who'd succumbed to their wounds or had died of postoperative infection had been removed from the ward almost as soon as they'd passed, mostly to free up the beds for incoming wounded, but also to avoid the more unpleasant aftereffects of death that would contaminate the beds and terrify the patients who were still clinging to life. Colin had explained the stages of decomposition, but, during the summer months, the estimate largely relied on whether the corpse had been left outdoors or kept in some cool place.

Tamzin must have been a lovely girl in life, but death had begun to ravage her body, and her features were becoming distorted, her skin marbling as putrefaction set in. Gemma felt overwhelming pity for the poor girl. She'd had so much living left to do, but instead here she was, a specimen to be studied, her body dissected, and her organs examined before she was finally buried and her remains no longer had anything to reveal. Gemma could give in to emotion as a woman, but not as a surgeon, so she steeled her heart and turned her attention to the task at hand.

She began by gently lifting up Tamzin's eyelids. The eyes that had been blue and might have twinkled with good humor or filled with tears when she was upset were now expressionless and opaque. Her tongue protruded slightly between parted teeth, and her lips were stretched into a grotesque half-smile. When Gemma held the oil lamp close to Tamzin's face, she noticed that reddish froth had gathered in the nostrils and at the corners of her mouth. Her fair hair was thick and lustrous, and her skin must have been clear and supple before her death. There was no evidence of scurvy or malnutrition, and she still had all her teeth. The only thing that was out of place was the seam that ran just below the hairline and was smooth and neatly stitched. Whoever had performed the postmortem had been skilled and careful in their work.

Finished with the head, Gemma undid the buttons of the bodice and moved on to the torso. Postmortem gasses had already begun to build up inside and might have accounted for Tamzin's distended belly if it weren't already so enormous. The corset, over a well-made chemise, was loosely laced below the waist, and when Gemma placed her hands on the stomach she could feel the baby's head and the smooth curve of its back. Curious, she lifted Tamzin's skirts and moved down the waistband of her bloomers to reveal the swollen abdomen. As she had suspected, a thick seam bisected the belly, and for a second Gemma allowed herself to believe that someone had tried to save the baby—but, given that they had left it in utero, they had either been too late or had never cared about the child at all.

Gemma looked at Tamzin's hands one after the other. They were the hands of a woman who did housework and probably spent hours sewing, but there was nothing unusual about the clean, gently rounded fingernails or the mildly calloused palms. If Tamzin had fought for her life, whoever had worked on her body had cleaned her hands and made certain that nothing was left beneath the nails. Which once again begged the questions—who had autopsied her, and why had they left her corpse for her father to find? It couldn't be a coincidence that her body had been left next to the tavern, which meant that they had known who she was and who her people were.

Gemma rearranged Tamzin's skirts and buttoned the bodice before rolling the body onto its side. She couldn't see a wound, and there were no bloodstains or tears in Tamzin's gown or undergarments. How had she died? Perhaps she had suffered a cardiac infarction, or maybe she'd had some sort of cerebral seizure, but surely she had been too healthy and young to die so suddenly. And even if she had died unexpectedly, what had happened to her after her passing was impossible to explain. The condition of her body was most disturbing and absolutely heartbreaking for her family, who had lost a wife, daughter, and sister, and would be left with questions about her final moments that would haunt them all for years to come.

Suddenly deeply uneasy, Gemma returned the body to a supine position and pulled up the sheet to cover Tamzin's face. She had successfully assisted Sebastian in several complex murder investigations, but, as she turned out the oil lamp and trudged up the stairs, she felt convinced that this case would be like nothing either of them had undertaken before.

CHAPTER 6

Sebastian was determined to get to the truth, but before he delved any further into the case he needed to speak to Superintendent Ransome. For one, he had to impress on Ransome that he had to assign the case to Sebastian, and for another he was certain he had heard something just yesterday that might have direct bearing on the investigation. Sebastian pulled open the heavy door and strode into the duty room. He was greeted by raucous laughter; one of the constables was poking fun at a woman who had been hanged just that morning, convicted of murdering her abusive husband. Policemen often resorted to levity to minimize the horror of the things they had seen, but, although Sebastian could understand the need to dispel the darkness, he couldn't countenance the crude jibes made at the expense of people who could no longer defend themselves.

"Inspector Bell," Sergeant Meadows called after him, but Sebastian raised a hand in greeting and continued on his way, unwilling to watch the gruesome pantomime of the woman's final moments.

Ransome's door was open, the superintendent's head obscured by an open newspaper. When Sebastian knocked on the doorjamb, Ransome folded the paper, set it aside, and gestured to the guest chair.

"They never stop," he said with a shake of his head. "Do away with the Metropolitan Police Service and form private militias. What bilge. Do they really believe they will be safer?"

Ransome clearly didn't expect a reply, so Sebastian didn't bother to answer. This was a conversation they'd had many times before and would have again before long. There were always those who called for the abolition of the police, relying on the tired argument that the service drained valuable resources that could be better spent on improving the lives of the poor. What these firebrands neglected to consider was that, even if the police service were no more, there was no guarantee that the freed-up funds would be used to benefit anyone other than the wealthy and the powerful. People were hopelessly naive and epically misguided. Without the police service, most victims would never get justice, and countless murderers would remain at liberty, free to kill again and again.

"Didn't you have the morning off?" Ransome asked and peered at Sebastian curiously. Few men would come to work when they didn't need to.

"I did, but I was drawn into a case."

"Were you, indeed? Go on, then. I need something to take my mind off this tommyrot."

Sebastian relayed the details and watched Ransome's eyebrows lift in astonishment.

"She was autopsied, you say? And her a respectable woman? You're absolutely right, Bell, this outrage cannot be ignored. Even if the chit died of natural causes, to cut her open and dump her in an alleyway for her kin to find is quite beyond the pale."

"What happened to the dwarf?" Sebastian asked as a thought occurred to him.

Ransome leaned back in his chair and studied Sebastian with renewed interest. "Heard about that, did you?"

"I did."

There were times when duty room twaddle served a purpose, even if it was in bad taste, and oft-times downright cruel.

"You think the two cases might be related?" Ransome asked.

"They may be. I believe there are similarities?"

Ransome nodded. "The case was assigned to Inspector Warren, but he wasn't able to make much headway."

"Tell me what happened."

"The body was discovered on the foreshore near Vauxhall Bridge a fortnight ago. The woman was with child, and her body bore the scars of an autopsy."

"Who found her?" Sebastian asked.

"A pair of mudlarkers. Not the haul they were hoping for, but that's what you get when you live off the river. One day the Thames blesses you with an ancient coin, and the next you get a bloated corpse."

"Where's the body now?"

"I expect it was taken to a dead house."

"Was Warren able to learn anything at all?" Sebastian asked.

Inspector Warren was an experienced copper, if experience was judged in years on the job, but, although he was willing to put in the time, he lacked imagination and the ability to look at a problem from a different angle. The obvious answer was always the right one where Warren was concerned, and he never bothered to look for an alternative explanation, even in cases where the evidence didn't quite fit his assumptions.

"You'd have to ask Warren," Ransome said.

"I will, if you assign the case to me."

Ransome scoffed. "Do you imagine anyone else would want it? It's all yours, Bell. I only hope you get further in your inquiries than Warren did. One victim is regrettable. Two is concerning. Three is the makings of mass hysteria. Let's not get to three."

"Unless the third victim is already out there, I will do my best," Sebastian replied, and took his leave.

He found Timothy Warren in the office he shared with Inspector Blake, whose desk was unoccupied at present. The inspector had been enjoying a mug of tea and what looked like a ham sandwich, but he set both down when Sebastian walked in and stared at him in mute inquiry. Warren was tall, broad, and bad-tempered. It was common knowledge that the constables dreaded working with him, and he was never invited to join the men for a well-deserved pint after work. Warren knew he wasn't liked, but despite his investigative skills he couldn't seem to figure out why, and his manner had become even more pugnacious as a result.

"Bell," he drawled. "To what do I owe the pleasure?"

"This morning, the remains of a young woman were discovered in Pimlico. The woman was with child, and her body was autopsied before it was disposed of."

"Like the midget," Warren said, and smiled unpleasantly to reveal tobacco-stained teeth.

"What can you tell me about the victim?"

"Not much. I had Constable Burrows ask around, but no one recognized her, and no one had reported her missing, at least not to Scotland Yard."

"Did you take down the names of the mudlarkers who found her?" Sebastian asked.

"A pair of silly old biddies, Leticia and Leda Spires."

"Address?"

Warren shrugged. "No idea, but I expect they prowl the shore every day for lack of anything better to do."

"Did you order a postmortem?" Sebastian asked.

"Didn't seem much point."

"It would help to know the cause of death."

"Given that she was found by the river, I'd say death by drowning is a safe bet."

"Did you follow any other lines of inquiry?"

"Like what? Ask at every carnival if one of their freaks was missing?" Warren replied with a nasty smile.

"That's uncalled for," Sebastian said angrily.

"Nothing wrong with calling a spade a spade."

"Or a cretin a cretin," Sebastian replied, and turned to leave.

"You'll regret that, Bell," Warren hissed to his retreating back.

"It's rather telling how you immediately assumed I was talking about you," Sebastian tossed over his shoulder, and walked out.

CHAPTER 7

Sebastian didn't expect to learn much about the unidentified woman, but he thought he should begin his inquiries at the city mortuary. The attendant, Mr. Stubbs, was with an elderly couple, who'd come to claim their daughter's remains and stood over her body now, weeping quietly as they looked upon her still face. Mr. Stubbs greeted Sebastian by name as soon as the necessary arrangements for the collection of the body had been completed and the grieving parents had finally left.

Mr. Stubbs immediately recalled the case of the autopsied dwarf and told Sebastian that the body had been transferred to the old watchhouse in St. Anne's parish. Sebastian was familiar with the place, since it had once been the residence of a rather unpopular police surgeon he had met on several occasions. The surgeon had been evicted after the Burial Act of 1852 had been passed, and the building had been converted into a dead house, one of several properties allocated to the storage of deceased individuals who were either unidentified, scheduled to be displayed at upcoming inquests, or remained unclaimed by kin who couldn't afford the price of a burial.

The prohibitive cost of funerals and the shortage of burial grounds had created a health crisis, since many families kept their dead at home, the bodies decomposing in rooms where the families ate and slept. The unsanitary conditions had ultimately forced the government to step in and propose a cemetery system that included public dead houses and newly consecrated cemeteries in the heart of London.

"Can you tell me anything about the deceased, Mr. Stubbs?" Sebastian asked.

"I'm afraid there isn't very much to tell," the attendant replied. "Inspector Warren wasn't able to identify her, and no one had come in search of the body. I had to make room for new arrivals, so I sent her on."

"What about the cause of death?"

Mr. Stubbs wasn't a surgeon, but he had been the attendant at the city mortuary for years and examined each body upon arrival. Ascertaining the cause of death when one wasn't immediately obvious was something of a hobby with him, probably because he had little else to stimulate his mind and needed to do something to pass the time between visits from policemen and bereaved relations.

"The woman had undergone a postmortem before her remains were discovered, but I didn't see anything that might have been a fatal wound," Mr. Stubbs said. "I'll tell you something odd though. Her clothes and hair didn't smell of river water, and there was no evidence of bloating, but when I turned the body over in the course of my duties water leaked from the deceased's mouth."

"And what did you make of that?" Sebastian asked.

"I think she may have drowned."

"But not in the Thames."

Mr. Stubbs shook his head. "I don't believe so."

"And the postmortem?"

"I would venture to guess that someone sold the body to resurrection men, who sold it on to a medical school."

"Medical schools don't dump the bodies once they're finished with them," Sebastian pointed out.

"No, they don't," Mr. Stubbs conceded. "Perhaps the graverobbers sold the body to a private tutor. I doubt you will learn anything from the remains, especially after all this time, Inspector."

"You're probably correct, but I would still like to see the body for myself."

"There was something else," Mr. Stubbs suddenly said. He looked mildly uncomfortable, and his gaze slid towards the room where the bodies were kept. "I'm not a surgeon, so I'm rarely asked for my opinion, but I have handled enough bodies to notice when something is not as it should be."

"Go on," Sebastian prompted when Mr. Stubbs lapsed into thoughtful silence.

"The woman's head was abnormally light. Now, I know there are some who would say that might be on account of her being a dwarf, but I don't believe that to be the case."

"What do you believe?" Sebastian asked.

"I think her brain was removed."

Sebastian did not find this as shocking as Mr. Stubbs might have expected. He supposed the attendant only ever saw bodies that had not been tampered with, but Sebastian knew of surgeons and certain self-proclaimed criminologists who believed that a person's character could be determined by the shape of their skull and that the brain of a criminal or a person born with a marked disability had to be different from the brain of a healthy person. Even Colin found the theory intriguing, and kept a brain preserved in formaldehyde on a shelf in the cellar, the organ floating in a jar like a pickled cauliflower. Sebastian had never asked who the brain had belonged to; he wasn't sure he wanted to know, but now that Mr. Stubbs had mentioned it he was certain it had to be the brain of someone Colin knew to have been deviant in some way and in need of further study.

"Thank you for telling me, Mr. Stubbs. That's a very helpful observation."

"Is it?" Mr. Stubbs asked, clearly gratified by the compliment. "I thought since you had asked about her, you might wish to know."

Mr. Stubbs ushered Sebastian out of his office when the bell above the front door chimed to announce a visitor.

"Take precautions, Inspector Bell. The dead house is a foul place."

"Thank you, I will," Sebastian promised.

He tipped his hat to a white-faced couple who clutched each other's hands in obvious terror as they advanced into the waiting room, then stepped outside, thinking for the second time that day that he was blessed to be free and still alive.

CHAPTER 8

The dead house was a two-room stone structure with a door at the center and a window on either side. There was no need for a sign, since the reek of death was enough to inform anyone who came too close what the building was used for. No one who didn't need to go inside would dare set foot on the premises, but the door was still kept locked. Sebastian knocked and was admitted by an elderly attendant, who was as pale as the corpses he watched over.

"Are you here to identify a relation?" the man wheezed.

Sebastian held his handkerchief over his nose and mouth with one gloved hand and produced his warrant card with the other. "I need to see the remains of the woman found near Vauxhall Bridge."

"You're in luck," the attendant said. "That one is due to be buried tomorrow."

He pointed to a pallet by the far wall. There were at least a dozen bodies between Sebastian and the nameless woman, and the floor was slick with substances he didn't care to identify. He crossed the room in four long strides and pulled down the grubby sheet to reveal the body of a short, stocky woman who could have been anywhere between fifteen and fifty. Even with the handkerchief, the stench was eyewatering, and Sebastian kept it pressed to his mouth and nose to keep out the noxious fumes. He was glad he'd pulled on his gloves before entering. He wasn't about to touch a corpse that was in an advanced state of decomposition with his bare hands.

The woman's dark hair was long and matted, and her forehead protruded slightly over slanted eyes and an upturned nose. She had a generous mouth that was curved faintly upward at the corners, and a dimple in her chin. Having seen his share of bodies, Sebastian could usually see past the ravages of death to imagine what the person had looked like in life. He thought this woman must have looked impish and might have been quick to smile.

He used his free hand to lift the woman's head off the pallet, and, as Mr. Stubbs had said, it felt unusually light, like a melon whose flesh had been scooped out, leaving nothing but the rind. Sebastian set the head down and turned his attention to the body. Like the rest of the individuals in the dead house, the woman had a distended belly, the abdominal cavity filled with gasses that built up after death, but besides the bloating she was also clearly pregnant. The clothing had been removed, and the deceased was dressed in nothing but a soiled shift that was draped over her belly like a dustsheet over an ottoman. Sebastian mentally braced himself for the unpleasant task and pulled up the hem.

She had died a fortnight ago, and the view that greeted him wasn't for the faint of heart. Sebastian didn't spot any wounds, but the roughly stitched scars were clearly visible, the Y incision extending all the way to the woman's pubis. Whoever had performed the postmortem had probably cut open her womb and examined the child within. Now that he was aware that the brain had most likely been removed, Sebastian thought that, if the surgeon was a student of anatomy, he might have wanted to know if the child the woman carried was also a dwarf, or if a dwarf could conceive a child that was normal in appearance.

He would have to ask Colin about that when he stopped by for the postmortem results on Tamzin Norris.

Unable to tolerate the sight a moment longer and feeling more than a little bilious, Sebastian readjusted the shift and sprinted outside, where he gulped fresh air until the smell finally left his nostrils and the queasiness passed. There was a pump around the side of the house, and he scrubbed his leather gloves and wiped the soles of his boots on the grass until he was certain they were clean. He would have liked a drink, but was afraid the water was tainted and would make him ill.

Having now seen the body of the dwarf, Sebastian was convinced the two cases were connected. It would be immensely helpful if Colin could autopsy the woman, but he could hardly send a two-week-old corpse to his friend's home and ask him to handle the putrid remains. Sebastian also couldn't keep referring to the deceased as *the woman* or *the dwarf*. It seemed wrong, even though she must have heard the term every day and had probably been called some unflattering names in her time. He had to come up with a suitable name for her.

Sebastian looked around and was surprised to see colorful blooms clinging to the crumbling stone wall behind the dead house. It was a timely reminder that where there was death there was also life, and everything was part of a natural cycle that shouldn't be feared but accepted. Sebastian's mother had loved her garden, and, whereas his brother had only been interested in farming, Sebastian had been fascinated by horticulture and had been willing to help his mum to weed and dig. She had spoken to him of the plants and their properties while they worked. Sebastian had not touched a trowel since his mother had died nearly twenty years before, but he still recalled everything she had taught him.

Hollyhocks, he thought as he recognized the pretty flowers. *Holly*. That would be the woman's name for the duration of the case. Satisfied with his choice, Sebastian headed to the nearest cab stand.

CHAPTER 9

"Most perplexing," Colin said as he looked down at the body of Tamzin Norris. He ran his finger along the seam on her forehead and nodded with approval. "Very neat and clean."

"So not some self-taught amateur?" Gemma inquired.

"Definitely not, unless the man had turned his back on a career in tailoring in order to become a surgeon."

Gemma chose not to point out that the stitching could have been done by a woman. Colin might allow her to learn at his side, but he wasn't ready to accept that there might be other women with an interest in pathology. She also decided not to remind him that through the centuries it had been the women who'd nursed the sick and wounded, laid out the dead, and stitched on severed heads and hacked-off limbs in order to make the body whole for burial.

Colin turned away from Tamzin and fixed Gemma with a quizzical look. "Did you already examine the remains?"

"Yes," she admitted. "I didn't think you'd object."

He chuckled and shook his head. "When it comes to you, Gemma dear, there's little point in objecting. Your inquisitive nature defies all the dictates of genteel upbringing."

"I don't believe the two are mutually exclusive," Gemma replied with a shrug.

This was an argument she and Colin had all too often. He seemed torn between his admiration for her need to learn and his dismay at her insistence that a woman could aspire to the same goals as a man. Colin could accept that a woman could be a competent nurse, a chemist even, but he still had difficulty believing that the females of the species possessed the necessary intelligence or the temperament to become a surgeon. Gemma's composure in the face of an open body amazed him, and he attributed her lack of fear to her time in Crimea, where he believed she had become desensitized to the horrors that would send any respectable woman reaching for her smelling salts.

"Sebastian is a brave man," Colin muttered under his breath.

"Don't feel sorry for Sebastian," Gemma replied with a grin. "He knows what he's in for."

"I don't," he replied with a smile of his own. "I quite envy him. Now, let's open her up and see what we can discover, shall we? We'll compare notes once we have finished."

Colin reached for the leather apron he wore to shield his clothes and tied it behind his back. Gemma put on the smock she kept in the cellar for just this purpose and took her place.

"Would you like to do the honors?" he asked.

She suspected he was only inviting her to make the first incision because all she had to do was follow the path of the scars, but as far as she was concerned this was a step in the right direction, and she would be glad of whatever experience she could gain from the victim.

Gemma picked up the scalpel, pressed it beneath the clavicle, and drove the tip into the unyielding flesh. She no longer saw the woman on the table as a wife or a daughter. Tamzin was a puzzle to be solved, and in order to decipher the clues Gemma had to have all the pertinent pieces of information. After a while, Colin took the scalpel from her and began on his usual show-and-tell method of instruction, but she didn't mind. She had scored a victory today and was stunned when he suddenly stepped aside.

"Go on," he said, and pointed to Tamzin's belly.

Gemma's first thought was that Colin wanted her to extract the child because he thought the sight of the infant might shock her and sway her from her chosen course, but he didn't look smug or make any comments to that effect. Perhaps he realized that this was a teaching opportunity neither of them was likely to encounter again soon, so she would take it and say thank you. Gemma braced herself and sliced into the woman's belly. She refused to give in to her sadness when she saw the sweet face of the tiny girl, and didn't flinch when she pulled the infant from the womb and laid it alongside its mother. It was only once she had cleaned the baby with a linen towel that the horror of what she was seeing finally breached her shield of determination and Gemma cried out, unable to control her emotions any longer.

CHAPTER 10

Sebastian alighted near the entrance to Vauxhall Bridge and walked along the Thames foreshore. It hadn't rained in two days, but the bank was still damp, and the mud sucked at his boots. Several barefoot children walked slowly near the waterline, their heads bowed and their gazes glued to the ground beneath their feet. For many children, mudlarking was a way of life. They spent their days searching the bank for anything of value that might have washed up on the tide and often found coins, buttons, bits of metal, and bones, all of which they sold or traded for food and coal. Sometimes, the mudlarkers came upon a body, and those who were less squeamish or simply more desperate would pick the corpse clean, relieving the deceased of anything that could be used or sold. Holly's gown and shoes, for example, might have been cleaned and brought to a rag-and-bone man, and her jewelry, if she'd had any, might already be being worn by another woman who had no idea where the items had come from.

"Oi," Sebastian called to a boy of about ten who'd just pocketed a coin and looked very pleased with himself. The child was thin, and his ankles and wrists were very pale, unlike his face, which was bronzed from the sun. The boy's clothes were tatty, and his mop of hair and widely spaced eyes were the same color as the river mud that caked his bare feet.

"It's mine," the boy snarled, and balled his hands into tight fists. "I found it."

"I'm not after your treasure, son." Sebastian took a step back. "I'm looking for Leticia and Leda Spires. Do you know them?"

The boy nodded, clearly relieved that Sebastian wasn't trying to steal his find. "They're 'ere most days."

"Do you know where they live?"

The boy shook his head, then studied Sebastian, his brown eyes narrowed with suspicion. "What ye want wif 'em?"

Sebastian showed the boy his warrant card, even though he didn't think the boy could read it. "Inspector Bell, Scotland Yard. I want to speak to them about the body they found."

"The midget?" the boy exclaimed, his earlier reservations already forgotten.

"Yes, the midget."

"She were just there." The boy pointed to the stone abutment of the bridge.

"What's your name?" Sebastian asked.

"Rolly," the boy replied with obvious hesitation.

"Were you there when they found her, Rolly?"

The boy nodded enthusiastically. "I tell ye, Inspectah, she were a fright with those scars on 'er noggin."

"Was she wet?"

"'Course she were wet. She were in the mud."

"Did she look like she had drowned?" Sebastian clarified.

"Nah," Rolly said with a shake of his head. "She weren't bloated like them floaters as jumped off a bridge. And she still 'ad 'er ring." He went pale and began to back away, no doubt ready to break into a run should the situation call for it.

"I don't care what you took off the corpse. I just want to know what she had on her, and what she was wearing," Sebastian said.

"She were wearing a fancy gown and leather boots, and she had the ring."

"What sort of ring?"

"A wedding ring."

"Which you palmed before anyone spotted it?"

The boy nodded guiltily. "She didn't need it no more."

"And the boots?"

"Miss Lettie pulled 'em off before she went for the constable. She 'as small feet, Miss Lettie does, and 'er boots were worn through."

"What about the gown? Did anyone try to get it off?"

Rolly shook his head. "No one wanted to touch 'er, and it were too short anyhow. She were a midget, remembah?"

"So, what do you reckon, Rolly?" Sebastian asked. "You think someone dumped the body?"

"For sure they did," the boy replied, his narrow chest swelling with pride at being asked for his opinion. "She weren't there the night afore, and I were 'ere at first light, so someone left 'er in the night."

"Did you tell the constable?"

"I weren't going to 'ang about, was I?"

"Did the Misses Spires tell the constable, do you think?" Sebastian asked.

"I'm sure they did. They're smart, and they notice things."

Like good boots, Sebastian thought, but kept the criticism to himself. "Do they find much?" he asked, his gaze raking the sucking mud along the shore.

"'Nough to keep 'em coming back. I reckon they was born gentry, but they fell on 'ard times. 'Appens more often than ye think," Rolly said wisely.

There was something endearing about the little urchin, so Sebastian pulled out a twopence and handed it to the boy. "For your assistance."

"Thank ye kindly, guv." Rolly took a small bow. "I'll be going now, if ye don't mind."

"Happy hunting," Sebastian said, and watched the boy dash off.

Once Rolly had disappeared from view, Sebastian continued walking along the shore. He asked a few more mudlarkers if they could direct him to the Spires sisters, but no one knew where they lived. Two adolescent girls, who were as scrawny and dirty as Rolly, informed him that they hadn't seen the old ladies in days, but they weren't worried. The ladies always came back after a few days' rest.

No one knew anything about Holly either. A few people had been there when the body had been found, but they had kept their distance from both the victim and the constable, who might question their right to their finds or take the valuables for himself. It wasn't until Sebastian came upon an old man, whose reddened skin hung in folds around his scrawny neck, that he finally got a lead on the Spires sisters. Armed with an address, Sebastian hoped he'd find the ladies at home. He couldn't afford to wait until they turned up on the shore.

CHAPTER 11

The Misses Spires lived in the squalid end of Carmelite Lane in Whitefriars. The tall building across the street blocked the light from entering their ground-floor lodgings, and the room was in deep shadow, even so early in the day. There was one bed, covered with a faded flowery quilt, a scuffed round table and two chairs, and a rickety cabinet filled with mismatched china and well-thumbed books. A half-eaten loaf of bread, a tea tin, and a wedge of cheese were lined up on a wooden shelf. The floorboards were bare, the leather trunk at the foot of the bed smelled of mildew, and the curtains, which must have been dark green damask embroidered with tiny pink flowers when they were new, now resembled lumpy pea soup with chunks of overcooked ham.

The ladies looked just as worn. Their light brown hair was streaked with gray, and they were rail-thin, their faces stretched tight over the skulls. The sisters' gowns were years out of fashion, the fabric threadbare at the elbows. On first impression, Sebastian thought the women were in their sixties, but on closer inspection he realized they were probably twenty years younger. Constant worry and the daily struggle to keep going was enough to age anyone, especially unmarried women, who had no means to earn a living unless they had some desirable skill. Rolly was right; the sisters did not look like they had been born to poverty, rather that their current situation was the result of drastically reduced circumstances, and they were doing their utmost to survive.

Sebastian briefly wondered why they hadn't hired themselves out as tutors or paid companions, then thought that it might be that they refused to be separated.

"How can we help you, Inspector?" Leda Spires asked once Sebastian had presented his identification and asked if he might speak to them for a few minutes. She appeared to be the older of the two and the one more comfortable taking charge.

"Would you care for some tea and a slice of bread?" Leticia asked nervously.

Sebastian wouldn't have minded; he hadn't had anything since breakfast, and his stomach reminded him that it was time to eat, but if he accepted the ladies would probably have to go without, and he couldn't permit himself to further deplete their meager supplies.

"Thank you, no," he said, and saw the relief in Leticia's eyes. "I was told you summoned a constable when you found the body near Vauxhall Bridge."

Leticia paled and took a step back, as if she could somehow hide from Sebastian in the tiny room.

"Miss Spires, I have no interest in the woman's possessions. I only want to know if you might have seen anything that would help me to track down the individuals who dumped the body."

Leda reached for her sister's hand and squeezed it reassuringly. "Please, sit down, Inspector," she invited him.

Sebastian sat at the table with Leda, while Leticia perched on the bed for lack of anywhere else to sit and used her foot to push the chamber pot further beneath the bed.

"Lettie and I go out first thing each morning," Leda said. "It's still dark when we leave."

Sebastian didn't need to ask why the ladies wanted to arrive at the foreshore at the crack of dawn. They wanted to have first pick of anything that might have been deposited on the bank overnight and might have resale value.

"We're usually the first ones there," Leticia said softly.

"And were you there first that day?"

"Rolly was there," Leticia said. "He's a young boy who comes every day. I saw him in the distance."

"I've already spoken to Rolly," Sebastian said.

Letitia seemed to shrink even further into herself, and hid her feet beneath the bed, even though Sebastian had reassured her that he hadn't come for Holly's things.

"We also saw two men," Leda said. "They were on the bridge."

"Were they on foot?" Sebastian asked.

"No, they had a wagon. I think they were going to drive out to the middle of the bridge, but something spooked them. They tossed the body over the side and continued across. By the time we reached the poor woman, Rolly was already there, checking the corpse for valuables."

"Is there anything you call tell me about these men?"

"We didn't get a clear look since they were above us, on the bridge, but they looked like laborers," Leda replied. "Both wore dark coats and caps pulled low over their eyes."

"One man had red hair," Leticia said. "When the wagon passed beneath a lamp, his hair gleamed like copper. And he wore a red kerchief around his neck."

"Did you get a good look at him?" Sebastian asked. "Was he young, old, thin, stout?"

She shook her head. "I really couldn't say with any certainty, Inspector. I think he may have been around forty and broad through the shoulders, but I only saw him for a second."

"What about the deceased? Is there anything you can tell me about her?"

"At first I thought she was a child, but when I saw her face I realized she was a fully grown woman. And she was enceinte," Leda said.

The fact that she used a French term to say that the deceased had been pregnant further supported the likelihood that the sisters had had a genteel upbringing. The most obvious scenario was that their father or legal guardian had left them with nothing when he'd died, and they had been scrounging ever since.

"There was a black seam just below the woman's hairline," Leticia said. "It put me in mind of Frankenstein's monster."

"That's unkind, Lettie," Leda admonished her.

"Well, it's true," Leticia protested. "Someone had cut her open and sewn her back together. I wager it was because she had trusted the wrong man. You can never put your faith in men. They will raise you up and cut you down," she said solemnly.

"Not everyone has the same experience, dear," Leda said warily. "My Charles was a good man. You can't lump him in with his wicked brother."

"Charles left you just the same," Leticia scoffed.

Sebastian didn't think he should remain while the women squabbled over who had been treated worse. Given their current situation, it didn't much matter.

"Thank you, ladies. You have been most helpful," he said, and made for the door.

Leda stood, ready to see him out, but Leticia remained where she was, her stolen boots safely hidden beneath the counterpane.

CHAPTER 12

Sebastian was hungry but, even though he'd spotted several street vendors, he was hesitant to purchase food that had been sitting out in the summer sun for what could have been hours. The odor of rancid grease from a tray of sheep's trotters helped to make up his mind, and he stopped in to a chophouse in New Bridge Street. He considered his next move over steak and ale pie but decided there was no one he had to speak to urgently, not until he had the results of the postmortem and knew precisely how Tamzin had died. Colin probably hadn't yet had an opportunity to carry out the postmortem, but, even if Sebastian wasn't going to get any answers until tomorrow, he needed to see Gemma. She had been deeply upset by the sight of Tamzin's remains, and their plan to view the house had been interrupted so unexpectedly, he hadn't had a chance to reassure her that he would write to the owner and reschedule their appointment for next week.

When Sebastian arrived at Colin's house, he expected a friendly greeting from Mabel, but when the maidservant answered the door her gaze was cold, and she fairly bristled with disapproval as she silently held out her arms for Sebastian's things.

"They're in the cellar," she announced, and walked away without another word.

Sebastian wondered if he had done something to annoy her, then decided that her sour mood most likely had nothing to do with him. She had plenty to be disgruntled about. Sebastian had heard from Gemma that Jacob, the object of Mabel's affections, had been stepping out with a parlormaid from across the street.

The coachman was a striking young man, no doubt with a string of admirers from the houses along the street, but Sebastian had thought that Jacob reciprocated Mabel's feelings. She deserved better than a man who'd trifle with her feelings, but he didn't suppose Mabel had many opportunities to meet eligible men and was terribly disappointed to have been thrown over.

As he descended the steps to the cellar, Sebastian tried not to dwell on the past, but every time he walked down those steps he recalled the circumstances that had led to Anne Ramsey's grievous injuries and blamed himself anew for his failure to apprehend the person responsible before he had been able to inflict so much damage. The man was gone now, hanged only last week before a crowd of hundreds, but that was cold comfort for Anne, who was still suffering, and for Sebastian, whose personal life was in limbo until Colin finally found a new nurse for his ailing mother, a task he kept putting off.

It suddenly dawned on Sebastian that it was too quiet. Perhaps Mabel had been mistaken, and Colin and Gemma had come upstairs since Mabel had checked on them last? But a flicker from an oil lamp signified that someone was down there. Colin never left the lamp on if he left the cellar, for fear that it might accidentally tip over and the cellar would become engulfed with flames, the fire fed by the formaldehyde he used to preserve his specimens.

When he reached the bottom step, the first thing Sebastian saw was Gemma. She wore her smock and was seated in the corner, her hands clasped in her lap. Her face was the color of whey, and her staring gaze was fixed on nothing in particular. Colin was in the act of closing the body, and, even though he'd calmly performed this task many times before, he looked furious, his movements jerky and unnecessarily forceful as he stabbed the needle into the pale flesh. Ignoring Colin, Sebastian went to Gemma and knelt before her.

"Gemma? What's wrong?" he asked as he covered her cold hands with his own.

Her gaze met his, and her eyes brimmed with tears. "It's awful, Sebastian. Truly awful," she whimpered.

"I've never seen anything like it," Colin said as he tied off the thread. "Barbaric doesn't begin to describe what was done to this woman."

"And the baby," Gemma choked out as tears spilled down her cheeks. "Oh, the baby…"

"I think you had better explain," Sebastian said, directing his request to Colin since he didn't want Gemma to have to put her horror into words.

What he did want was to draw her to him and hold her until the storm of emotion passed, but this was neither the time nor the place for such an intimate gesture. He would have to wait until they were alone, which might not happen for a while.

Gemma sprang to her feet and swept past Sebastian, coming to stand across from Colin. Her hand shook as she pointed at a linen-wrapped bundle on the worktop.

"Show him," she cried, her voice trembling with rage.

Colin nodded and unwrapped the second body. Thick black stitches covered the child's translucent skin, the evidence of a recent postmortem somehow more horrifying on one so tiny. Colin wrapped the body once again, and Gemma breathed a barely audible sigh of relief once she could no longer see the infant.

"Talk me through it," Sebastian said. He would have preferred that Gemma go upstairs and have a calming cup of tea, but he knew she wouldn't leave and would be deeply offended if he suggested she step away.

"My initial assumption was that, despite the evidence of the autopsy, Tamzin died of natural causes," Colin began. "I did not locate a fatal wound or any evidence of poisoning or strangulation. It was only once I opened the body that I realized the victim's lungs were filled with water. While drowning could have been accidental, I had my doubts, so I went back with a view to finding the evidence needed to support my suspicions."

"What did you discover?" Sebastian asked.

Colin turned the body onto its side and lifted Tamzin's hair to expose the back of her neck. The pale column was flanked by livid bruises, one on the left, four on the right. Colin wordlessly placed his hand over Tamzin's neck. His fingers aligned with the bruises, which framed his fingertips, since his hands were smaller than those of the man who'd held Tamzin down.

Removing his hand, Colin rolled the body back onto its back and continued. "I found bits of straw in Tamzin's hair, and traces of mud and horse manure on the hem of her gown and the soles of her shoes."

"She was drowned in a horse trough," Sebastian surmised.

"Yes, I think so. But killing her wasn't enough," Colin said with disgust. "The surgeon then autopsied both mother and child."

"Perhaps the surgeon was not the killer. They don't tend to work in stables. Could the killer have sold the body to someone who wasn't inclined to ask too many questions about where it'd come from?"

"Yes, I suppose they could," Colin allowed. He peered at Sebastian. "Do you have any leads?"

Sebastian shook his head. "I spoke to Tamzin's father and interviewed her husband, who works at Millbank Prison. Jonah

Norris admitted to having an argument with his wife in the days before she died, but I don't think he killed her. Neither man was able to offer any theories on how Tamzin died. I did not speak to her sister, Alice."

"So, a dead end, then?"

"Not necessarily. There was a similar case a few weeks ago," Sebastian said. "A woman's body was dumped near Vauxhall Bridge. She was also with child and had been autopsied before her remains were disposed of."

"And the child?" Gemma asked quietly.

"I don't know. Inspector Warren did not order a postmortem." Sebastian sucked in a sharp breath and continued, "The attendant at the city mortuary thought the woman's brain had been removed, though. Was that the case with Tamzin Norris?"

"No," Colin replied, and shot an apologetic look in Gemma's direction. "But her brain had been dissected, as was the brain of the infant."

"The other woman—I named her Holly, since she was never identified—was a dwarf," Sebastian said.

Colin nodded. "That explains the brain, then. The surgeon would want to compare it to the brain of a normal person. And, if this is the handiwork of the same individual, then I expect her baby was autopsied as well."

"You're probably right."

"Has Holly been buried?"

"Not yet."

"Where is the body?" Colin asked.

"The old watchhouse in St. Anne's. She is scheduled to be buried tomorrow. Colin, the body is in an advanced state of decomposition," Sebastian warned.

"I'm sure I've seen worse," Colin said as he set about gathering his instruments and placing them in a leather satchel he'd taken from a shelf. "Let's go."

"I'm coming with you," Gemma cried, and made ready to follow, before Sebastian took hold of her arms.

"No," he said firmly.

"You can't forbid me to go," she snapped. *You're not my husband* hung in the air between them.

"I cannot forbid you, and I wouldn't dare try, but I can implore you to wait here. Gemma, you will never be able to erase those awful images from your mind."

Gemma hesitated. "Are you saying it's worse than the things I saw in Crimea? Worse than this?" Her gaze slid to the swaddled baby.

"Much worse," Sebastian replied, and hoped she would take his word for it.

Colin finally came to his rescue. "Gemma, I won't require your assistance. I will perform a cursory examination and share my findings with Sebastian. Besides, Mother has been on her own for hours," he reminded her. "She could use some company."

Gemma gave a silent nod of acknowledgement, then turned back to Sebastian, her eyes brimming with feeling. "You must find the person who did this, Sebastian. I beseech you."

"I will," he replied, but his mind wasn't on his hasty promise. It was on the questions that had arisen during Colin's explanation and the horror he knew they would encounter at the dead house.

CHAPTER 13

After Gemma had spent an hour with Anne and made sure she was tidy, well fed, and comfortable, she returned downstairs and asked Mabel for a cup of tea. Mabel had been sulking for days and had been taking out her despondency on the pots and pans and occasionally on Colin and Gemma, but she made the tea without complaint and even brought Gemma a few ginger biscuits to tide her over until supper. Sickened by what she had witnessed, Gemma didn't think she would be able to eat, but she hadn't eaten since breakfast and the ginger biscuits helped to settle her stomach. The hot tea made her feel pleasantly warm, and she looked out the window at the street beyond as her mind tried to make sense of what she had learned.

The facts of the case, or cases, if the two deaths were connected, were truly grim, but it was the events following Tamzin's death that troubled Gemma the most. Someone, presumably a man given the size of their hands, had killed Tamzin Norris—an act that had been the result of either careful planning or a fit of anger. The killer had then left the body for someone else to find, or, if he was mercenary in nature, had sold it to whoever had carried out the postmortem. Perhaps he'd thought that was the best way to avoid detection, since the body would never be tied to him, but then how had Tamzin's remains ended up in the alley behind the Rose and Thorn? It couldn't be a coincidence that her body had been left for Hume Macklemore or someone who worked at the tavern to find. Had returning Tamzin to her family been an act of kindness or a vicious taunt? And who would have reason to want her dead?

In a case of a woman's violent death, the husband was always a suspect, but Sebastian did not suspect Jonah Norris. Which didn't mean Norris hadn't murdered his wife, only that if he was guilty the evidence against him had yet to surface. He worked at the prison and came in contact with unscrupulous individuals. If he'd wanted to dispose of his wife's remains, he was sure to know someone he could turn to, which might also explain why Tamzin's corpse had been delivered to her father's tavern. Perhaps Jonah had wanted to see his wife and child decently buried, but only once he felt safe in the knowledge that there was no proof of his guilt.

And why would a man murder his pregnant wife? The obvious reason was betrayal. Had Tamzin been unfaithful to Jonah? Had the child she'd carried been fathered by another man? Was that why the little girl had been subjected to a postmortem, as an act of revenge against Tamzin and her lover? Or was it possible that Tamzin's death had nothing to do with her marriage? Might she have unwittingly threatened someone? Or maybe she had rejected an ardent suitor who couldn't bear to see her happy with another man.

And what about the second casualty, Holly? Gemma was touched that Sebastian had taken the time to name the unidentified woman. He had wanted to humanize her and to give her the respect she probably hadn't received in life. Was she a random victim, or had she known Tamzin Norris? The spot where Holly's body had been dumped wasn't very far from the Rose and Thorn, and the bridge was extremely close to Millbank Prison. Colin had established that Tamzin had drowned. Had Holly been drowned as well before her body was dissected? And had she been dumped in a place where she had been known? Although she hadn't been identified, that didn't mean she wasn't a local. Might Tamzin and Holly have put their trust in the same man and met with a similar fate? Gemma didn't know anything about Holly's life, but she knew something of Tamzin's, even if it was precious little. She didn't think Tamzin would have divulged her secrets to her father or her husband, especially if they involved another man, but there was someone Gemma could speak to. Tamzin had a younger sister, and, if she had shared her innermost thoughts with anyone, it might have been her.

Gemma couldn't expect Mabel to look after Mrs. Ramsey while she traveled to Pimlico, not when Mabel was dealing with her own troubles, so she decided to ask her friend, Poppy Bright, if she might look after Anne for a few hours before Poppy headed to work at the infirmary in Lambeth. She was always happy to help, partly because she was sincerely fond of Anne, and partly because caring for Anne gave her a chance to see Colin. Poppy admired Colin, who seemed oblivious to her tender feelings and treated her as he would any other friend. Gemma could hardly chastise Colin for not noticing Poppy, but she could bring the two together and hope that he would finally come to see her friend for the wonderful, kind, and intelligent woman she was.

Gemma set aside her empty teacup and walked over to the writing desk where Colin kept the stationery. She penned a quick note to Poppy and stepped outside. Neighborhood children usually congregated at the corner, and the boys were always willing to deliver a message or fetch something from the shops for minimal recompense. Gemma waved, and one of them, Paul, came running towards her, his round face wreathed in smiles.

"How can I help ye, Miss Tate?"

"Would you deliver this to Miss Bright?" Gemma handed the child tuppence. Paul had delivered several messages to Poppy in the past and knew where she lived.

"Will there be a reply, miss?"

"Yes, I expect there will be."

"Very good, miss. I'll be back as soon as," Paul promised, and dashed off.

Gemma watched as he disappeared around the corner then went back inside. There wasn't much more she could accomplish today, but she hoped tomorrow would prove more productive.

CHAPTER 14

"I wonder if you could spare me a few minutes this evening, Inspector."

Bertram Quince materialized in the foyer as soon as Sebastian walked in the door, probably because the man had been waiting for him. Sebastian almost missed the days when Mrs. Poole had stalked him in the shadows, but she was married to Quince now, and the only thing that interested her about Sebastian was his cat, who kept the boarding house nearly free of vermin in exchange for the fish heads and tails she fed him.

"I don't think that will be possible," Sebastian replied, and headed for the stairs, but Quince stepped into his path.

"You can't avoid me forever."

"I'm not avoiding you, Mr. Quince, but I've had rather a trying day."

A murder, two visits to a dead house, and two autopsies were enough to test any man's mettle, and Sebastian thought that the things he'd seen today would haunt both his waking hours and his dreams, but it seemed the day's trials were not yet at an end.

"Really?" Quince asked, sidling uncomfortably close to him. "Are you investigating a new case, or is it Miss Tate who's been trying your patience?"

Sebastian glared at Quince. When not attending to the duties of a landlord, the penny dreadful writer was working on a novel, the first of its kind, as he liked to remind everyone, in which he hoped to have his clever inspector solve an impenetrable mystery.

Problem was that Mr. Quince's imagination didn't stretch to inventing a gripping scenario, so he accosted Sebastian at every opportunity in the hope that Sebastian would furnish him with a good idea.

On the whole, Sebastian thought the novel wasn't a terrible idea and might be quite entertaining. He would be especially in favor of such a project if Quince were to actually spend time writing and keep from haunting him like a restless spirit, but he did resent the thinly veiled reference to himself in the guise of Inspector Knell and wasn't about to spoon-feed Quince the premise and the clues just so he could finally fulfill his long-cherished dream of literary greatness.

"Have you eaten?" Quince asked.

All Sebastian wanted was to go up to his room, shut the door, and try to put this awful day from his mind, but he had missed supper and could do with a stiff drink.

"No," he admitted. "I haven't eaten."

Quince smiled happily. "Then allow me to make you a sandwich and pour you a drink, my dear Inspector. A few minutes of your time in exchange for sustenance, what do you say?"

Sebastian nodded and made his way to the parlor. Quince disappeared into the kitchen and returned a few minutes later with a plate bearing a ham sandwich. He'd even remembered to bring a napkin. Had Mrs. Quince made the sandwich, it would have been half the size and mostly bread, but Quince was clearly feeling generous, and a thick wedge of ham peeked from between slices of brown bread. He set the plate on a low table before Sebastian, then poured him a liberal measure of brandy and handed him the glass.

"Thank you," Sebastian said, and set the glass down next to his plate.

"I have been engaging in factual research," Quince said once he'd taken a sip of his own drink and set it aside.

"What does factual research entail?"

"Searching for inspiration," Quince replied. "I have visited various public houses and conversed with the barkeeps and the patrons in the hopes of hitting upon a promising idea."

"And have you had any luck?" Sebastian asked with genuine interest. He was enjoying his sandwich and feeling more favorably disposed towards Quince.

"Yes and no," Quince admitted.

"Where have you been searching?" Sebastian asked, and took a small sip of brandy.

He'd agreed to one drink, and he'd meant it, since he knew how easy it would be to hold out his glass for a refill and then another, until his senses had been sufficiently dulled by alcohol to forget the faces of the dead mothers and their babies, at least until tomorrow.

"I've visited public houses from Seven Dials to Piccadilly in search of a worthy plot," Quince said. "Sadly, although there's no shortage of crime, most cases are disappointingly pedestrian in their planning and execution."

"What sort of case were you hoping for?"

"Something deliciously shocking," Quince said with a sly grin. "Surely you've come across murders that were gruesome enough to chill your blood."

"I have." *Today*, Sebastian added inwardly. "But I am not at liberty to discuss investigations with you."

That wasn't strictly true. Police officers routinely sold stories to the papers to supplement their incomes, but, unless Sebastian had no choice but to run a public appeal, he did not go to the papers or reveal the names of those involved. And he wasn't about to tell Quince about the cases that had left a permanent scar on his heart. For one, he thought it unfair to the victims and their families to share the details with a writer, and for another, he simply didn't trust Bertram Quince.

Quince sighed with disappointment and settled more comfortably in his chair. "Three people were killed and at least a dozen badly injured when a brawl broke out at a cockfight in Spitalfields last week. And a gentleman who has strong, one might say almost familial, ties to the royal family beat a harlot to death in a Covent Garden brothel, but, although gory, neither case is intriguing enough to capture the attention of the reader."

"No," Sebastian agreed absentmindedly, his thoughts circling back to his own case. "Have you heard about any unusual killings?"

"Unusual?" Quince's gaze narrowed as he studied Sebastian. "Unusual how?"

"Someone murdering expectant women and selling the bodies to an anatomist."

Quince shook his head. "Nothing like that. Oh, but that would make for a fascinating case," he exclaimed. "Thank you, Inspector. You've given me a brilliant idea."

"You are not to write about this," Sebastian growled. He was furious with himself for giving so much away but also disappointed by the response. He had half hoped that Quince might have heard something that could provide a lead.

Quince inhaled sharply and sat up straighter, his eyes alight with excitement. "There was a case a few months back. The victim wasn't an expectant woman, but the body had been autopsied and dumped."

Sebastian sat up straighter as well, his copper's instinct vibrating like a tuning fork. "What do you know about the victim?"

"Victims," Quince corrected him. "They were with Petroni's Circus, his most famous freaks."

Sebastian cringed at Quince's description. He had been to a freak show only once, when he was a child, but the memory of the monkey boy who'd been covered in hair and had worn nothing but a loincloth and been kept in a cage had stayed with him. His innate sense of justice rebelled against treating human beings who'd been born with some terrible affliction so cruelly, but he also acknowledged that those unfortunates rarely had another way to earn a living and would perish otherwise. As members of a circus troupe, they had a family of sorts and were at least paid to put themselves on display and entertain curious onlookers, who jeered and pointed fingers at them, considering them not quite human and unworthy of compassion.

"Tell me about them," Sebastian asked, since Quince was clearly familiar with the case and eager to divulge the details.

"The victims were identical twin boys. I think they were about fourteen at the time. Their bodies were fused from chest to hip, but otherwise they were fully formed. Petroni dressed them in Roman togas and made them look in opposite directions. He called them his Janus. You are familiar with the Roman god Janus, are you not?" Quince didn't wait for an answer. "He was the god of beginnings and endings, transition, and duality. The month of January is named after him, so Petroni advertised the act as the Two Faces of January. The twins were the biggest draw in his menagerie of oddities. Have you really never heard of them?"

"I don't frequent freak shows."

"Maybe you should. You might learn something. It was said that Petroni was devastated and that ticket sales continued to decline until he found his new star. I saw the act for myself, and let me tell you, Inspector, Mother Nature really does have an odd sense of humor."

Sebastian doubted Holly had been the main attraction, but it was important to rule out the possibility. "What's so special about the current attraction?" he asked.

"Ho-ho," Quince exclaimed. "You have to see it to believe it."

"Just tell me," Sebastian snapped. His patience was wearing thin.

"The man's name is Enrico Rossi. He's the son of Italian immigrants. The poor git was born with three legs, four feet, and two working cocks, one in front, one on the side. Petroni wouldn't dare display his pet's more shocking attributes, but word gets around, and I heard it said that Rossi is open to private viewings. For a price."

"How old is this man?" Sebastian asked, wondering if he was old enough to know that he was being exploited.

"Late twenties. He is married and has two children. There's a lid for every pot, isn't there?" Quince said with a shake of his head. "I wonder if his wife rides both cocks or if she has a preference."

"Is Petroni's Circus here now?"

"No," Quince replied. "I don't think Petroni is due back for several weeks. I'm going to take Mathilda when they come. She's never been. I think she will enjoy herself. I might even pay for a private viewing," he said with a lewd grin.

"Tell me about the twins," Sebastian said. If Petroni's Circus wasn't due back until next month, he had no reason to worry about Rossi. "Where were the bodies dumped?"

"In Kennington Common, I believe. Near one of the tents."

"What was the cause of death?"

Quince shrugged. "Damned if I know."

"How did you even hear about the murder?" Sebastian asked. He was surprised he hadn't heard about the case from one of his colleagues, since this was just the sort of thing that would get the tongues wagging in the duty room.

"I read about it in *Lloyd's Weekly*," Quince said. "I sometimes purchase a copy if the headline grabs my attention. For the purposes of research, you understand."

Sebastian never bothered with *Lloyd's*, since the broadsheet frequently resorted to lurid scandalmongering that was meant to appeal to the lowest orders of society and individuals like Bertram Quince, who was always on the lookout for sensational stories that could be incorporated into his series of penny dreadfuls.

"Did you write about the case?" Sebastian asked.

He knew from previous conversations with Quince that the writer submitted the manuscripts to his publisher on the first of each month, but the stories were written well in advance, and he sometimes had as many as three installments ready and awaiting publication.

Quince had the decency to look shamefaced. "I submitted the story last week. 'The Two Faces of January' will hit the streets on Saturday." His gaze turned defiant. "It was too good a story to pass on, and I have to maintain my reader base until my novel comes out."

"Were there any similar cases that you know of?"

Sebastian had finished his sandwich and his glass was empty, but he couldn't leave now. The information might have nothing to do with Holly and Tamzin, but there could be a connection, and, if Quince could point Sebastian in the right direction, he would gladly repay him for his help.

"Not that I know of," Quince said.

"Were any carnivals in town a fortnight ago?"

"Sanger's Circus held several performances on Hampstead Heath, and there was a smaller act in Smithfield, but both have moved on. Why the sudden interest? Is your victim a freak?"

"Do you still have the article about the Janus murder?"

"I do."

"May I see it?" Sebastian asked.

Quince nodded and reluctantly heaved himself to his feet. He nipped to the tiny back room he used as his study and returned with the newspaper. "I'll need that back."

"You'll have it tomorrow. Thank you for the sandwich."

Sebastian gathered his coat and hat and headed for the stairs. Quince didn't try to stop him, since Sebastian had clearly given him enough to think about. Knowing Quince, he probably regretted writing about Janus in his penny dreadful. Now that there could be a bigger story, he just might have what he needed for a full-length novel.

CHAPTER 15

Gustav weaved between Sebastian's ankles and purred contently as soon as Sebastian entered his rooms.

"Sorry, old son, no treat for you today," Sebastian said. He didn't feel overly guilty since Mrs. Quince kept the cat well supplied. He didn't think Gustav would miss her too much, though, since Gemma was sure to spoil him rotten once they moved in together. The cat gave him the gimlet eye and went to sulk in the corner.

Sebastian set the paper aside, hung up his coat and hat, then removed his tie and the stiff detachable collar, and undid the top two buttons of his shirt. It was too warm for a fire and still bright enough that there was no need to light a lamp. He picked up the newspaper and settled in a chair by the hearth. Gustav must have forgiven him because he jumped into Sebastian's lap, and Sebastian absentmindedly stroked the silky black fur as he read the article. The author had drawn out and embroidered the story as much as he reasonably could, but the nearly half-page article was thin on information. No one had seen or heard anything, and the members of the troupe hadn't realized the boys were missing until their bodies were discovered the following morning. The only details of note that caught Sebastian's attention were that, aside from the autopsy scars, there were no visible wounds on the bodies, and that the performer who'd discovered the bodies had thought that the boys' heads felt strangely light. The paper also mentioned that the twins' real names were Elias and Silas

Pruitt and that they had been sold to Giacomo Petroni by their mother when they were two years old.

Sebastian sighed and set the newspaper aside. He had seen so much death in his years on the job, but most murders were the result of fear, jealousy, greed, and sometimes even love. This case was something else entirely. A pattern was beginning to emerge, but Sebastian wasn't yet sure if Tamzin's murder was directly related to the deaths of Holly, Elias, and Silas. Tamzin had been with child and been autopsied and dumped, but she hadn't been born with any obvious deformities and had not been part of a traveling carnival. The only explanation that came to mind was that Tamzin's killer might have heard about the other murders and thought that by copying the method he might be spared the hangman's noose. The only thing Sebastian was sure of was that, if he was correct in his estimation, more victims would turn up in the coming days.

More than anything, he wished he could speak to Gemma and get her point of view, but, even if she were there now, how could he share the gruesome facts he'd just learned when he knew how much the news would upset her? Sebastian chuckled mirthlessly. He knew precisely what she would say in response to his misguided attempt at chivalry. Failure to get justice for the victims would upset her much more. As a policeman, he had to acknowledge the validity of such an argument, but as a man who loved her all he wanted was to protect Gemma from the ugliness of the world and spare her the horrors that lurked around every corner and claimed innocent victims every day.

Gustav suddenly meowed, jumped off Sebastian's lap, and raced to the door. His desertion was followed by a loud knock. Sebastian thought it might be Bertram Quince, come to ask more questions, but when he answered the door he found his landlady outside.

"You have a visitor," she announced, and retreated down the stairs before Sebastian could ask who'd come calling.

CHAPTER 16

Sebastian did up the buttons of his shirt, decided he could see whoever it was in his shirtsleeves, then glanced in his shaving mirror to make sure he was presentable before going downstairs. He experienced a moment of panic followed by pure joy when he saw Gemma, who sat perched on the edge of the settee, her reticule in her hands and her expression one of hard-won forbearance rather than distress. Mrs. Quince stood by the door, guarding the entrance to the parlor should Gemma decide to throw caution to the wind and invite herself to Sebastian's rooms. Women were strictly forbidden at the boarding house, so it was a kindness that the landlady had allowed Gemma to wait inside instead of leaving her on the step, but she wasn't about to let either one of them forget it.

"Thank you, Mrs. Quince," Sebastian said as he joined her in the doorway.

"You are to leave the door open, and Miss Tate is not to go upstairs," Mrs. Quince said, loudly enough for Gemma to hear.

"I'm well aware of the rules," he replied.

She made a noise that was probably meant to convey that she didn't trust him to follow the rules, and then muttered under her breath that some women were no better than they should be and were bold as brass as she headed to the kitchen. Sebastian was in no doubt that she would stand by the door, listening in on his conversation with Gemma, and then share what she had heard with her husband, who now had a vested interest in Sebastian's investigation. Tempted as he was to defend Gemma's honor, he let Mrs. Quince's slight pass. He wouldn't have to deal with her for much longer and there was no point in engaging in an altercation, not when Gemma obviously needed to speak to him.

She sprang to her feet as soon as he entered the room. "Have you eaten?" she asked.

"Not yet," Sebastian lied. If Gemma was hungry, he wouldn't deny her the chance to get something to eat, and it was always more pleasant to talk over a meal than to wander the darkening streets.

Gemma smiled ruefully as her cheeks turned a lovely shade of pink. "I had to see you," she whispered. "Perhaps I shouldn't have given in to the impulse, but I'm here now, so get your coat and let's go."

Sebastian did not need to be asked twice. He raced upstairs, reattached his collar, and grabbed his coat and hat, and a few minutes later they were on their way to Mann's Tavern. It was a respectable establishment that served excellent food and had a separate dining room for couples who didn't wish to dine in the taproom. The owner knew Sebastian well and showed them to a table in the corner. Sebastian held out a chair for Gemma, and she sank into it gratefully, then set aside her reticule and pulled off her gloves. He removed his hat and settled across from her. He experienced a pang of guilt at feeling so happy when faced with such unspeakable brutality only a few hours before, but one had to take pleasure where one could, and he was excited to spend a few hours with his intrepid bride-to-be.

"Does Colin know you left?" Sebastian asked once they'd ordered their drinks and heard the day's specials from the publican's daughter, Trixie.

"Colin retired early. He said he was feeling bilious and had developed a megrim."

"I can't say I blame him." Sebastian pushed away memories of the dead house.

"Colin told me everything," Gemma said, her expression turning grim.

Holly's baby had been autopsied as well as his mother and then deposited inside the womb before the body was closed post-mortem. The child had to have been dead by the time it was torn from its mother, but that knowledge didn't make it any easier to accept what had been done to him. Mr. Stubbs had been correct: Holly's skull was empty of its brain, as was the baby's. The brains had either been dissected or were even now floating in a jar of formaldehyde in someone's lab. And perhaps the most telling of all was that Holly's lungs had been half full of fresh water and there were bruises on her neck. The woman had been drowned on dry land before her body had been cut open and taken apart.

"Who is this predator?" Gemma asked once Trixie had delivered a tray loaded with Sebastian's ale, Gemma's cider, and two orders of fried sole. "Clearly these poor women weren't random victims. The killer must have chosen them because they were with child. And then he disposed of their bodies once they were no longer of any use to him. Or paid someone else to do it, possibly even the person who had procured them."

"I'm afraid there may have been other victims," Sebastian said.

"Other women?" she exclaimed.

"Conjoined male twins, Elias and Silas Pruitt, were found in Kennington Common two months ago. Their act was called the Two Faces of January, and they were dressed as Janus, the two-faced Roman god. They had been autopsied and their bodies were dumped near their tent. The individual who found the Pruitts thought their heads felt unnaturally light when he tried to lift them."

Gemma's hand flew to her breast. "Dear God, what sort of monster are we dealing with, Sebastian?"

"I don't know, but whoever did this had clearly chosen the twins for their oddity. And although dwarfism is not uncommon, it still made Holly different, more so because she was with child."

"Because the killer wanted to see if her baby was developing normally and to study it if it wasn't," she concluded.

"That's the only theory that makes sense."

"Man is capable of great evil, but surely even the most awful human being has not been driven by such evil intent before."

"Unfortunately, they have," Sebastian admitted reluctantly.

"What, here? In London?"

"In Edinburgh. Sixteen people were murdered, and their bodies sold to a surgeon who used them for public dissection."

"How recent was this?" Gemma looked horrified, and Sebastian wished he hadn't brought up the case just as they were about to eat, but he could hardly backtrack now.

"It happened thirty years ago, but any surgeon working today would have heard of Burke and Hare and the surgeon, Mr. Knox, who purchased the bodies in good faith."

"Are you suggesting that someone is murdering these people and selling their bodies to surgeons?" she asked.

Sebastian sighed heavily. "I think it's even worse than that."

"How can it possibly be worse?"

"I think the surgeon might be choosing his marks, and he's either doing the killing himself, or the more likely possibility is that he's paying someone to do it for him."

"How do we stop them?" Gemma asked. Her shock had distilled into cold determination, and she was clearly ready to do whatever it took to save the next intended victim.

"I don't know, and I'm not one hundred percent sure that Tamzin was part of the plan," Sebastian admitted. "The deaths of Holly and the twins fit the same pattern, but Tamzin was an ordinary woman who happened to be with child. Perhaps she was chosen as a comparison to Holly and her baby."

Gemma nodded in acknowledgement. "The killer might have spotted Holly and the twins when he visited the attractions, but how would he come across Tamzin?"

"Perhaps he'd seen her at the Rose and Thorn."

"The killer might live nearby," Gemma suggested.

"We don't even know if this person is local," Sebastian replied. "He might have come from any other city—but even if he is London bred there are hundreds of surgeons in this city, and not all of them are registered with the Royal College of Surgeons or hold positions at local hospitals. And since the circuses have moved on, it's now impossible to locate an eyewitness."

"Petroni's is coming back," Gemma said.

"When?"

"Next Saturday. Colin saw a flyer advertising a new attraction and tried to cajole Anne into going. It seems she and the late Mr. Ramsey used to go to the carnivals quite often in their younger days."

"What new attraction, did he say?" Sebastian asked, wondering if she was referring to Enrico Rossi.

"The Mermaid," Gemma said. "The advertisement claimed that the last surviving mermaid had been captured off the coast of the Cape of Good Hope and brought to London in a fishtank."

"And Colin thought this possible?"

"Of course not. It's likely some poor woman who is forced to sit in a tank of water all day while wearing a fancy fishtail, but he hoped to ignite a spark of interest in Anne. She has been so apathetic lately."

"And has Anne agreed to go?"

"She said she might, but of course she forgot all about it a few minutes later. I expect Colin will try again once the troupe arrives."

"Do you know if they will set up in Kennington again?"

"Hampstead Heath. Shall we visit the circus?"

"I think we might have to."

Gemma clearly had little inclination to attend the circus, but he knew she would go if the visit might yield some insight into this troubling case. "What will you do until then?" she asked.

"Tomorrow, I will visit the offices of *Lloyd's Weekly*. I would like to speak to the journalist who reported on the Janus murder and check the back copies going back to the start of the year. Perhaps I will find other victims."

"Why is it that no other newspaper reported these deaths?" Gemma asked.

"If I had to guess, I'd say it was because no one else knew. The journalist on the Janus case might have visited the attraction or had some sort of personal connection to the troupe or the site, but no one seemed to know about Holly, and Tamzin's murder has yet to be reported. People like the Pruitt twins and Holly usually exist on the fringes of society and don't have an accepting family or a fixed abode. They're travelers, and the individuals who monetize their uniqueness see no point in reporting their deaths, since they generally prefer to avoid visits from the police. If the murders are reported, the added publicity might stir up curiosity, but the gruesome descriptions might also deter spectators from attending the shows. And the owners will not make their money back even if the case is solved. The public will simply find a new attraction."

"What a cruel world we live in where a parent would sell their children to a freak show to make a profit," Gemma said sadly. "Those poor boys probably likely didn't even remember their mother or know any sort of love."

"I'm not sure the parents are driven solely by profit," Sebastian said. "I imagine it's very difficult to look after disabled children, especially once they become mobile and can no longer be hidden from the world. The cruel comments and possible physical attacks would be enough to drive any parent to despair."

"Yes, I suppose they would. A healthy child is never to be taken for granted."

There didn't seem to be anything left to say on the subject, so they talked of other, less unsettling things until they finished their meal. Then Sebastian found a hansom and escorted Gemma home before returning to the boarding house, where he successfully avoided both Quinces and sought solace in the quiet of his rooms.

CHAPTER 17

Gemma was still flushed with desire, her neck tingling where Sebastian's lips had brushed against the delicate skin and her insides quivering after his ardent goodnight kiss when he'd escorted her home. She had expected to be on her own when she let herself into the house and was surprised to find Colin in the parlor. He was clad in his embroidered dressing gown and slippers, and his hands were wrapped around a cup of steaming milk.

"I couldn't rest," he said miserably. "And as I sat here on my own, I realized just how quiet this house will be once you leave for good."

Gemma sat across from him and smiled sympathetically. "It doesn't have to be," she reminded him.

Colin sighed heavily. "I know what you're going to suggest, but you simply don't understand."

"What don't I understand, Colin?"

He shook his head, and his shoulders drooped even lower. "If I employ Poppy as Mother's nurse, then it will be inappropriate for me to court her. And if I court her, she will think the only reason I'm interested in her is because I want someone to take care of Mother."

As absurd as Colin's explanation sounded, Gemma had to acknowledge that there was a grain of truth to his logic. She had received a marriage proposal from her former employer days after her brother Victor had died, and she had thought much the same thing. Mr. Gadd was a bachelor in his early forties, and, although he had openly admired Gemma, she'd feared that his sudden interest in marriage had been precipitated by his need for round-the-clock care for his mother. It was cheaper to marry than to hire a live-in nurse and continue to pay her wages for years. And although marriage afforded stability and financial security for the wife if she married a man of means, it was the husband who profited from the arrangement, since he gained not only a nurse but also someone to look after him and see to his every need. And since Gemma's own circumstances had changed drastically and she no longer had a male guardian to protect and support her, Mr. Gadd had thought she might be more inclined to accept.

"Colin, Poppy knows you hold her in high regard and would never take advantage," Gemma said.

"Perhaps, but I must behave honorably."

"Is it honorable to deny yourself and Poppy the happiness you deserve because you think she might erroneously assume that your only objective is free care for your mother? Poppy cares for you, and you obviously care for her. Why not act on your feelings?"

Colin stared into the depths of his cooling milk. "Perhaps I'm afraid," he muttered. "I have loved before, but I wasn't loved in return. What if Poppy thinks me a disappointment?"

"And why would she think that?" Gemma exclaimed.

"I'm not handsome or dashing, or even particularly successful."

He had the look of a puppy who was hoping for a bone, and Gemma felt a wave of affection for him. He really had no idea what a prize he was. "Colin, you are attractive, wonderfully kind, and incredibly loyal. What more can a woman ask for?"

"Love," he replied softly.

"Love is not lightning. It doesn't suddenly strike. It must be cultivated, nourished, and cherished."

"Did you not fall in love with Sebastian the moment you met him?"

"No, I did not. I was devastated by the death of my brother and consumed with fears for the future. And I'm sure Sebastian wasn't struck by Cupid's arrow when he met a sad, grieving spinster who defied him at every turn."

Colin smiled, his eyes glowing with good humor. "Well, when you put it that way."

"Colin, there are only so many chances life gives us. Don't let happiness slip through your fingers."

He nodded, and his smile was one of affection and gratitude. "Thank you, Gemma. What will I do without your wisdom once you leave?"

"I will visit often and dispense sage advice at every opportunity."

"Do you promise?"

"If you keep tutoring me. And now I'm in need of assistance."

Colin set aside his cup and leaned forward. "I will help in any way I can."

"Then tell me about Burke and Hare."

He sat back, his mouth falling open in surprise. "Why on earth would you want to know about them?"

"Because their crimes might have a bearing on the current case."

"Is that so? Did Sebastian learn something after we parted ways?"

Gemma relayed everything she had learned about the Pruitts. "Have you ever heard of conjoined twins?" she asked.

"I have, but I have never seen a pair myself. Such births are rare, and if the children survive the delivery they rarely live long."

"The Pruitts lived," she pointed out.

"Which is a miracle in itself. I can't say for certain, not having examined the bodies for myself, but the twins likely shared a heart, as well as other vital organs. I would wager a guess that there was great strain on the heart, since it had to sustain two fully grown individuals, and the lungs, kidneys, and liver would also have to work twice as hard to keep the body functional. Their act was actually ingenious, because it not only attracted paying customers, but it also worked to their advantage since they didn't have to perform any physical feats. As long as all they had to do was sit and stare in opposite directions, they were protected from organ failure."

"I can't begin to imagine how they got through the day," Gemma said. "The abilities we take for granted would make every task an ordeal for someone whose mobility was so compromised."

"Yes, I expect you're correct, but those boys never knew any other life, so I suppose they learned to compensate for their limitations. In fact, the lecture I attended at the Royal College of Surgeons was on the subject of birth defects."

"Really? You never said."

Colin smiled wryly. "I never got the chance."

"Can you tell me about it?" Gemma asked, Burke and Hare forgotten for the moment.

"It was presented by Spencer Ellis, a surgeon who has devoted several years to studying congenital anomalies."

"Here in London? Is his research funded by one of the teaching hospitals?"

"Mr. Ellis recently returned from abroad," Colin explained. "His interest was initially piqued by the writings of William Smellie, a Scottish accoucheur who documented deformities in stillbirths and infants. Mr. Ellis continued his research in Paris, where he worked closely with Isidore Geoffroy Saint-Hilaire."

"I'm sorry, but I'm not familiar with the name," Gemma said when he looked at her expectantly.

"Isidore is the son of Étienne Geoffroy Saint-Hilaire, who compiled extensive accounts that detailed various malformations in humans and animals. His conclusions were quite revolutionary, in fact."

"How so?"

"He treated the deformities as natural phenomena rather than evidence of divine punishment."

Gemma could see how such an approach might be seen as radical, since most doctors believed that children born with physical or intellectual defects were the result of their mothers' immoral behavior, a terrible fright experienced during the pregnancy, or simply bad blood, and saw no reason to find treatments that might make the lives of those affected easier or safer. The majority of children born with defects either died from neglect or were sold to traveling shows, much like the Pruitt twins.

"And does the son subscribe to the same conclusions as the father?" she asked.

"I believe so. Isidore Geoffroy Saint-Hilaire has yet to visit London, which I imagine suits Mr. Ellis, since he wants to be the first to publish in England and doesn't care to share the credit."

"What sort of anomalies does Mr. Ellis study?"

"Missing or deformed limbs, an abnormally small head that causes cognitive impairment, also deafness, mutism, and retardation," Colin replied.

"And what is his opinion on these conditions? Does he share the view that these are natural occurrences, or does he see them as examples of divine retribution?"

"Mr. Ellis believes that the defects are nature's mistakes, not a punishment visited on the mother. In fact, he goes so far as to suggest that the anomalies might be the result of mutations in the blood or in the father's seed. He thinks that each mutation causes a particular set of disabilities."

"That sounds plausible," Gemma said, impressed. "Does Mr. Ellis work alone?"

"He seems a solitary man," Colin said. "But he did befriend a French physician he met on the crossing. Mr. Allard is affianced to an Englishwoman and has agreed to live in London for a time since the lady's mother is unwell and cannot travel to France to visit her daughter once they marry. Mr. Ellis introduced me to Mr. Allard after the lecture. Charming man. I believe Mr. Ellis had hoped to convince Mr. Allard to aid him in his research, but Mr. Allard prefers to focus on surgery at present."

"And how was Mr. Ellis's lecture received?" Gemma asked.

"With great skepticism. English medical men are not quite ready for such radical theories, but there were several attendees, myself included, who enjoyed the lecture and were interested in hearing these new theories."

Gemma sighed dejectedly. "I would have loved to attend the lecture," she confessed. "This topic is of great interest to me."

Women were not permitted at the Royal Academy of Surgeons, not even as guests, so there was no way she could ever learn anything firsthand. All her knowledge was funneled through Colin and depended on what he felt was appropriate to share.

"You can, actually," Colin said, taking her by surprise. "Mr. Ellis's lecture at the RCS was exclusively for his colleagues, but he will also be presenting his findings at the Westminster Hospital tomorrow morning. I can bring you as my guest."

A schedule of upcoming surgeries and lectures was posted at the Royal College of Surgeons daily, and any surgeon or medical student could attend an event they were interested in, regardless of their affiliation. It was a way for the students to gain exposure to multiple lecturers and observe a variety of operating techniques. Gemma didn't think a woman had ever attended a lecture or a surgery, but as Colin's guest she would be permitted inside, if not exactly welcomed.

"Would you really do that for me?" she exclaimed excitedly.

He smiled indulgently. "There's no harm in you attending a talk, but I wouldn't dare bring you to an operating theater, so don't even ask."

"What time is the lecture scheduled for? I asked Poppy to look after your mother for a few hours," Gemma said wistfully. "I have an errand I need to run."

"The lecture is scheduled for eight o'clock and should last about forty-five minutes, with fifteen minutes allocated for questions. You should be back in time."

"And you wouldn't mind going again?"

"I didn't have an opportunity to speak to Mr. Ellis after the talk, and I have a few questions I would like to put to him."

"What sort of questions?" she asked.

"I'm intrigued by the idea that an anomaly can be caused by a hematological mutation, and I would be deeply interested in a comparative study of the blood between a normal and an afflicted specimen, but I don't expect one will ever be carried out in England, at least not in my lifetime. You see, sometimes science goes too far, but at other times, it doesn't go far enough," Colin observed. "What Burke and Hare did was truly unconscionable, but, believe it or not, some good has come from their actions."

"What good can possibly come from murdering innocent people?"

"The surgeon, Mr. Knox, used the bodies Burke and Hare had obtained to conduct public dissections. He sometimes performed two autopsies a day and drew as many as four hundred students to his lectures. The students were able to learn by watching, not simply by reading outdated texts. Knox's lectures allowed the current generation of surgeons to acquire practical knowledge and attempt new techniques that hadn't been tried before due to a lack of understanding of the human body. As it happens, a few of my tutors in Edinburgh were disciples of Mr. Knox, and they spoke very highly of him. Burke and Hare murdered sixteen people, but the deaths of those victims led to countless lives being saved."

"That doesn't justify what they did," Gemma argued.

"No, of course not, but there are men who believe that a few human lives are a small price to pay when it comes to the greater good of humanity."

"So do you think a surgeon might order victims the way a restaurant patron orders items off a menu?"

"They need to study certain conditions in order to understand what caused them."

"Even if that means murdering expectant mothers?"

"Murdering pregnant women is unforgivable, but think how many women die in childbirth or immediately after, and how many children are stillborn or die in infancy. We know precious little about the stages of gestation and what really happens in the body during birth, since we can only observe what happens from the outside."

"That doesn't make killing in the name of science less of a crime."

"No, it does not," Colin agreed. "And I will do everything in my power to help Sebastian solve this case."

"Do you know any doctor who is so ambitious that he would kill just to achieve his goals?" Gemma asked.

"No, I'm happy to say I don't, but I doubt this man would freely admit to selecting his subjects."

"What about your students? Has anyone ever mentioned tutors who are willing to cross a line?"

Colin shook his head. "Not to me."

"So, how do we find this man?"

"By following the evidence," he replied.

"Of which we have none," Gemma reminded him.

"It's early days, but I'm certain Sebastian will find the proof he needs."

"Not every case gets solved. In fact, many criminals walk free because they're daring and clever."

"Sooner or later, the person who performed the postmortems will present his findings, and then he will reveal himself."

"And how many people will die in the interim?" Gemma exclaimed. "This man can't be allowed to continue with his work."

Colin nodded tiredly and got to his feet. "You've given me much to think about. I will now wish you goodnight, Gemma."

"Sleep well," she replied, but her mind wasn't on peaceful slumber.

CHAPTER 18

Thursday, July 21

The cobblestones in Salisbury Square glistened darkly as Sebastian approached the offices of *Lloyd's Weekly*. He was glad to get out of the rain and determined to speak to the author of the article about the Pruitt twins. He was asked to wait in the tiny waiting room and hoped that the editor-in-chief would not be as obstructive as Marshall Lawrence of the *Telegraph*, but, if he had learned anything since he'd left the family farm and come to London at the age of eighteen, it was that few people gave something for nothing, so he had to be prepared to negotiate.

When Sebastian was finally invited to come inside, he saw that the editor, Mr. Graves, was younger than he had expected. He was a stout, raspy-voiced man of about thirty, who didn't bother to tame his bushy dark hair with pomade or wax his bristly moustache. Despite the early hour, a cheroot dangled from the corner of his mouth, a curl of smoke rising towards the yellowed ceiling. Mr. Graves shuffled the papers on his desk as he seemingly searched for something he had misplaced, and nearly knocked over a cup of milky tea, before he finally turned his attention to Sebastian.

"What is it that I can do for you, Inspector?" Graves asked once Sebastian had introduced himself and settled in the proffered chair.

"I would like to see the back copies of your paper and speak to the journalist who wrote the piece about the Janus case."

"Why?"

"Because I'm investigating a similar case, and I believe there may have been other victims."

"Have there, indeed? Are you saying there's a mad killer on the loose in London?" Mr. Graves seemed excited by the prospect and was probably already imagining the headline and the sales such a claim would generate.

"I cannot speak to the sanity of the man, but I do think one individual might be behind several killings."

"I will be happy to allow you to peruse the back issues, Inspector Bell, but I will need something in return."

And there it is, Sebastian thought. "I'm prepared to give you an exclusive on one of this butcher's unfortunate victims," he offered.

"Go on, then," Graves invited him, and reached for his pen.

Sebastian shared everything he knew about Holly, which wasn't very much but enough to pique Graves's curiosity. In itself, the article would hardly make for more than a few paragraphs, but if tied to the article about the Pruitt twins the story could take on a life of its own. Sebastian had needed something he could trade, but he had his own reasons for telling Graves about Holly. She had worn a wedding band, so presumably she'd had a husband. And maybe more family and friends. Sebastian hoped someone might recognize her from the description and come forward to claim her remains. And if she had already been buried, then at least they would know what had happened to her and her child.

"I would like to speak to the journalist," Sebastian reminded Graves.

"That might prove difficult," Graves replied. "Mr. Haskell was never an employee, even though I have offered him a permanent position several times. He enjoys his autonomy and doesn't care to be told what to write. He submits a piece he's written, and if I refuse it he simply tries somewhere else."

"You printed the Janus piece."

"And why wouldn't I? It had all the elements of a great story. And I would remember if anything else of that nature had crossed my desk."

"So, you don't think there were other victims?" Sebastian asked.

"If there were, their deaths weren't brought to my attention." Graves looked thoughtful. "Come to think of it, I haven't seen Haskell in more than a fortnight, which is unusual. He usually stops in every few days. Haskell is a prolific writer and pens several articles a week, some of them utter tripe, but we all need to eat, don't we?"

"Do you have an address for Mr. Haskell?" Sebastian asked.

"Erm, yes, somewhere. I'll have it for you by the time you're finished in the archives." Graves took hold of his cheroot and used it to point to a door in the back wall. "Through there. The binders are in chronological order. Help yourself."

Since Sebastian could see only one other employee, he thought *Lloyd's* had a small staff and probably relied on freelancers like Mr. Haskell. He supposed it was a way to reduce operating costs, but also rather an uncertain way to run a business. But since *Lloyd's* was a weekly publication, Graves had time to gather enough printable material to fill an issue, and if he didn't he could always print a serialized penny dreadful that would take up an entire page.

The archive room was small and windowless, and smelled of dust, paper, and ink. Sebastian used a lucifer match to light the oil lamp on the only desk, and found a binder labeled January–March 1859. He carefully examined each issue, then moved on to the next binder, which covered the second quarter. It was in an issue from late April that he came across a short article written by Haskell. The article centered on Henry Boyd, who was known to the public as Wolf Man and had vanished from his tent at Mr. Reed's traveling carnival on the night of April the twenty-first. The article did not say what had happened to Boyd, but, if a man with an unusual condition that had clearly been used to draw crowds of paying customers had disappeared, it was worth investigating, since the victim fit with both the Pruitt twins' and Holly's general profile.

Sebastian scoured the remaining issues but did not find any further instances of strange disappearances or bodies that had undergone a postmortem and been left in a public place. The two issues for July were at the back of the binder, ready to be filed once the archive for July to September was added, but there was nothing of relevance in either. He replaced the binders on the shelf, turned out the lamp, and returned to the main office.

Graves didn't bother to look up from his writing, and Sebastian thought he might be composing an article about Holly. A slip of paper rested at the edge of the desk, Ronald Haskell's address copied out in a bold hand. Sebastian folded the paper and put it in his pocket, then left the office without another word.

CHAPTER 19

The address turned out to be for the Swan and Quill Inn in Water Lane. It was a convenient choice of lodgings for Haskell, its proximity to Fleet Street meaning it was within walking distance of all the newspaper offices where he could peddle his work. Sebastian thought that the taproom probably provided a constant source of information and leads about possible stories, since Water Lane was home to numerous publishers, printers, and small legal chambers. The building stood near the river's edge, close to a modest boatyard just upstream from Blackfriars Bridge.

The rain had stopped, and watery sunshine dazzled the river and bathed the building in mellow morning light. When Sebastian approached, members of a local rowing club were in the process of getting ready for a race on the river, and there was much competitive posturing and plans to meet for a pint after the race. Sebastian planned to be long gone by the time the rowers descended on the inn.

Inside, the taproom was dim, the wooden beams blackened by centuries of smoke and the wavy panes in the mullioned windows diffusing the meager light. The yeasty smell of hops wasn't unpleasant, and an aroma of stewing meat wafted from the kitchen. A few patrons sat at the bar, but all the tables were unoccupied. A girl of about twelve was sweeping the floor with a twig broom, and a boy who was no older than seven was wiping the tables. They both bore a resemblance to the plump, motherly woman who'd just bustled out of the kitchen and blessed Sebastian with a gap-toothed smile.

"Good day to ye, sir. Are you in search of lodgings, ale, or vittles? Hopefully, all three," the woman added with a throaty laugh.

"I was actually hoping to speak to Mr. Haskell."

"Well, then ye're in luck because he'll be down in a few minutes. Ye're welcome to wait. Might I tempt ye with a jar of ale, or maybe a plate of kippers or a couple of fried eggs?"

"A jar of ale would be most welcome," Sebastian replied, and settled at one of the tables the boy had cleaned.

The landlady brought him his drink and kept an eye on the stairs until a man of about twenty-five appeared on the landing. He was tall and thin, and gave the impression of movement even when standing still. His dark hair was parted on the side and carefully pomaded into place, and his blue eyes scanned the room as if he expected to be ambushed.

"A visitor for ye, Mr. Haskell," the landlady announced joyfully. "He passed on breakfast, but I reckon ye will enjoy a lovely fry-up this morning."

"I surely will, Mrs. Grimm." Haskell smiled at the landlady, who beamed at him in return. "And I'll take a pot of coffee, if you have any left."

"Can't abide the stuff meself, but I always keep a bag of beans on hand, Mr. Haskell," she said. "I'll ask Mr. Grimm to grind them for ye."

Mrs. Grimm disappeared into the kitchen, leaving the two men to take each other's measure. Haskell descended the steps and walked over to Sebastian's table, but did not sit down.

"You have the look of a copper about you," he said.

"Inspector Bell of Scotland Yard."

"How can I help you, Inspector?"

"Would you care for a jar of ale while you wait for your breakfast?" Sebastian asked.

Haskell shook his head. "Can't drink ale in the morning. It sours my stomach, but thank you." He pulled out a chair and sat down, his expression quizzical. "So, what's this about, then?"

"I'm investigating the murders of two women, who were drowned, then autopsied and dumped. My neighbor directed me to an article you had written about—"

"The Pruitt twins," Haskell cut in.

"Yes, there appears to be a connection."

Haskell's cool indifference instantly turned into keen interest, and his gaze fixed on Sebastian as he unabashedly studied him, and no doubt formulated an opinion on his competence.

"I stopped by the offices of *Lloyd's Weekly*," Sebastian said, "and came across another of your articles, about the Wolf Man, who vanished from his tent." Haskell nodded in acknowledgement but remained silent. "The story was never followed up. Do you know what became of Henry Boyd? I expect you've looked into his disappearance."

"I have," Haskell admitted with some reluctance.

"I take it Mr. Boyd did not meet with a similar end to the Pruitt twins."

Haskell shook his head, and his lip curled with derision. "The Wolf Man was a fake. He was some poor boy Reed picked up on the street. Reed used an adhesive paste to attach patches of hair to the boy's face and hands. Henry was happy enough to prowl his cage in a loincloth and growl at the spectators as long as he got a warm bed and daily meals, but once he got older he found that he couldn't simply leave, since Mr. Reed was afraid Henry would reveal the truth of his profitable attraction and drive him into bankruptcy."

"So Henry ran away?" Sebastian asked, disappointed that Henry Boyd wasn't connected to the investigation but also glad to hear that the lad hadn't been murdered.

"He didn't, actually," Haskell said. "He was abducted. Two men took him to a stable yard, where they tried to drown him in a horse trough. As a result of their efforts, the hair came off his face, and they realized that he was nothing more than your average adolescent boy."

"So they let him go?"

"Not before they gave him a thorough beating and threatened to gut him if he ever told anyone what had happened to him. Henry took his opportunity and ran for it."

"And how do you know this, Mr. Haskell? Surely the boy did not report to you after he had been kidnapped and beaten."

Haskell smiled, revealing slightly crooked teeth. "I don't know if you are aware, Inspector, but traveling shows cannot simply set up where they please. They require a performance license, which can be obtained from the parish council or the metropolitan board, and the Metropolitan Police Act of 1839 granted the police the right to regulate public gatherings and to inspect show grounds, most especially when dangerous animals are displayed."

"Yes, I'm aware," Sebastian replied. "And am I to assume that you have made useful connections with individuals who can inform you if something goes awry?"

"You assume correctly. As a journalist, I need to be where the stories are, and I cannot wander the streets in search of a newsworthy catastrophe. I have friends at several police stations, who notify me when there's a lead worth investigating."

"Fair enough, but how do you know what happened to Henry Boyd?"

"Henry reported the kidnapping to the Bridewell station."

"And I wouldn't have heard about it because Bridewell is part of the City of London Police," Sebastian concluded.

"Precisely. The duty sergeant is an acquaintance of mine and told me what happened but made me promise not to write about Henry. He's got a kind heart, said the lad deserved a fresh start after the way he'd been exploited since he was a child."

"Where is he now?"

Haskell grinned sheepishly. "At Bridewell. He's their youngest recruit."

"And has Mr. Reed not tried to get him back? Surely he would have spotted him in Smithfield."

"Mr. Reed has a new attraction—the Monkey Boy of the Serengeti. Reed found an abandoned Negro infant at the docks and made good use of him. I reckon once the child gets older, the name of the attraction will change to reflect his size. But cruel as it might seem, the child is actually lucky," Haskell mused. "He would have died of starvation or exposure had Reed not taken him in. At least now he has a chance at life, like Henry Boyd."

"True, I suppose," Sebastian agreed. "Did you see the bodies of the Pruitt twins?"

Haskell nodded, and the smile slid off his face. "It was a grim sight."

"Do you believe they were murdered?"

"Undoubtedly. Murdered, dissected, and thrown away like trash."

"Any guess to the cause of death?"

"There were no obvious wounds aside from the postmortem scars, but when the bodies were lifted—and it was an awkward business, you understand—a bit of water leaked from Silas's mouth."

The same as Mr. Stubbs had noticed with Holly. It seemed odd to Sebastian that the surgeon who performed the autopsy would not drain the water from his victims' lungs, but perhaps he'd had no interest in their lungs if they were normally developed. If the victims had been chosen for their uniqueness, the surgeon might only focus on those attributes that made them different from the average corpse. Holly's lungs were child-sized, according to Colin, but they were in proportion to her body, so seemingly of no interest to the individual who had autopsied her.

"Mr. Haskell, why do you suppose the bodies were dumped close to where they were taken from?" Sebastian asked.

"Perhaps it's an act of atonement," Haskell theorized.

"How so?"

"I doubt the men who kidnapped and murdered these poor souls are the same ones who carried out the postmortems. They were probably instructed to dispose of the corpse once it was no longer of use," the journalist replied. "Perhaps leaving them where they might be discovered and identified was a way to ensure they received a proper burial and let their families know what happened to them."

That made a sort of sense but clearly didn't apply to Holly, whose body had been tossed off the bridge.

"There will be more victims," Haskell said. "Whoever is doing this got a taste for it, and they have a goal in mind, I am sure. They will not stop until their mission is accomplished."

"I wholeheartedly agree with you, Mr. Haskell," Sebastian said. "Unfortunately, I have precious little to go on in order to stop them."

"So, what will you do, Inspector?"

"I'm going to speak to Henry Boyd. Perhaps he remembers something that might prove useful." Sebastian pushed away from the table. “Enjoy your breakfast, Mr. Haskell, and please contact me if you hear of any similar incidents.”

“I will,” Haskell promised, but, even if the journalist kept his word, the summons would come too late to save the next mark.

CHAPTER 20

The butterflies in Gemma's belly had morphed into giant swallowtails by the time she and Colin walked into the auditorium. There were about three dozen attendees, all male and ranging in age from very young to quite mature. She tried to blend into her surroundings, but heads turned nonetheless when the men spotted a woman in their midst. Several students recognized Colin and bowed stiffly from the neck before taking their seats, but Gemma saw them making comments behind their hands as their eyes followed her progress. Colin found them seats at the end of a row at the back. Had this been a mixed audience, she would have removed her bonnet and cape, but she kept them on, the outer garments providing a sort of shield, since the men kept eyeing her sidelong when she turned to speak to Colin. They would have probably felt less scandalized had he brought a monkey.

Still, Gemma was in, and she ceased being the focus of unwelcome male attention as soon as Spencer Ellis took his place behind a lectern and addressed the audience. She wasn't sure what she had expected a groundbreaking medical researcher to look like, but Mr. Ellis was neither imposing nor particularly attractive. With his slim physique, wavy brown hair, dark eyes, and bushy muttonchop whiskers, he was entirely nondescript, the sort of man one would hardly notice if one passed him in the street. He noticed her, though, and his forehead wrinkled in consternation before he finally looked away.

Gemma once again questioned the wisdom of attending the lecture, but, once the introductions were out of the way and Mr. Ellis began in earnest, her reservations fell away. She listened intently, both repelled and fascinated by the anomalies the researcher described and how they affected the sufferer's daily existence. The time flew by, and before she knew it the members of the audience were collecting their belongings and filing out of the auditorium, and Mr. Ellis was putting away his notes and preparing to walk off the stage.

When Colin called out a greeting, Mr. Ellis paused and waited for Colin and Gemma to join him.

"Mr. Ramsey, a great pleasure to see you again," Spencer Ellis said, but his gaze was on Gemma. "And who is your *companion*?" he asked, placing emphasis on the last word as if she were Colin's pet.

His attitude was galling but not unexpected. Spencer Ellis seemed certain that Colin wouldn't bring his fiancée or wife to a lecture on congenital abnormalities, so was assuming that Gemma was some sort of paid employee, which wasn't far from the truth.

"May I present Miss Tate," Colin said. "She was one of the brave souls who went out to nurse our men in Crimea, and she now looks after my mother."

He didn't tell Mr. Ellis that Gemma was also studying anatomy, routinely attending postmortems, and investigating cases of murder with her inspector fiancé. The less said, the better, Colin's apologetic smile seemed to say when he turned to her, and she was certain he wished her to remain as unobtrusive as possible. If her reticence meant that he might take her along to other lectures, she was happy to comply, so she smiled meekly to foster the impression that she was intimidated by both the venue and the great man.

"A pleasure, Miss Tate," Spencer Ellis said, and reached for her hand. He brought it to his lips and looked up into Gemma's eyes as he brushed a kiss across her gloved knuckles. "I do hope the lecture didn't bore you too much."

"Not at all, but I do have questions," she said. "There were several points in particular—"

She didn't get to finish the sentence because Mr. Ellis let out a guffaw of laughter. "You can't pick apart a lecture, Miss Tate. It's not presented à la carte."

"I'm not familiar with that term," she said, and hoped she didn't sound put out. She was sure Mr. Ellis would not have dismissed her so abruptly were she a man.

"Apologies, dear lady," he replied pompously. "It's French. It means to pick from a menu, and with my lectures you cannot simply pick and choose what you wish to expand on."

Colin was about to do just that, and Gemma was sure that Mr. Ellis would reply considerately to his every question, but she could hardly call the man out on his rudeness. "Forgive me," she replied. "I must have misunderstood the purpose of this presentation."

Mr. Ellis smiled back, but there was no amusement in his eyes, only irritation. He turned away, effectively shutting Gemma out of the conversation. Thus dismissed, she had no alternative but to let the men talk. She found a seat far enough from the lectern that she wouldn't look like she was eavesdropping on the conversation.

She looked up when a man she hadn't noticed at the lecture approached and stood before her. He was tall and broad, and his curling fair hair fell into the bluest eyes Gemma had ever seen. He had enviable bone structure and wore a pencil moustache that seemed to accentuate his full lips and square chin.

"Please excuse my colleague's boorish behavior," the man said, and she instantly understood whom she was speaking to. The man's French accent wasn't so thick that he was difficult to understand; rather, it made him sound foreign and debonair. "François Allard at your service," he said with a courteous bow.

"Gemma Tate."

"Enchanté, Miss Tate. May I?" He pointed to the seat next to her.

"Of course."

"Personally, I find it refreshing to see a female face at one of these lectures. What did you think of Mr. Ellis's address?" Mr. Allard asked once he'd settled next to Gemma.

"I found it thought-provoking," she replied truthfully.

"Mr. Ellis is very dedicated to his research and takes great interest in anyone he finds worthy of study."

"Such as?" Gemma asked carefully.

"Many people are born with disabilities, madame, both physical and mental. It is a great shame that our countries do not show an interest in either helping these people or studying their conditions in order to prevent them in others."

"Do you believe they are preventable?"

Mr. Allard smiled indulgently, as if Gemma were an adorable child who had just asked a clever question.

"That is what Mr. Ellis is trying to figure out. Me, I would hazard a guess that many congenital conditions cannot be eradicated and the only way for an afflicted individual to avoid passing them on to their children is to not procreate, but there are some conditions that might be prevented as a result of further study."

"What sort of conditions do you think can be treated?" she asked.

"I don't believe physical afflictions can be foreseen or reversed, but madness is something that might be prevented with the appropriate tools."

"And what would be the appropriate tools?"

"Some individuals are more emotionally fragile than others, do you not agree?" Mr. Allard did not wait for Gemma to answer. "Perhaps if they are treated with more patience and understanding, they might not suffer a nervous collapse should a situation that's beyond their control drive them to the point of madness. A British surgeon, Walter Cooper Dendy, introduced the term 'psychotherapy' in 1853. He believes that a healer can have a beneficial influence on the sufferer through helpful suggestion."

"And do you think such therapy can truly help a person who's predisposed to madness?" Gemma asked.

"I think it can perhaps help in those whose affliction is mild."

"And are you currently conducting your own research, Mr. Allard?"

"No," he replied with a slow smile. "I'm a guest in your country and not a particularly welcome one. Despite our countries' brief alliance during the Crimean War, the English and the French are still deeply suspicious of each other and do not seek to engage in joint scientific research. As long as I'm on sufferance here at the hospital, I perform a service I'm tasked with and spend the rest of my time with my beautiful fiancée."

"When is the wedding to be?" Gemma asked, suddenly eager to confide in Mr. Allard that she too was getting married.

"The fourth of September, at St. Gabriel's Church in Pimlico. It will be followed by a modest wedding breakfast hosted by my future mother-in-law."

"St. Gabriel's is lovely," she exclaimed. "And new. It was completed only a few years ago."

Mr. Allard's gaze betrayed his sadness. "I had hoped to get married in the church I was baptized in and attended all my life, but unless Beatrice converts to Catholicism our union will not be sanctioned by the diocese."

"And the vicar of St. Gabriel's has not raised objections to the marriage?"

"According to the Marriage Act of 1836, interfaith couples can only marry in a civil service, but an Anglican priest can perform the ceremony if the banns are read and a special license has been granted. Reverend Lewis has known Beatrice her whole life, and although he thinks I'm a poor choice of husband he has agreed to perform the ceremony as a favor to Beatrice and her mother."

"I'm sorry. That must be difficult," Gemma said, imagining all the obstacles an interfaith couple would have to overcome.

"Life is difficult, Miss Tate, but love should never be hard. And I love Beatrice with all my heart. To me, religion is simply the many different ways we choose to worship Our Lord. None of them wrong, all of them right."

"I suppose that makes it easier."

"It does, and Beatrice has no objection to settling in my hometown."

Gemma was just about to ask where that might be when Colin and Mr. Ellis came over to join them.

"Thank you for keeping Miss Tate company, Mr. Allard," Colin said, and shot her an apologetic look.

"It was my pleasure," Allard replied, and the smile he gave Gemma was warm and genuine. "We enjoyed a most stimulating discussion."

Mr. Ellis looked doubtful, but Colin nodded. "Miss Tate and I have many interesting discussions," he said. "She has a keen mind." *For a woman* seemed to hang in the air between them. "I'm afraid we must be going," he continued. "Previous engagement, you understand."

"Of course. Of course. Always a pleasure to see you, Mr. Ramsey," Mr. Ellis said. "Miss Tate, I hope we'll meet again, but perhaps under more appropriate circumstances."

"Good morning, gentlemen," she said, and allowed Colin to escort her from the auditorium. She was more than ready to leave, and, given Colin's closed expression, she thought he was too.

"Did Mr. Ellis answer your questions?" she inquired once they'd stepped outside.

"He did, but he raised several new ones."

"Oh?" Gemma asked nonchalantly, and hoped Colin would fill her in.

"He believes that during the gestational period, the child absorbs the feelings of its mother, and, if she's angry or particularly fixated on some aspect of her life, the child's development might be affected, and once it's born it might display a propensity for violence or unnatural obsessions."

"So, Mr. Ellis's theory is that madness is not so much inherited as acquired?"

"He thinks there are different types of madness, the sort some families are afflicted with and the kind that's developed and which causes an inability to govern one's reactions and results in mindless rage. He is convinced that the insanity shows in the subject's brain in the form of deviant pathways. And then, of course, there's the madness some develop later in life as a result of tragic circumstances, which has nothing to do with hereditary factors."

"I suppose it's possible that there are different forms of emotional instability caused by a variety of factors, but, until modern science takes an interest in a person's mind and begins to study it seriously, we'll never truly know, will we?"

Colin smiled and nodded enthusiastically. "That is exactly what I said. And Mr. Ellis said that every branch of science began by people asking questions and seeking answers."

"It seems Mr. Allard is interested in madness as well," Gemma said.

"He's a clever man, but he seems to have lost interest in research," Colin said.

"What makes you say so?"

"Mr. Ellis claims he invited Mr. Allard to collaborate with him, but Allard refused. He said he would prefer not to engage in further research until he returns to France. I daresay he doesn't feel he can hold his own with his British colleagues due to the language barrier."

"But Mr. Allard speaks beautiful English," Gemma replied.

"Speaking and writing are two different things. Scientific turns of phrase are quite specific and can mean different things if not expressed correctly. Perhaps he doesn't care to ask Mr. Ellis to check his work."

"Perhaps," Gemma agreed as Colin placed a hand on her lower back and guided her across the street and towards a cab stand at the far corner.

He handed her into a cab and gave the driver his address. "I have an appointment at the bank. I will see you later."

"Thank you again for taking me," Gemma said just before the conveyance pulled away from the curb. "It was marvelous."

She wasn't sure Colin had heard her, but she'd thank him again once she saw him tonight. The lecture and the conversation that had followed had been a truly eye-opening experience and made her realize she could never go back to nursing, not in the true sense. She had questions, and she needed answers, and today had been the first step towards being admitted to a society where she might find some.

CHAPTER 21

Gemma was going to leave for the Rose and Thorn as soon as Poppy had arrived to look after Anne, but when she noticed the shadows beneath Poppy's eyes and her sluggish gait she set her own plans aside and asked her friend if she would like a cup of coffee. Poppy nodded tiredly and settled in the parlor. Once the coffee was ready, Gemma brought in the tray and poured them each a cup.

"Poppy, is something wrong?" she asked when her friend stared grimly into her cup.

"I've been sacked."

"Sacked? Why?"

Poppy sighed with her entire being. "The infirmary is funded by donations, and generous benefactors have been thin on the ground these past few years. The governor must cut costs, or the infirmary will be forced to close. It was agreed that one night nurse is enough, and the governor decided to keep Ada."

Gemma didn't need to ask why Ada had been chosen, since she'd heard enough about Poppy's coworker to have formed an impression. At only seventeen, Ada had been hardly more than a child when Poppy and Gemma had served in Crimea, and she lacked the expertise and the audacity to voice her opinions and question the doctors. She was probably also paid less than Poppy, on account of her youth and inexperience.

"I'm sorry, Poppy. What will you do?"

"The rent is paid until the fifteenth of August. I must find a new position by then, or I will have to move in with my sister and her husband. They will expect me to work at Harbor Drugs, of course. Where Mary will lord it over me, and my brother-in-law will be thrilled to have free labor."

"You don't have to work at the pharmacy. There are other options. What about applying to teach at Miss Nightingale's nursing school?" Gemma suggested.

"The school is still in the planning stages and will not open until next year," Poppy replied. "And if I'm honest, that's not what I want."

"Why not?"

"Because it will be a live-in position," Poppy explained.

Gemma nodded. She could understand Poppy's reservations. Miss Nightingale would welcome someone like Poppy onto her staff, but an afternoon off would be the extent of her personal freedom. At nearly thirty, Poppy craved a life of her own. She longed for a husband and children. If she joined the school, unless she caught the attention of one of the doctors at St. Thomas's Hospital, where the school would be based, she would be sure to end up a spinster.

"What about asking the others? They might have heard about an open position," Gemma suggested.

Neither she nor Poppy kept in regular contact with the women they'd served with in Crimea, but there was the occasional letter or serendipitous meeting that usually led to a cup of tea and a bit of a chinwag. Of the thirty-six women who'd sailed to Crimea with Gemma and Poppy, only a few were still employed. Anglican and Catholic nuns had made up nearly half the group, and had returned to their religious houses after the armistice, and more than a dozen women had either returned to their parents' homes or got married since they'd come back to England. And a few had died, including Gemma's friend Lydia, who had been brutally murdered and who Gemma thought of often, and sadly not always in the most flattering terms.

Of the women who were employed, there was Mary Frisk, who worked at Clerkenwell Prison, Ellen Packard, who was a private nurse to a wealthy dowager, Amelia Hormel, who worked the night shift at St. George's Hospital, and Veronica Saxe, who Gemma knew had recently moved from the London to the Westminster Hospital.

"What about approaching Godfrey Price?" Gemma exclaimed, amazed she hadn't thought of him right away. "He's head of surgery at St. Thomas's now, and he always held you in high regard at Scutari."

"That's a wonderful idea, but I will have to wait to call on Mr. Price. Since I've lost my position anyway, I almost wish the governor had sacked me effective yesterday," Poppy said, "but I must go in today and tomorrow if I'm to receive my wages for this week."

"Why don't you want to go?" Gemma asked. "Are you ashamed because you were asked to leave?"

Poppy shook her head. "It's not that. Mr. Evans—one of the surgeons I work with—told us just yesterday that a dangerous lunatic has escaped from the Lambeth Marsh Asylum. That's less than half a mile from the infirmary, and by all accounts the man will murder anyone who gets in his way. Lambeth Marsh is a good distance from St. Thomas's, but if I'm honest I would rather not go across the river at all just now."

"Good Lord," Gemma exclaimed. "How did he manage to escape?"

"I don't know. Mr. Evans claims the place is like a fortress. He brought me home in his carriage last night, but if the inmate is still in the area and I have to get home on my own at the end of my shift…" Poppy shuddered. "I'm really frightened, Gemma. The streets are deserted when I leave, and I can't afford to pay for cabs, not when I will be out of a job come Sunday."

"Then don't go back," Gemma said. "I'm sure the governor will understand."

Poppy shook her head again. "If I don't go, not only will I forfeit this week's wages, but the governor will also not give me a character. I won't be able to secure another position without a reference."

"Perhaps you won't need one?"

"Gemma, I know what you're thinking, and you are not to exert pressure on Colin. I won't be taken on as a charity case," Poppy stated firmly.

"You are not in need of charity. You are perfectly capable of finding a new situation, especially when you already have a reference from Miss Nightingale herself."

"That is from three years ago, and, even though Mr. Price knows me personally, he might need to show his superiors an updated reference if he is to offer me a position," Poppy reasoned.

"Well, if you must return to the infirmary, what about Mr. Evans? Would he mind taking you home again?"

"He probably wouldn't, but I would really rather not ask."

"Has he been making a nuisance of himself?" Gemma asked worriedly.

"He kissed me last night. I didn't push him away, which as far as he is concerned only confirms his assumptions."

"What assumptions are those?"

"The ones where he imagines that a sad spinster just might be lonely enough to warm his bed until he finds some innocent young miss to marry. He's not the sort to take no for an answer, either, so I'll have to take my chances with the lunatic."

"Wait just a moment." Gemma retrieved her reticule from the console table in the foyer and took out several coins, which she held out to Poppy. "To pay for a hansom there and back."

"Absolutely not," Poppy exclaimed.

"Poppy, you have come to my rescue more times than I can count. Please, allow me to help you. It's the least I can do."

"But Gemma—"

"I can spare the money, but I cannot risk you. Please take it."

"All right," Poppy conceded. "Thank you. I will pay you back."

"Arrange with the cabbie who brings you to the infirmary to collect you when you're done. That way, you won't have to look for a cab once you finish your shift."

Poppy nodded and pocketed the coins. "You should get going," she said. "You only have a few hours until I have to leave."

Gemma hurried upstairs, where she put on her bonnet, pulled on kid gloves, then reached for her cape. The rain had stopped, but a strong breeze blew off the river, and the new cape was perfect for the changeable weather. It was cut just to the elbows and fashioned from deep-garnet velvet that was gently rounded at the shoulders but flared slightly towards the hem to allow freedom of movement. Gemma hadn't purchased many things since she had returned from Crimea and had worn her mourning weeds until mid-May, but as she had managed to save most of her wages since coming to work for Colin she'd thought she deserved to splurge on something that was not only practical but also very beautiful. The edge was trimmed with a narrow braid of black jet beading and lined with black silk taffeta, and an embroidered pattern in the shape of a vine picked out in silver thread adorned the back and shoulders.

The cape fastened with a pair of silken cords drawn through a silver clasp in the shape of a rosette. Gemma arranged it about her shoulders, then returned downstairs, called out to Poppy that she was leaving, and stepped outside. As she walked to the cab stand near St. Paul's, she felt pleased to have helped Poppy in a small way but also deeply irritated with Colin for being so gallant. This was his chance to snap Poppy up, but Gemma was sure he would allow her wonderful friend to slip through his fingers.

CHAPTER 22

Despite Tamzin's death, the Rose and Thorn was open for business. Hume Macklemore didn't appear to be about, but a barmaid of mature years stood behind the bar and did not ask Gemma to leave when she entered. The few customers didn't seem put out by an unaccompanied woman in their midst, and the barmaid wasn't too busy for a chat. When Gemma asked, the woman introduced herself as Tessa Garrett and said she'd been working at the Rose and Thorn since the New Year.

"And what's your interest in this?" Tessa asked once Gemma had explained the reason for her visit.

"I'm assisting Inspector Bell in his inquiries."

"You? A woman?" The barmaid looked scandalized.

"Yes, me," Gemma replied defensively. She was used to this type of reaction from the men, but she had hoped that a woman who worked in a tavern might see her way to being less judgmental. "I'm a nurse. I served in Crimea."

"You're a brave one, then," Tessa said. "You couldn't pay me enough to go to a war zone. Life is hard enough at home."

"How is Mr. Macklemore bearing up?" Gemma asked.

"Much as you'd expect. The man just lost a daughter and a grandchild."

"And Alice?"

"How do you know about her?" Tessa asked.

"Her father mentioned her."

"Alice is grieving her sister. She's devastated, the poor mite."

"Did you know Tamzin well?" Gemma asked. She thought it might help to learn something about the victim. There had to be a reason Tamzin had been chosen. Perhaps her death had been the result of an unsavory association, or maybe it had been directly linked to her husband and his position at the prison.

"Not really," Tessa replied with a shrug. "I saw her from time to time, but she just said how d'ye do and went straight up. A tavern is no place for a married woman unless her man is the publican."

"Did you always work in this area?"

Tessa smiled sadly. "This is my first ever job."

The barmaid wore a wedding ring and didn't appear to be in mourning, but that didn't mean she wasn't widowed. Perhaps her period of mourning was over, or maybe she simply couldn't afford to give in to grief when she had a family to support.

"I would like to speak to Alice," Gemma said, and peered up the dim stairs. She hoped Alice was up there and not staying with relatives until her father could learn more about what had happened to Tamzin.

"I doubt Alice will talk to you, but it doesn't hurt to ask, does it? It's up the stairs, last room on the right."

Gemma thanked Tessa and hurried upstairs. The corridor was in shadow, all the shutters closed against the light. Gemma approached the room Tessa had indicated and stood listening for a moment, but didn't hear anyone moving about. She knocked lightly, but there was no reply. She knocked a little louder and thought she heard the creaking of bedsprings.

"Alice," she called softly. "My name is Gemma Tate. I'm a nurse. I'm working with Inspector Bell to find out what happened to your sister and would like to speak to you for a moment, if that's all right."

Nothing moved, but she was certain Alice had heard her and was debating whether to let the visitor in. After a few moments, the bedsprings moaned again and then the door opened a crack. An adolescent girl peered at Gemma through the opening. Her fair hair tumbled about her shoulders, and her pale blue eyes were moist and red-rimmed. She was still in her nightdress, and her feet were bare, her toes very white against the dark floorboards.

"How can you possibly help?" Alice asked tearfully.

"By learning more about Tamzin and the sort of people she associated with."

"Are you suggesting that what happened was Tamzin's fault?"

"No, I didn't mean that at all. It's only that someone has been targeting women who are with child, and I thought they might have come here."

That was a bit of an overstatement, since there had been only one other pregnant victim to date, but Gemma needed to convince the girl to speak to her. Alice considered what Gemma had said, then stepped away from the door and gestured for her to come inside. She shut the door, pointed to the only chair in the room, sat down on the bed, and pulled the blanket about her hunched shoulders.

"Alice, did Tamzin say anything to you?" Gemma asked. "Was she afraid? Might someone have been watching her?"

Alice shook her head. "Tamzin was her usual self the last time I saw her." She frowned as she seemed to recall something important. "She was angry with Jonah—that's her husband."

"Why was she angry?"

"Tamzin didn't like him working at the prison."

"Why not?"

"She was worried about him," Alice said.

"Was someone harassing him? The other guards, or the governor?" Gemma pressed.

"It wasn't anyone who worked at the prison. Most prisoners are awaiting deportation to Botany Bay. Their families know they will never see them again, so they try to pass them letters and supplies for the journey. Some just beg the guards for help or try to bribe them, but there are those who use threats to get what they want."

"Was Jonah threatened?"

Alice nodded. "There was one man. Jonah never mentioned his name, but his wife, Glory, was with child. She was to be transported on the next outbound ship. The man followed Jonah home."

"What did he want?"

"He wanted Jonah to take Glory's name off the list."

"But she would be shipped out eventually, even if no one realized that her name had been removed," Gemma reasoned.

"Yes, but after her baby was born," Alice said. "Glory would have a better chance of survival if she wasn't forced to have her baby aboard the ship, and the baby would remain with its family." She was silent for a moment, then added, "Babies don't survive in Botany Bay."

"Did this man threaten Jonah?"

Alice nodded.

"What exactly did he say?" Gemma asked.

"I don't know."

"Was Glory shipped out as intended?"

Alice shrugged. "Tamzin never said. But she felt pity for Glory and said she couldn't think of anything worse than getting shipped to the other side of the world, knowing all the while that you and your baby would probably die before you even got there." Her eyes swam with tears, and she huddled deeper into the blanket. "I wish I could help you find Tamzin's killer, but I don't know anything, Miss Tate. I had no idea anything was wrong until I heard Father weeping."

"I'm so very sorry for your loss, Alice," Gemma said. "Losing a sibling is very hard."

The girl sniffed loudly. "At least we got Tamzin back," she said. "Archie Peck's wife went missing a few weeks ago, and he still doesn't know what happened to her. I reckon he never will."

"Is Archie Peck a customer?"

"He's a regular. Or was until Deb disappeared. He walked the streets looking for her, and then he just holed up in the house for days and days."

"What about his job?" Gemma asked. Few people could afford not to work for weeks on end, unless they had family money to rely on.

"Archie can't work without Deb," Alice said. "They're street performers." She gave Gemma a watery smile. "They do a Punch and Judy show, only in person, not with puppets."

"That's unusual," Gemma remarked, but she supposed watching two grown people pummel each other could be entertaining to some.

"They are very funny. They always make people laugh."

"Alice, where can I find Archie?"

"What do you want him for?" she asked.

"I want to ask him about Deb."

Alice nodded her understanding. "Archie and Deb rent a room above the tobacco shop. It's at the corner of Vauxhall Bridge Road and Chapter Street."

"Thank you."

"Must you leave?" Alice moaned plaintively. "No one tells me anything, and I miss Tamzin so much."

Gemma laid a gentle hand on the girl's arm. "I know what it is to lose a beloved sibling. It will get a little easier. With time."

Alice nodded and stared at her feet, her tears dripping onto the blanket and leaving dark spots on the blue wool.

CHAPTER 23

When Sebastian arrived at the Bridewell station, the duty sergeant informed him that Constable Boyd was out on patrol and wouldn't be back for several hours. The sergeant did specify where the constable might be found, so Sebastian decided to walk Boyd's patch until he located him. Unlike the Metropolitan Police, which had jurisdiction over the entire Greater London area, the City of London Police patrolled the square mile that comprised the City, so it wasn't long before Sebastian spotted a tall bobby with the City of London crest on his hat.

"Henry Boyd?" Sebastian asked as soon as he was within speaking distance of the young man.

"Who's askin'?"

Sebastian showed Henry his warrant card. "May I ask you a few questions?"

"'Bout what?"

"A case I'm working on. We can talk in the street, but I'd be happy to buy you a drink."

Henry's face instantly brightened. "I could go for a pint. I'm due a break."

"Let's go, then."

Henry led Sebastian to a nearby public house and found a table while Sebastian walked up to the bar and ordered two pints. He set one before Henry, then settled on a stool and took a sip of his own ale. It was robust and cool, and slid down his throat with ease.

"Thank ye kindly," Henry said, and took a long pull of his ale. "Policing is thirsty work."

"Yes, it is," Sebastian agreed. "Henry, can you tell me about Mr. Reed's carnival?"

Henry's shock was obvious. "Know about that, do you?" he asked and set down his tankard. His hand trembled slightly. "It were a 'orrible place, Inspector, but better than life on the streets. I were six or thereabouts when Mr. Reed found me sleeping in a doorway. I reckon I looked feral enough to suit 'is needs. 'E fixed patches of 'air to me face and told me to growl and 'owl and act like a wolf. I'd never seen a wolf, but I did what I were told, and 'e said I'd do. For the first few years, I were locked in me cage, even at night, but after a time, once Mr. Reed figured I wouldn't bolt, the door were left unlocked. I got breakfast and supper, and a pallet and blanket of me own, so I stayed. And before I knew it, ten years 'ad passed."

"The night you were taken, do you remember anything about the men who kidnapped you?" Sebastian asked.

Henry's face clouded at the mention of his ordeal. "I were sleeping, and then suddenly there were a gag in me mouth, a sack over me 'ead, and someone were twisting me arms and tying them with cords. I were dragged and forced into a cart. I didn't see the men as took me, not then."

"What happened next?" Sebastian asked.

"I were brought to a stable. Can't tell ye where it were, Inspector. I reckon all stables look alike. The men took off the sack and pulled out the gag. I could see them then, but they wore dark caps and kerchiefs over their faces, so all I were able to make out were their eyes. And mean eyes they was, at least on the older one," Henry said with a shudder. "There were no pity in them, only purpose."

“Could you gauge their ages?”

“The one as were in charge were much older, but strong. I couldn’t see ’is ’air, but ’is eyebrows were bushy and red. And the other one was young. Maybe eighteen.”

Sebastian waited for Henry to take a sip of his ale and summon his determination until he was able to continue.

“The older one pushed me to me knees and forced me ’ead in the trough. The water were murky and had bits of straw in it. I thrashed and kicked and was able to lift me ’ead enough to draw breath. That were when they saw the ’air on me face come loose. The younger one yanked at it, and the patches came right off.”

Henry took another sip. “They pulled all the ’air off, and then the older one slapped me, hard. Like it were my fault I weren’t really a wolf. ’E wanted to finish what ’e’d started, but the young one said, ‘Let ’im live, Ed. I reckon ’e’s suffered enough.’ Ed weren’t keen, but ’is partner said, ‘We won’t be paid for this ’un, so why take on the sin?’”

“So they let you go?” Sebastian asked.

Henry smiled wryly. “Ed gave me a kicking first, but yeah, they let me go. I stumbled out of the stable and ran, and I kept running till the sun came up.”

“What did they sound like, Henry?”

Henry made a show of thinking. “Ed ’ad a deep voice, raspy like. And the other one ’ad a bit of a lisp.”

“Did Ed ever call him by name?” Sebastian asked.

“Nah, ’e were more careful.”

“Did you see anything that looked familiar after you left the stable?”

Henry shook his head. “I ’adn’t been out of me cage in ten years, guv. That were all I knew—the cage and the tent.”

"But were there any buildings or landmarks that stood out?" Sebastian pressed. He was desperate for a clue.

He now knew that one of the men had red hair. And he was called Ed, but so were hundreds if not thousands of other men. Ed could be Edward, Edgar, Edwin, or Edmund. Or some other name that didn't even start with Ed. And the other man had a lisp. Hardly a breakthrough in the investigation.

"There were a castle," Henry announced.

Sebastian tried to think of a structure that might resemble a castle, but the only building that came to mind was the White Tower. "Was it the Tower of London, do you think?" he asked, even though at the time Henry probably wouldn't have recognized the Tower even if he had seen it when he was a child.

"No," Henry said. "Definitely not the Tower of London."

"So, what did this castle look like?"

"It were enormous. And it 'ad lots of towers. Two dozen or more."

"Was it surrounded by a brick wall?"

Henry nodded. "Like a fortress, it were."

"And you haven't seen this building since?" Sebastian asked.

"I don't venture too far from me beat, guv," Henry admitted. "I reckon it's daft, but I'm still scared I'll be taken back to Reed's."

"Surely you're too big to pass for a wolf boy now."

"But not for a werewolf," Henry said. "That were always Reed's plan once I got bigger."

"Thank you, Henry. I'm very glad you survived and that you don't have to pretend to be a werewolf for the rest of your days," Sebastian said.

"Not as glad as I am," Henry quipped. He gulped the remainder of his ale and stood. "I'd best be getting back. Wouldn't want to lose me job on account of slacking. But I do wish I could 'ave 'elped ye more, guv."

"You helped me more than you know," Sebastian assured him.

CHAPTER 24

Gemma had no difficulty locating the shop. The pungent odor of tobacco wafted through the open doorway and was actually one of the more pleasant smells, since the reek of horse manure, urine, and rotting vegetables mingled to create a rather overpowering miasma. She didn't go into the shop but pushed open the door to the right of the bay window. The dark, narrow stairs creaked pitifully beneath her weight, and the walls on either side were covered with spidery cracks and peeling paint. The landing smelled of cooked cabbage and rancid grease, and a baby cried behind the door on the right. Since there was only one other door, Gemma decided to try that one.

She knocked several times, but no one answered. The other door opened, and the neighbor stepped out onto the landing. The baby on her hip wore a damp smock, and its cheeks and chin were covered with an angry rash, the skin slimy with drool. The woman looked annoyed.

"Will you stop banging on that door," she said irritably. "I have enough to deal with listening to this one wail day and night without having to listen to that racket."

The baby was obviously teething and deserved sympathy, not anger, but the woman looked so worn, Gemma thought she was barely holding on.

"I'm sorry to have disturbed you," Gemma said. "I was looking for Mr. Peck."

"Well, you won't find him here."

"Do you know where he is?"

"At the Gun Tavern, in Lupus Street. That's where Archie and Deb put on their show," the woman said, and her expression softened. "Deb's gone now, but Archie keeps hoping she'll turn up."

"Were you friendly with Deb?"

"I don't have time for friends," the woman said wearily, and glanced at the child, who was watching Gemma through puffy eyes.

"If you rub a little clove oil on the gums, it will help. Also cold cloths soaked in chamomile tea. Soothes the area."

"Thanks. I'll try that. I can't afford those expensive remedies," the woman admitted. "My sister swears by Mrs. Winslow's Soothing Syrup. Says it got her three children through teething with nary a peep."

"That's because the syrup is mostly morphine," Gemma said. "It can be quite dangerous."

The woman gave Gemma a narrow-eyed look that seemed to say, *and what do you know?*

"I'm a nurse," she explained. "I was in Crimea."

The woman smirked. "Ministered to a lot of teething babies, did you? Anyhow, no amount of nursing could have helped those two, but Deb was a good sort, all things considered. Archie too, before all this."

"What sort was she?"

The neighbor shook her head, as if she didn't care to explain, then returned to her flat without another word and shut the door firmly behind her. Gemma wished the woman had been more forthcoming, but at least she had told her where she might find Archie Peck, so the visit hadn't been a complete waste of time.

CHAPTER 25

Gemma picked out Archie Peck before she even approached the Gun Tavern. He was sitting on the ground, near the door, his shoulders slumped and his back against the wall of the pub. His curly brown hair was matted with sweat, and his clothes looked like he'd been sleeping in them for weeks, which he probably had. And he had clearly got an early start on his drinking. But the one thing that made Archie Peck stand out on a crowded street was that he was a dwarf. And now Gemma understood what the neighbor had meant. *She was a good sort, all things considered.* Deb must have been a dwarf as well, and the woman had resented having to live next door to a couple she clearly thought beneath her, even if she could grudgingly admit that they were good people.

And now the Punch and Judy act made more sense. The sight of two people going at each other would probably draw a crowd, but the onlookers would hardly feel compelled to pay for the pleasure of watching an average couple fight; however, if such a scene were enacted by little people, the crowd would find it hilarious and gladly throw pennies into a jar, happy to pay for a few minutes' entertainment.

"Mr. Peck?" Gemma asked as she approached the man.

"Who are you?" Archie smelled strongly of gin and slurred his words, but she didn't think he was too drunk to carry on a conversation.

"My name is Gemma Tate. I'm investigating the murder of Tamzin Norris."

"Yeah, I heard about that," he said. "She was a kind person."

"Mr. Peck, Alice told me your wife has gone missing." Speaking to Archie was awkward, since Gemma had no choice but to tower over him, but he made no move to get up and seemed content to remain on the ground.

"Deb didn't go missing. She was taken," he said, and his eyes glistened with tears. "Deb would never leave. We'd been together since we were children—us two against the world. We were the only two of our kind at the workhouse orphanage and..."

Archie's voice trailed away, but Gemma could guess what he had been about to say. He and Deb must have been treated cruelly, not only by the other children but also by members of staff, who would have seen them as physically and intellectually inferior. Not that intellect mattered much in a place like that. Archie and Deb would have been put to work, and the tasks that were difficult for a healthy child would have been doubly taxing for someone with a physical disability.

"The master sold us to a traveling freak show when we were around six. I reckon we'd still be there, clowning for the amusement of the masses, but the owner was killed a few years ago, knifed by his business partner. The partner fled, and all the performers dispersed," he said. "Deb and I had no idea how to fend for ourselves, but we were dead set against joining another troupe. The Punch and Judy show was Deb's idea." Archie smiled through the tears. "She was clever, Deb was. And strong. She would give me a swift kick in the rear when I got down in the dumps and remind me we had much to be grateful for."

"She sounds like someone I would have liked to meet," Gemma said.

Archie looked up at her. "Would you? Most people want nothing to do with us. They think what we've got is catching."

Gemma didn't dare ply him with condescending platitudes. What he'd said was true. People were ignorant and superstitious and were quick to believe the worst. They might not think they would suddenly shrink if they interacted with people like Archie and Deb, but they might fear that they could be cursed, or imagine that their child would be born with dwarfism.

"When was the last time you saw Deb?" she asked instead.

"The first of the month. She went to pay the rent and never came back."

"Where did she pay the rent?"

"To the Rose and Thorn. Mr. Macklemore owns the building we live in, and the tobacco shop on the ground floor."

"Mr. Macklemore?"

Archie nodded. "He is an understanding landlord," he hastened to add. "He never threatened us with eviction when we were late with the rent, and he even sent Tessa over with some food when Deb fell ill in January."

"So, Deb would have known Tamzin," Gemma surmised.

"'Course she did, we both did."

"How long have you and Deb lived above the tobacco shop?"

"Six years now. It was our first real home. The place we would raise our family."

Archie began to cry in earnest, and Gemma wished she could say something that would comfort him, but what did one say to someone who'd lost their best friend as well as the love of their life?

"I'll never see Deb again; I know it. And I'll never meet our baby."

"Was Deb with child, Mr. Peck?" Gemma asked, suddenly chilled despite the warmth of the early afternoon.

"Eight months gone," he confided. "Deb longed to be a mother and give our baby the love neither one of us had ever known."

"I'm so sorry. Is there anything I can do to help?"

"Find my Debbie," Archie wailed through the tears. "If only so that I can bury her."

Gemma couldn't bring herself to tell Archie about the nameless woman at the dead house. It would only cause him more pain, especially if she turned out not to be Deb. She managed to get around the corner of the building before tears spilled down her cheeks and a sob tore from her bosom. She pulled a handkerchief from her sleeve and pressed it to her mouth, acutely aware of Archie Peck, who was only a few feet away and could probably hear her crying.

Deb Peck had to be Holly though. She had been with child, and the timeline of the kidnapping and murder fit. And Deb had known Tamzin Norris, and had visited the Rose and Thorn on more than one occasion. Both women had been in a state of advanced pregnancy at the time of their deaths, and their bodies had been left close to where they had lived.

Tamzin had been identified by her father, but if Archie and Deb hadn't gone down to the river no one there would recognize Deb, especially without her Judy costume and exaggerated makeup. The Pruitt twins had been taken from a fairground in Kennington, which was across the river, so it was possible that the men who'd tossed Deb's body off the bridge had either been heading in that direction or coming back. Could the surgeon who had autopsied the bodies maintain premises in Southwark and work at one of the teaching hospitals? It was possible, but how did one isolate a single man when there were hundreds of surgeons in London? Unless that surgeon was brazen enough to give talks on congenital birth defects and eager to share his superior knowledge with his colleagues.

Gemma needed to speak to Sebastian, but he wouldn't be at Scotland Yard. He was out there somewhere, following his own leads and formulating his own theories, so she wouldn't get the chance to tell him what she had learned until she saw him later today. She prayed it wouldn't be too late for the next victim.

Taking a moment to compose herself, she dabbed at her eyes, blew her nose, and stuffed her handkerchief back into her sleeve. When she walked around the corner, she saw that Archie Peck had gone, and the spot where he had sat was now occupied by an elderly beggar.

CHAPTER 26

Sebastian didn't bother to search for a cab. It would take less than an hour to walk from Bridewell to Pimlico, and he needed the time to organize his thoughts. He was certain that what Henry Boyd had seen when he'd escaped from the men who had taken him was Millbank Prison. It was the only building Sebastian could think of that had two dozen towers and with its curtain wall and moat resembled a medieval castle. The prison was a stone's throw from Vauxhall Bridge, where Holly's body had been discovered, and a few streets from the Rose and Thorn, where Tamzin Norris's body had been left. It was also where Jonah Norris worked.

Likewise, the prison wasn't that far from Smithfield or Hampstead Heath if one had access to a wagon. That didn't necessarily mean that whoever had worked on the bodies lived in Pimlico, but the area figured prominently in three of the four cases. The victims were a pregnant dwarf, a pair of conjoined twins, a phony wolf boy, and Tamzin Norris. Ordinarily, Sebastian would be hesitant to conclude that the cases were connected, but given the state of the bodies he had to assume that the autopsies were the handiwork of one man, or a group of men, who were working towards a similar goal.

The problem was that, as far as Sebastian was aware, even the ones who were similar in the sense of all being unusual had not known each other or been taken from the same area or the same traveling troupe. He could understand why Holly and the twins had been of interest, and how a wolf boy might fit with the rest, but Tamzin did not meet the criteria. Why had she been murdered? The only answer that made sense was that she had been chosen to punish her husband, who came in contact with the criminal element every day and had perhaps refused to comply with some dodgy demand. Sebastian thought there were probably other victims whose deaths had not been reported to the police or mentioned in the papers, but even if he discovered a dozen dead bodies he would be hard-pressed to find a connection that pointed him to the orchestrator of this ruthless scheme. All he could hope to do was to find the killers, who might in turn lead him to whoever was pulling the strings.

Sebastian was just about to cross the road when he spotted a newsboy clutching a thick stack of leaflets. The child held one out to Sebastian, but he shook his head and kept going, until he heard the boy's shrill shout. "Shut your windows. Lock your doors. There's an escaped lunatic on the loose."

Sebastian retraced his steps and held out his hand for a leaflet. It showed a grainy photograph of a thickset man in his twenties. The subject stared into the camera, his face contorted with pent-up rage. The man's shaved head bristled with dark stubble, and a wide nose and thick lips dominated his fleshy face. He had small, closely spaced eyes and heavy brows.

"If you see this man, run for your life. He's killed before, and he'll kill again," the boy screeched.

Sebastian examined the leaflet, but the information provided was scant. The inmate's name was Algernon Stager, and he had escaped from the Lambeth Marsh Asylum on the previous night. The leaflet did not call upon the public to try to apprehend Stager or to inform the police if the man was seen, only to proceed to a place of safety if they spotted him. This meant the inmate was not only deranged but extremely dangerous, and, although the police must have been notified, it was imperative to warn the public. The governors of the asylum had gone to the expense of printing the leaflets, which, although a responsible thing to do, was probably also a way to limit their culpability should there be any casualties of their negligence.

The one fact that stood out was that Stager had escaped the previous night. By now he could be anywhere. Assuming the man had any sense—and he had to be capable of reasonable thought if he had managed to escape a locked and guarded facility—he wouldn't cross the river but would head for areas that were sparsely populated and offered plenty of places to hide. But if he had gone the other way in the hope of getting lost in the crowds, the nearest crossing would be Vauxhall Bridge. And if Gemma had gone to the Rose and Thorn, as she had mentioned she might do just before they parted last night, then she was just the other side of the bridge.

Logically, Sebastian acknowledged that the odds of Stager coming upon Gemma were slim, but he wasn't about to take any chances, not when the woman he loved might be in danger. He jumped into an empty hansom and instructed the driver to take him to the Rose and Thorn.

CHAPTER 27

When Gemma returned to the Rose and Thorn, she immediately spotted Hume Macklemore, in his office with two men. The older man stared at Macklemore defiantly, while the younger one hung back, his head bowed. The door was partially open and Gemma, as well as the rest of the patrons, could hear Macklemore and the middle-aged man arguing. The dispute centered around barrels of ale that were too light to contain the full load, for which Hume refused to pay the full price.

"Get out," Macklemore said to the young man irritably, "and shut the door."

The man seemed visibly relieved, and muttered, "I'll see you later, mam," as he walked past Tessa Garrett and out the door.

As Gemma stepped up to the bar, she reflected that even in his grief the publican seemed entirely focused on business. That might change, she thought, when Tamzin's body was delivered to her father later today and he was once again confronted by his tragic loss.

"I can't serve you here," Tessa said when Gemma tried to order a half pint of cider.

"I would like to speak to Mr. Macklemore."

"Lord, you don't give up, do you?" Tessa remarked with a shake of her head.

"Not if I can help it," Gemma replied.

"I'll tell him you're here when his business is done. In the meantime, if you want a drink, you'll have to sit in the snug. I'll bring it over," the barmaid threw over her shoulder impatiently as she turned to get a clean glass.

Gemma found the snug, shut the door behind her, and sat down at one of the two tables. The snug was partitioned from the taproom by a half wall, the top constructed of frosted glass that allowed the light and the noise from the taproom to filter in. It was actually quite cozy, and, as Gemma set aside her reticule and took off her cape, she began to relax. Tessa arrived a few minutes later with a glass of cider and a plate of bread and cheese.

"I thought you might be hungry, and it looks like Mr. Macklemore might be a minute. The dispute appears to be heating up," she said with a shrug.

"Is he always like this?" Gemma asked.

"Like what?"

"So immovable."

The man Hume Macklemore was arguing with had to be a driver. He likely didn't have the authority to offer the publican a discount or accept less than a full payment before leaving the load. It seemed that Tessa's son worked for him or was employed by the brewery.

Tessa shook her head. "People show grief in different ways. Alice has barely left her room, but with Mr. Macklemore it's all blazing anger."

That didn't bode well for Gemma, but she had already committed to this course of action, and she was hungry and thirsty. She took a sip of cider and reached for a piece of bread.

She had finished everything on her plate when Hume Macklemore walked into the snug.

"What is it you want with me, Miss Tate?" he demanded.

"I'm assisting Inspector Bell, and I would like to ask you a few questions," she said, and jutted her chin forward in her desire to appear determined.

Macklemore chuckled. "Assisting Inspector Bell? In what capacity, may I ask?"

Gemma was certain the publican remembered her, since she'd been the one to take Tamzin's body away, but he'd either dismissed her from his mind in his grief or had assumed that she was Sebastian's companion and had simply been doing his bidding.

"I'm a nurse, and there are times when a medical examination is necessary," she reminded him.

"Isn't that why your inspector sent my girl to a surgeon?" Macklemore asked warily.

"Yes, but there are clues men sometimes miss."

Macklemore pulled out a chair and sat across from her. He clearly didn't care to be reminded of the state his daughter had been found in, but he also wanted her killer caught and seemed resigned to answering Gemma's questions.

"Go on, then. I have a business to run," he snapped.

"I believe you knew Deb Peck."

"Yes. Deb and Archie Peck were my tenants. Deb ran off a few weeks ago."

"Why do you think she ran off?" Gemma asked.

Macklemore shrugged. "Found a better man, I expect. Someone who could provide for her and her sprog. Archie is a good lad, but he's stupid and lazy. If not for Deb mothering him, he'd have drunk himself to death years ago. What's this to do with Tamzin?"

"Mr. Macklemore, Deb's body was discovered near Vauxhall Bridge a fortnight ago. She had been—that is to say—well, the same thing had been done to her as to Tamzin." Gemma couldn't bring herself to say "autopsied." Abrasive as the man was, he was hurting enough already as he grieved his daughter.

Macklemore's eyes widened, and his eyebrows lifted in surprise. "Deb had been butchered too?"

"She had," Gemma confirmed, but kept the more disturbing details to herself.

"But why haven't I heard about this? Or Archie been notified? He's been going out of his mind."

"A constable was summoned. But the individuals who came upon Deb's body weren't able to identify her, and if Archie Peck never reported Deb missing no one was likely to make the connection."

Hume Macklemore nodded in acknowledgement of this truth.

"Mr. Macklemore, Archie said Deb went missing on the first of July, when she set off to deliver the rent. Did she ever arrive?"

"She did. She handed over the rent, had a chat with Tessa while Alice prepared the crock of stew she'd ordered, and then Deb collected the food and left."

"And that was the last time you saw her?"

"Yes."

"How did she seem?" Gemma asked.

"Like her usual self." Macklemore smiled wistfully. "For such a small person, Deb was large as life. She had quite the personality. I expect when she met Archie she decided right then and there what her life was going to look like."

"And they were expecting their first child," Gemma said, and her voice quavered with emotion.

His eyes reflected his grief. "Like my Tamzin."

"Mr. Macklemore, can you think of any other women that have gone missing from this area?"

"You think there were others," he said. It was obvious he hadn't considered the possibility until that moment.

"I think there may have been. Or will be."

"I haven't heard of anyone else," the publican said. "Why would I?"

"Both Tamzin and Deb Peck had a connection to the Rose and Thorn. Have you seen any unsavory characters hanging about the tavern?"

"Plenty who come in here are unsavory, Miss Tate. That's the nature of a public house's clientele. That's why we have a family room and the snug, so respectable patrons don't have to mix with the riffraff."

"So, no one stood out?" Gemma pressed.

"No."

"Thank you for your time." She reached into her reticule and extracted her coin purse, but Macklemore waved her money away.

"I don't want your money. Just help that man of yours find my daughter's killer."

He stood and walked to the door. When he pulled it open, he nearly collided with Sebastian, who smiled in obvious relief when he spotted Gemma.

"Have you any news, Inspector?" Macklemore asked, his voice trembling with hope, or more likely dread.

"Not yet, but new information has come to light," Sebastian assured the man. "I'd like a word with Miss Tate, if you don't mind."

Macklemore shut the door behind him, leaving Sebastian and Gemma alone in the snug.

"I have much to tell you," Sebastian said as he set his hat on the chair beside him and settled across from Gemma.

"And I have something to tell you too," she replied. "I have identified Holly."

CHAPTER 28

Sebastian listened carefully, then filled Gemma in on his own findings and the theories he had arrived at on his way to Pimlico. "Unless there were earlier, unreported cases, these abductions seem to have begun in the spring," he said, "but I can't see how Tamzin Norris fits in. The only plausible explanation is that someone held a grudge against Jonah Norris or Hume Macklemore, and used Tamzin to get revenge."

"That would make sense if Tamzin had just been murdered, but her body underwent a postmortem," Gemma reminded him. "The cases have to be connected. Alice told me that Jonah Norris was followed home and threatened by an inmate's husband. The woman was due to be transported to Botany Bay, and she was with child. The man, whose name Alice did not know, begged Jonah to take his wife Glory off the deportation list. When Jonah said he couldn't help, the husband became angry and abusive."

"You think Tamzin's death might be the result of Jonah's refusal?"

"If it is, then the man in question would have to have ties to whoever carried out the postmortems on the other bodies," Gemma replied.

"Which doesn't seem very likely," Sebastian said, but he thought it was an avenue of inquiry worth pursuing. Perhaps the man did not know the surgeon personally, but, if he had murdered Tamzin and then sold her remains out of spite toward Jonah, there remained a faint possibility that her body had found its way to the surgeon. Assuming, of course, that the Pimlico connection was more than a figment of Sebastian's imagination.

"There's another possibility I've been considering," Gemma said.

She seemed unsure, so he wasted no time in encouraging her. "Anything you think relevant could be of help."

She sighed. "It could be relevant, or it might be a coincidence. But my suspicions could destroy a man's life."

"You know I would never charge anyone unless I had evidence of their involvement," Sebastian said.

Gemma nodded.

"Whom do you suspect?"

"Mr. Ellis."

"And who's Mr. Ellis?" This was not a name he had heard before, and he wondered how she had come to know the man.

"Mr. Ellis is a surgeon who spent years studying congenital birth defects. He recently returned from abroad, and he delivered a lecture at the Royal College of Surgeons just this week. He currently teaches at the Westminster Hospital medical school. Colin and I attended a talk he gave this morning. It was rather fascinating."

"Colin took you to a lecture?" Sebastian asked. He had to admit that he was impressed with Colin's commitment to Gemma's education. He had been reluctant at first, but he seemed to enjoy having a competent assistant.

"He did." She smiled happily. "The thing is that just because Mr. Ellis's area of expertise is congenital birth defects doesn't mean he's handpicking his subjects. But he might accept suitable remains, no questions asked, much like Mr. Knox, who trusted Burke and Hare and had no idea they were murdering people for profit."

"Westminster Hospital is very near here," Sebastian remarked. "It seems all roads lead to Pimlico."

"They do, don't they?"

"Including the crossing from Lambeth. Gemma, there's an escaped lunatic on the loose."

"I know. Poppy told me," she said. "She's been sacked. She's very worried."

"Surely Poppy can find another position. She's an experienced nurse. And someone we know is in need of just such an individual," Sebastian said.

To him, this felt like a sign from above, but knowing Colin he would probably hem and haw until Poppy was snapped up by another employer. Sebastian suspected that Colin's lack of initiative in finding a new nurse for Anne was driven by his hope that Gemma wouldn't really leave. Perhaps he thought she would give in to doubts about marrying a policeman, or Sebastian would get cold feet and break their engagement. Sebastian knew his own heart, but perhaps Gemma was having second thoughts now that the wedding was a few weeks away, and had shared her misgivings with Colin.

Much as he hated to consider the possibility, he would have second thoughts about marrying someone whose spouse had been murdered as a result of his actions. Gemma was the bravest woman he had ever met, but she wasn't foolhardy, and nor did she have a death wish, which was why he had to give her the space to examine her feelings and arrive at her own conclusions. He would be heartbroken if she changed her mind, but he would understand, and he would never blame her. But if the worst were to happen and he were to lose her, he knew he wouldn't remain in London another day.

Sebastian was distracted from his sad thoughts when he realized Gemma was speaking to him.

"If Colin doesn't offer Poppy the job, I'm going to write to Mr. Price," she announced. "He is sure to remember Poppy from

Scutari, and he's now the head of surgery at St. Thomas's. I'm certain he will be able to help."

"Excellent idea," Sebastian said, reassured by Gemma's desire to help her friend find a new position. "And it's a good thing Poppy won't need to travel to Lambeth in the coming days."

"But she does," Gemma said. "Her last day is tomorrow, and she will not receive her wages if she doesn't turn up. I made her promise to take a cab there and back."

"And speaking of cabs, I will see you off before I leave," he said, and reached for his hat.

"Where are you going?" Gemma asked as she collected her things.

"I'm going to have a word with Jonah Norris, then I will stop by the Westminster Hospital, and then I will have to update Ransome on the case before I go home."

"I don't suppose I will see you tonight, then," she said, her obvious disappointment music to Sebastian's ears.

"I'm sorry, sweetheart, but I won't have time tonight. But I will come by in the morning and update you. How does that sound?"

"It sounds like I will have something to look forward to." Gemma smiled up at him. "Is there anything I can do to help in the meantime?" she asked as Sebastian held the door open for her and she stepped out of the snug.

"You can go home and stay inside, where it's safe," he replied.

For once, Gemma didn't argue. Sebastian felt a sense of relief when she got into the cab, and he gave the driver Colin's address.

"Don't stop for anyone, and make certain she's safely inside before you leave," he told the cabbie.

"As ye say, guv," the man replied with a knowing grin. "I'll see yer lady safe."

CHAPTER 29

When Gemma arrived home, Poppy was waiting in the parlor with Anne, who was sitting in her favorite chair, staring vacantly out the window. Anne was in her dressing gown, her hair woven into a loose plait, but she had come downstairs, which was a significant step in her recovery.

"Well done," Gemma said.

Poppy grinned. "I promised her cake if she came downstairs."

"And did you deliver?"

Poppy nodded. "I asked Paul to fetch a slice of cake from the bakery."

Gemma hoped Poppy hadn't spent the money she had given her for a cab on the cake, but she could hardly ask.

"Hello." Mrs. Ramsey had turned away from the window and was looking at Gemma as though she were trying to place her. Then she recognized her and smiled. "Where have you been?"

"I went to see my fiancé, Sebastian," Gemma replied, not wishing to explain that she had been investigating a case.

"Sebastian?" Anne's brow furrowed in confusion. "You really should have consulted me if you mean to marry, Gemma," she said sternly. "And your young man should have given me the respect of asking for your hand. What sort of man is he?"

Anne sometimes thought Gemma was her daughter, and Gemma hated to remind her that she could no longer keep track of basic facts.

"You adore Sebastian," she replied. "You were pleased to hear our news and gave us your blessing."

"Did I?" Anne asked. "And who is this?" she asked, her gaze sliding to Poppy. "Are you the new parlormaid?"

"I'm Poppy. Poppy Bright."

"What a ridiculous name," Anne said with a huff. "Poppy Bright," she muttered under her breath.

"I really must get going," Poppy said. She glanced at the window. The sky had turned pewter and the wind had suddenly picked up. "I wish I had brought my cape. I think I might be cold this evening."

"Here, take mine," Gemma volunteered, and her hand immediately went to the rosette clasp.

"I couldn't possibly," Poppy protested. "It's too lovely."

"You can return it to me tomorrow. Or the day after. I have a spare one."

"So, give me that one."

Poppy still wore the serviceable cloak she'd had since her days in Crimea, and had expressed her admiration for Gemma's new cape several times since Gemma had shown off her splendid purchase.

"Poppy, I insist." Gemma held out the garment to her friend.

Poppy grinned. "Oh, all right. I will bring it back tomorrow."

Gemma walked Poppy to the foyer, where Poppy put on her wide-brimmed cottage bonnet and fastened the clasp of the cape at her throat. She opened the door and smiled at Colin, who was walking up the steps.

"Good afternoon, Mr. Ramsey."

"Lovely to see you, Miss Bright," Colin muttered, and averted his gaze in obvious embarrassment.

Poppy looked to Gemma for an explanation, but Gemma smiled and shrugged, then said goodbye and returned to the parlor.

Anne was looking around anxiously. "Why did everyone leave?"

"Poppy had to go to work," Gemma explained. "But Colin has just got home. He'll be so happy to see you up and about."

"Was Colin at the park with his nursemaid? I do hope he wore a cap. It wouldn't do for him to get sunburn on his face. And where's George?" Anne asked, peering through the doorway.

"Mr. Ramsey is out," Gemma replied. She had stopped reminding Anne that George Ramsey was dead. The news came as a shock to her every time, and she sometimes wept for the loss of her husband and lamented that her little boy would now grow up without a father.

"Well, I do hope he is home in time for luncheon. I had Cook prepare his favorite, mulligatawny soup," Anne announced.

Mulligatawny soup was Colin's favorite, but once again Gemma refrained from correcting Anne. There was little point, and she would no doubt forget the conversation moments later.

"Would you like to take luncheon in the dining room today, Mrs. Ramsey?"

Anne shook her head. "I'm not very hungry, and I'm hardly dressed for company, dear. I think I would like to lie down for a bit."

Gemma escorted Anne to her bedroom, helped her into bed, then stopped by her own room to freshen up and returned downstairs. Colin was already in the dining room, his gaze melancholy as he watched Gemma walk in and take her seat.

"I had hoped Mother would join us," he said.

"She came downstairs. That's progress."

"I suppose…"

"Colin, what do you know of Mr. Ellis?" Gemma asked once Mabel had brought in the soup, served it, and left.

"Why do you ask?"

"These killings started right around the time Mr. Ellis arrived in London, and his area of study happens to be congenital birth defects."

Colin sighed wearily. "Gemma, I know how eager you are to solve the case, but just because the man is interested in a particular branch of medicine doesn't mean he will procure subjects so he can study them at will."

"Well, why did he leave France?" she persisted.

"I really don't know. I suppose he had learned everything he could from Isidore Geoffroy Saint-Hilaire and wanted to continue his research at home."

"Is Mr. Ellis married?"

"Again, no idea," Colin said irritably.

"Why are men so incurious?" Gemma teased him. "I would know everything about him after the first meeting."

"I'm sure you would, which is why women are not allowed at the Royal College of Surgeons. They're too prone to gossip."

"Are you saying that men don't gossip?"

Colin smiled ruefully, no doubt recalling all the times the gentlemen of his acquaintance had discussed their colleagues behind their broadcloth-clad backs.

"Well, they do, sometimes," he admitted, "but gentlemen tend to maintain decorum when speaking of others' private lives."

"Do they?" Gemma huffed, but knew it was time to change the subject. "I was able to identify Holly," she told Colin.

"Were you, indeed?"

Gemma filled Colin in on the morning's happenings, then asked, "Why do you think Tamzin Norris was chosen?"

"I really couldn't say, except that maybe this person is interested in pregnant women. Perhaps he wanted to compare the development of Deb's baby with that of Tamzin's."

She hadn't thought of that, and the suggestion gave her pause. "Is it certain that Deb's child would be born with dwarfism?"

"I would think that would be the case, especially since the father is also a dwarf, but I don't believe anyone has conducted a study on the likelihood of such an outcome. Given that healthy parents can have a child that's afflicted with some sort of anomaly, perhaps it's possible that parents who were born with a disability can have a healthy child."

"Would Archie and Deb Peck be considered unhealthy?" Gemma asked.

"Well, as I said, no studies have been conducted on individuals with dwarfism, but I expect there are mobility issues that might affect the spine and the hips, and other lesser-known internal complications. I don't believe individuals with dwarfism have the same lifespan as people without the condition, but a shorter life might be the result of social difficulties rather than physical complications." Colin reached for a piece of bread and buttered it liberally. "Have you heard about the inmate who has escaped from the Lambeth Marsh Asylum?"

"Yes, I have."

He shook his head. "I cannot imagine how such a thing could be possible."

"Have you ever visited the asylum?"

"Not Lambeth Marsh, but I have been to other institutions as part of my training. What puzzles me is that persons who are that dangerous are rarely allowed out. In fact, most of them are fettered, even while they sleep."

"That seems rather cruel," Gemma remarked.

"It's for the safety of the staff," Colin said. "Such men cannot be permitted to roam about, not when they are ruled by violent impulses and will attack at will. Oh, I do hope Poppy will be safe, I should have offered to escort her."

"Even if you did, she would still have to return on her own."

"What time does she finish her shift?"

"Her shift is from three in the afternoon until five in the morning. That's when the day nurses arrive."

"And how does she normally get home?"

"She usually travels by omnibus, but I implored her to take a cab."

"That was good thinking," Colin said. "She'll be safer in a cab."

"She was fired from her job," Gemma said. "I'm going to write to Godfrey Price. Perhaps there's an open position at St. Thomas's." She fixed Colin with what she knew to be a loaded look. "If Poppy is able to secure a position at the hospital, she will probably move across the river."

That wasn't necessarily true, since Poppy had chosen to remain in Blackfriars instead of moving to Lambeth for her current position, but it was possible, and Gemma reasoned that her ruse was for a good cause, since Poppy needed to know if she should hold out hope or find the strength to move on.

Colin set down his spoon and placed the half-eaten bread on his plate. He didn't say anything, but Gemma could see that her arrow had finally found its mark.

CHAPTER 30

At Millbank Prison, Sebastian was informed that the warden had given Jonah Norris the rest of the week off on account of his loss. This was unusually sympathetic, more so because Jonah did not hold a high position and could be easily replaced if unable to do his job. Sebastian felt a brief pang of guilt about intruding on the poor man's grief, but it was important that he speak to Jonah, and it presented him with an opportunity to question Tamzin's friends, since he hadn't been able to call on them earlier.

When he arrived at the Norrises' address, he found the door unlocked. The rooms reeked of ale, provisions that had gone off, and stale sweat. Jonah was sprawled on the bed. He still wore his prison uniform and although dead to the world was thankfully not dead. Judging from the fumes that permeated the small bedroom, he was insensible with drink and might take hours to wake from his stupor.

"Mr. Norris," Sebastian called, but received no answer.

He tried again, then slapped Jonah lightly across the face. Jonah didn't budge. Sebastian slapped him a little harder, and Jonah moaned, "Hm?"

"Mr. Norris, it's time to wake up."

"What have I got to wake up for?" Jonah rasped, and covered his head with a pillow. "Tamzin is gone."

His words were muffled by the pillow, but Sebastian heard the agonizing pain in the man's voice. He knew how Jonah felt. He'd been in this very place himself not so long ago and recalled only too clearly how much he'd hated waking up, that first moment of awareness as painful as if someone had stabbed him through the heart. It had been like losing Louisa all over again, and he'd wished he'd die so he could be reunited with his wife and son.

"Do you want to catch Tamzin's killer?" Sebastian demanded. "Or do you want him to go free and live a long and happy life?"

"His death won't bring my Tamzin back," Jonah replied tearfully.

"No, it won't, but it might keep some other family safe."

"What do I care about other families?" Jonah cried. "I cared about mine, and now I'm alone. I wish I was dead too so I wouldn't have to feel this pain."

"There is life after the death of a loved one, Jonah," Sebastian said softly, and reflected on how far he'd come since those whisky-soaked days and nights when he had barely been able to get out of bed and hadn't eaten or washed for days. And then he'd discovered the opium pipe and could suddenly see Louisa again. It was as if she were there, beside him, holding his hand and stroking his brow. But the pipe had been a false friend, and it wasn't until he had met Gemma that he'd truly begun to heal.

"Not for me," Jonah muttered.

"You need to feel your grief, but you will come out the other side. I promise you," Sebastian said.

"How would you know?"

"I know because I lost my wife and child as well."

Sebastian rarely mentioned his loss to anyone. He didn't want their pity, and he had learned that it was best to keep one's sorrows as well as joys to oneself. But he didn't mind telling Jonah if it would help the younger man get through this terrible time.

Jonah threw off the pillow and sat up. Though he was bleary-eyed and his face was creased, there was a new awareness in his gaze.

"You did?" he asked.

Sebastian nodded. "Nearly four years ago. My wife was murdered. She was with child, just like your Tamzin."

"Was she…?" Jonah couldn't bear to say the words, but Sebastian knew what he meant.

"No, she wasn't autopsied, but she suffered a long, agonizing death, and died all alone. Her hand had been reaching for the door—her final hope of getting help."

Sebastian nearly choked on the words, but, although the memory of those days still had the power to wound him, there was now a little distance that had come with time and forgiveness. He didn't forgive the man who'd murdered Louisa to get back at Sebastian, not even in death. Sebastian had knocked him senseless and taken him outside the city walls, where he'd gutted the man like a fish and buried him in a pile of shit. But he had managed, if not to forgive himself, then at least to acknowledge that there was nothing more he could do and that Louisa would want him to be happy and live out what was left of his life with someone who loved him.

"Jonah, you will love again," he said softly. "If you let someone in."

Jonah nodded dumbly. Sebastian knew he couldn't see this painless future he spoke of, but also that the man wanted to believe that his pain would lessen and that he might even be willing to entertain the idea of a new family at some point in the future.

"I need to ask you about Glory," Sebastian said. He'd done his best to help Jonah, but this was as much comfort as he was willing to offer, especially when he had several murders to solve and time was getting away from him.

"Glory who?" Jonah stared at him in incomprehension.

"The expectant inmate who was sent to Botany Bay. I was told her husband had threatened you."

Jonah stood up abruptly, walked to the window, and opened it to allow in a welcome gust of fresh air. "You think that's relevant?"

"It may be."

Jonah's hand suddenly went to his stomach, and he nearly doubled over before choking out, "Wait." He bolted from the room and exploded into the tiny back garden. Sebastian could see through the window as he retched violently into a bush, then wiped his mouth with the back of his hand. Jonah returned to the bedroom, and sat heavily on the bed. His skin had a greenish tint, and he looked absolutely miserable.

"My head is pounding," he complained.

Sebastian walked into the kitchen, found a clean cup, and poured water into it from a jug. The water was tepid and looked a bit murky, and the bread he found was stale, but it was all there was. He carried the cup and a slice of bread into the bedroom and handed them to Jonah.

"The bread will soak up the bile," he said when Jonah gave him a puzzled look.

"Ta," the other man said once he'd drained the cup, and swallowed a few bites of bread, before setting both on the bedside table.

"Tell me about Glory."

Jonah exhaled heavily and nodded. "I remember her now. She was hardly more than a child. Sixteen, if that much."

"What was her crime?" Sebastian asked.

"Assault. She pushed her employer."

"Were there any mitigating circumstances?"

"Does it matter?" Jonah asked. "You know how these things go. It's the word of a gentleman against a helpless girl. He likely tried it on with her, and she rejected him, but the magistrates don't give a toss. If he laid his hands on her, they believed it was his God-given right. But Glory laid a hand on him, so she was judged guilty of assault. She fought back, and she was sentenced to transportation."

"And her husband? What was his name?"

"Toby Cates. He was just a boy himself. Couldn't have been a day over eighteen. He was distraught. He begged me to take Glory's name off the list, but I couldn't do that, could I? For one, I'd lose my job if the warden ever found out, and for another, Glory would get shipped off anyway."

"What did Toby threaten you with?"

"He said he'd teach me what it meant to lose my family," Jonah said with a sad smile. "And now I know."

"Did he mean it?" Sebastian asked.

"I thought it was just his grief talking, so I didn't pay him any mind."

Sebastian didn't think that was quite true, since Jonah had told Tamzin about it, and she had in turn told her little sister. Jonah must have been worried, or perhaps he'd felt bad for the condemned pair and had shared his feelings with his wife. Sebastian wondered what Tamzin had advised him to do. Probably nothing, since the loss of his position could mean financial ruin for them just when they had a child on the way.

"How long ago was Glory transported?" Sebastian asked.

Jonah's reddened eyes swam with tears. "She hanged herself in her cell the night before she was due to leave."

"When was this?"

"End of May."

"Was the body turned over to her husband?"

Jonah shook his head. "The warden was furious. A suicide on his watch doesn't look good in front of the prison governors."

"So Glory was buried at the prison?"

"That's what we were told," Jonah said, but Sebastian could see the young man didn't believe that.

"What do you think happened to the body?" Sebastian asked.

Jonah licked his lips nervously. "I heard there was an anatomist who came asking after bodies."

"Any bodies?"

Jonah shrugged. "I don't know, but if he was offering a fair price I wouldn't put it past the warden to make a little extra on the side."

That didn't sound like the same person who'd given Jonah several days off to nurse his grief, but perhaps the time off wasn't for Jonah's benefit but for the sake of appearances. If he turned up drunk or couldn't carry out his duties, the warden would look ineffectual before his superiors, who likely knew nothing of the trade in fresh corpses.

"Do you know anything about this anatomist?" Sebastian asked.

"I heard he was from the Westminster, but I don't know his name." Jonah chuckled mirthlessly. "And don't go asking the warden. He'll never admit to anything, and if he finds out it was me that told you it'll be my body on the slab."

"The warden won't hear it from me," Sebastian said. It was an easy promise to make, since he knew Jonah to be right. "Where can I find Toby Cates?"

Jonah made a show of thinking, then seemed to bring up the information. "He works at a livery at the junction of Grosvenor Road and Warwick Street."

"So, he's local," Sebastian said, surprised that the husband of an inmate was based so close to the prison.

"He wasn't before Glory was sentenced, but then he moved to be near her. I don't know if he's still in the area. I haven't seen him."

"Do you have any family besides the Macklemores?"

Jonah nodded. "My mother and sister live in Camden Town."

"Then do yourself a favor and go and be with people who love you," Sebastian said. He recalled how desperately he'd wished he could go home to Suffolk after Louisa had died, but when his estranged brother hadn't come for the funeral Sebastian had thought he could never go home again. He still couldn't believe Simian and he were now in regular contact, and he once again experienced a wave of gratitude.

"I'm not leaving until Tamzin's killer is caught," Jonah said.

"Then clean yourself up and tidy the house. Tamzin wouldn't want to see you like this."

"What would you know of what Tamzin would want?" Jonah retorted sullenly.

"Not a lot, but if she loved you, and I think she did, she wouldn't want to see you hit rock bottom."

Jonah stared at him. He probably wasn't familiar with the mining term, having lived in London all his life, but he took Sebastian's meaning.

"Thank you," he said with feeling. "But now I'd like to be alone, if you don't mind."

Sebastian stepped outside and checked the time. If Toby Cates still worked at the livery, he'd be there for a few more hours. And since Sebastian was already in Tamzin's street, he may as well call on her friends and see if he could learn anything useful. He consulted the addresses Jonah had provided on his first visit and then walked down the street.

He spent nearly an hour with June Lasker and Ruth Winn but came away with precious little. According to the two women, who were both devastated by Tamzin's death and claimed to have been close to her, Tamzin had been happy in her marriage, excited about the coming child, and not sad or worried about anything in particular. She'd had a good relationship with her father and sister, and often went to the tavern when Jonah worked late, eager for a bit of company and happy to help out if Hume was short-staffed and needed a hand in the kitchen or behind the bar.

This information helped Sebastian rule out Jonah Norris, but he didn't suspect the man anyway, not after everything he had learned. He didn't believe Tamzin Norris's murder had anything to do with whatever was happening in her life. Unbeknownst to her, she had been marked for death and had become the victim of someone who could benefit from her demise. But it was possible that Toby Cates, a young man who was angry and bereaved by the death of his young wife and unborn child, had found a way to influence the selection process.

CHAPTER 31

Sebastian had no difficulty finding Toby's place of work. The smell of manure and the sign proclaiming the stone building with its peaked slate roof to be the Premium Livery Stables were hard to miss. There was no one in the yard, but Sebastian noted the stone trough positioned against the front wall. If someone were drowned in the trough, the outer wall—constructed of brick and taller than Sebastian—would block the victim from view, and it was doubtful anyone would hear their struggle, since the buildings on either side were a good distance from the stables.

Inside, Sebastian was greeted by the familiar smells of horse and hay. For a moment, he was transported to his parents' farm in Suffolk, but their stable had been home to two tired Clydesdales, whereas the Premium Livery Stables housed a dozen sleek and expensive horses, each in its own clean, spacious stall. Two young men sat on bales of hay, their backs against the wall and their caps pushed back. A fair-haired lad was spooning stew from a metal crock. A man whose hair was as brown and smooth as the coat of the handsome bay in a nearby stall was munching on a sandwich and drinking from a leather flask.

Spotting Sebastian, the grooms sat up straighter, probably imagining he was a customer and they'd been caught slacking off.

"Which one of you is Toby Cates?" he asked. Since both lads were about the same age, it was hard to tell.

"I am," the brown-haired man replied. "Who are you?"

"Inspector Bell of Scotland Yard. May I have a word, Mr. Cates?"

"Would you give us a moment, Barry?"

The fair one nodded, fitted the lid on the crock, pulled down his cap, and jumped off the bale. He practically sprinted to the door. An inspector from Scotland Yard had that effect on people, especially people who had a guilty conscience.

Toby Cates remained where he was, but he carefully wrapped the remainder of his sandwich in brown paper and screwed the top onto the flask. He didn't appear worried, only mildly curious.

"Mr. Cates, the body of Tamzin Norris was discovered yesterday in the alleyway by the Rose and Thorn."

"Yeah, I heard someone was murdered," Cates said, and Sebastian thought he saw a spark of recognition in the man's dark eyes.

"I hear you're well acquainted with her husband."

Cates looked surprised. "Who's her husband?"

"Jonah Norris. He's a guard at Millbank Prison."

Cates's eyes narrowed, and although he looked puzzled he made no pretense at ignorance. "I know him, yeah."

"You asked Mr. Norris for help, then threatened him when he wouldn't deliver," Sebastian reminded the man.

"So, you think I murdered his wife to get back at him?"

"You lost your wife. And your child. I can see how you might blame Mr. Norris for your loss."

Cates lowered his head, and Sebastian could see how raw his grief still was, but when the man lifted his head once again his square chin jutted out defiantly, and his eyes blazed with anger. "My Glory did nothing wrong. Her employer got handsy with all the maids, but Glory dared to say no. And she paid for it with her life, and the life of our child. Tell me, Inspector, do you think that's just or fair? Would *your* lady be sentenced to a lifetime of hard labor on the other side of the world if she rejected her employer's advances? I think not."

"What happened to Glory was neither just nor fair," Sebastian agreed. "But Jonah Norris had no say in her sentence, nor could he do anything to counteract it."

"I know that. I didn't blame him, but I was desperate," Cates cried. "I had to try."

"I can understand that," Sebastian said, and he did. The poor man was visibly torn up, as any person would be so soon after losing the love of their life.

"I didn't hurt Tamzin. I had no idea she was the guard's wife, but I remember her from the tavern. She was a kind soul."

Sebastian was inclined to believe Cates, but there was still the fact that he worked in a livery within walking distance of the prison, the tavern, and the Norrises' home. It was also very close to Archie and Deb's lodgings and Vauxhall Bridge. That didn't make Cates guilty, but it was too much of a coincidence to ignore.

"Who owns the livery, Mr. Cates?" Sebastian asked.

"Mr. Brinley. Why? Do you think he has something to do with Tamzin's death?"

Sebastian ignored the question. "How often does Mr. Brinley visit the stables?"

"Normally, every day. But he's been away these few weeks," Cates said.

"Where did he go?"

"He has a country cottage. In Kent, I think. He took his family away for the summer."

"So, who looks after the business while he's away?" Sebastian asked.

"Mr. Brinley's nephew, but we haven't clapped eyes on him in days. Barry's uncle, Mr. Nader, is the head groom. He's worked for Mr. Brinley for years. He makes sure everything runs smoothly."

"Where's Mr. Nader now?"

"He took ill last night and fell down the stairs." Cates's smirk suggested that the fall was less due to any known illness and more to intoxication. "He should be in tomorrow."

"Is there anyone here at night?" Sebastian inquired.

Cates shook his head. "Mr. Nader locks up at eight. He puts a padlock on the stable door and locks the gate."

"Does anyone else have keys?"

"Mr. Brinley, his nephew, and today Barry. Mr. Nader gave him the keys so he could open up. Why are you so interested in the stables?"

"No reason," Sebastian said.

He wasn't about to tell Toby Cates that he thought Tamzin had been drowned in a horse trough. For now, it was a theory, and the victims could have been drowned at another yard or even in a bucket of water. As long as the water was deep enough to cover the mouth and nose, it'd do the job.

"Is he all right?" Cates suddenly asked.

"Who?"

"Jonah Norris. He's a good sort," Cates said. "He would have helped if he could. I saw it in his eyes."

"Why did you threaten him, then?" But Sebastian knew why. Toby would have said and done anything to save his wife.

"I swore to Glory I would protect her, but, in the end, I was helpless to do anything to help her. She was on her own in that prison, and she would be on her own in Botany Bay. If she even survived the voyage."

"I'm sorry, Toby," Sebastian said, and his voice sounded hoarse in the somnolent quiet of the stable.

Toby nodded and stared down at his hands, and Sebastian thought he was trying to hide his tears. There didn't seem anything more to say, so he left the young man to his memories and stepped outside. The sky was overcast, and he thought it might rain, but he couldn't go home just yet. He'd go to the Westminster Hospital, then stop by the Yard to give Ransome an update. Not that he had much to tell him.

CHAPTER 32

The hospital was housed in an old, dignified building near Westminster Abbey. Although it lacked the scope and grandeur of some of the newer hospitals that had been built across the river, it was a well-respected institution with a solid reputation for both teaching and caring for its patients. Having explained the purpose of his visit to the reception clerk, Sebastian was directed to the surgical floor, where he was immediately greeted by the matron. A forbidding woman in her forties, she introduced herself as Matron Rake and refused to answer any questions until she'd carefully examined Sebastian's warrant card and ascertained the reason for his visit.

"I'm afraid you just missed Mr. Ellis, Inspector," she said once he had answered the queries to her satisfaction. She could have said so before, but Sebastian got the impression that this woman liked to wield whatever tiny amount of power she had at every opportunity.

"Then I would like to speak to the head of surgery," he said.

The matron glared at him as if his request were highly unreasonable, then instructed him to wait while she consulted with Mr. Vance. She returned a few minutes later, her expression as she bid Sebastian to follow her worthy of someone who'd performed a minor miracle. She left him by the door, so he knocked, and was invited to come inside.

Mr. Vance had to be in his late forties. Even seated, it was obvious that he was extremely tall. His bony face, narrow nose, and thin lips gave the impression of someone who was easily annoyed, and Sebastian's hunch proved correct when the man instantly went on the offensive.

"What is it you imagine Mr. Ellis to have done, Inspector? I do not believe that any member of my staff can have anything to contribute to your investigation."

"Several victims have been autopsied and their bodies dumped, Mr. Vance," Sebastian reiterated.

"So I understand, but I really don't see what that has to do with this venerable institution," the man bristled. "We are and have been in compliance with the Anatomy Act of 1832 since it was passed, and all our cadavers are obtained legally."

The Anatomy Act had been passed in response to the shortage of bodies sought by the medical schools and the rise in body snatching that had been the result of the ever-increasing demand. Since then, unclaimed bodies of the poor, corpses of executed criminals, and remains donated by family members were distributed by a specially designated department of the Home Office; but, as with any law, there were those willing to break it. Grave-robbing continued to be an issue, and there were always those who were happy to pay for a fresh corpse.

"I'm not accusing you of anything, Mr. Vance," Sebastian backtracked, "but the victims are individuals who would be of interest to a surgeon whose particular area of study is birth defects and human development."

"Be that as it may, Inspector, Mr. Ellis is a highly respected member of staff who conducts his research openly and, above all, legally. It is not a crime to examine children afflicted with various disabilities or to dissect the remains of stillborn infants if their parents do not object. Our mission here at the Westminster Hospital is to expand our knowledge so that, in time, we may be able to prevent debilitating conditions before they occur."

"And that is a worthy goal, Mr. Vance, but it seems that someone has decided to expand their knowledge through the use of unsanctioned channels," Sebastian countered. "I have heard a rumor that a surgeon associated with the hospital has attempted to purchase bodies from Millbank Prison."

Mr. Vance didn't look as shocked as Sebastian might have expected. "Unless I'm made aware of any irregularities, I have to trust the men who work alongside me, Inspector. And no formal complaints have been lodged."

"Is there anyone you know of, besides Mr. Ellis, who's interested in researching inherent anomalies?"

"There are several individuals who are intrigued by that particular field of study but have not actively engaged in hands-on research. In fact, Mr. Ellis gave a talk only this morning that was very well attended. We in the medical community hope to inspire incoming professionals to study conditions that until now have seemed untreatable. And such an undertaking requires research and analysis, which for an administrator such as myself translates into funding."

"And is the hospital prepared to fund such research?"

Mr. Vance paused, then smiled thinly. "It's not at the top of the governors' list."

"Which means that if someone were dedicated to such a study, they would have to fund their own research."

"Yes, they would," Vance admitted.

"And you don't believe that person is Mr. Ellis."

"I categorically do not."

"Are there any new surgeons on your staff, or very ambitious pupils?" Sebastian asked.

"The only recent addition is Mr. Allard, who was highly recommended by Mr. Ellis and came to us with impeccable references from his native France."

"Does Mr. Allard hold a teaching post?"

"Mr. Allard is employed as a staff surgeon until such time as he returns to Paris." Mr. Vance looked uncertain for a moment. "Look, I'm not sure if this is relevant to your investigation, Inspector, but there was something of a scandal about six months ago. I am only privy to the facts because a close acquaintance is on the board of governors at St. George's Hospital and shared the details with me when we met at our club."

"Go on."

"Joss Stevens, a surgeon of some considerable skill, was accused of unethical practices and asked to leave St. George's. He was also barred from the Royal College of Surgeons, but the incident was kept quiet, and Mr. Stevens' colleagues were told that he was going abroad and would be away for some while."

"What sort of unethical practices would result in such drastic disciplinary action?" Sebastian asked. He realized he was leaning forward in his eagerness to hear the answer. He hoped this was the clue that would finally set him on the path to finding the culprit.

Sebastian knew from Colin that staff surgeons routinely made their own determinations and performed surgeries regardless of necessity or risk to the patient. Mortality rates were staggering, with roughly half the patients dying of complications or postoperative infections. The surgeons' decisions were rarely questioned or condemned, and the men were so confident in their opinions that they rarely took advice or showed any interest in learning new techniques or familiarizing themselves with the most recent studies. To dismiss a respected surgeon and bar him from the Royal College of Surgeons would require a transgression of unspeakable ineptitude—or cruelty.

Mr. Vance sighed, acting the part of the reluctant informer, when it was blatantly clear that all he wanted to do was point

Sebastian in another direction, far away from his precious institution.

"Mr. Stevens volunteered his time at a parish-run infirmary in Seven Dials. The majority of his patients came from a nearby workhouse and ranged in age from very young to quite aged. In December, the director of the infirmary informed the parish council that he was certain Mr. Stevens was experimenting on the patients and performing procedures that ultimately led to their deaths."

"What sort of procedures?" Sebastian asked.

"Mr. Stevens had a particular interest in childhood illnesses and open-heart surgery."

"Is open-heart surgery even possible?"

"It has been attempted but not successfully accomplished. There has yet to be a patient who survived. And most of the children he'd operated on died as a result."

"So, what happened to him?" Sebastian asked when Mr. Vance went quiet as he seemingly contemplated the magnitude of Mr. Stevens' transgressions.

"An inquiry was carried out by the RCS, and they found sufficient proof to back the accusation. Mr. Stevens apologized and offered to pay for the most recently deceased patients' burials. But instead of burying his victims, he had their remains delivered to his surgery, where he performed dissections for the benefit of private students. He then had the remains brought to various dead houses."

"Bloody hell," Sebastian exclaimed.

Mr. Vance nodded. He had the look of a man who had just shed a heavy burden. "Such skullduggery could not continue, nor could it be made public for fear of an outcry against the medical community. Patients die, Inspector, most often through no fault of the operating surgeon. They die of shock, hemorrhaging, or infection. If members of patients' families were to imagine that surgeons use their loved ones for the purposes of experimentation, the surgeons would become fair game."

"So Stevens' actions were hushed up, and the dead were made to disappear," Sebastian summed up.

"It was too late to help the dead, Inspector Bell, but not too late to protect the courageous men who toil tirelessly to help those in need."

Sebastian inwardly made a vow never to submit to the courageous men who'd toil tirelessly to kill him. He'd rather die on his own terms.

"Where is Mr. Stevens now?" he asked.

"Last I heard, he had sold his house in Knightsbridge and found lodgings in Pimlico. If he is practicing medicine, it's not under his own name."

"So, how would I find him?"

"I have no idea," Mr. Vance replied with a sorrowful shrug, then instantly brightened. "I do have a photograph of him, if you think that might be helpful."

That seemed an odd coincidence, but Mr. Vance was able to provide an explanation. He stood, walked around his desk to the wall behind Sebastian, and removed a framed photograph from the wall. He held it out. "This was taken at last year's Royal Medical and Chirurgical Society Christmas luncheon."

The photograph was of three dozen men, arranged in two rows. The men in front were seated, while the guests at the back stood behind them. Vance pointed to a man in the back row. "I must admit, Mr. Stevens was jovial company. I enjoyed meeting him, and I was shocked to hear the accusations against him. I had hoped they had been exaggerated, but alas…" Vance shrugged and handed the photograph to Sebastian.

Joss Stevens looked to be in his mid-thirties and was possessed of pleasing features that were easy to discern since, unlike a number of his counterparts, he was cleanly shaven. Although he was not smiling in the photograph, his dark eyes twinkled with good humor, and he looked comfortable and relaxed. Not at all like someone who would use human beings for his experiments, then dissect their remains to line his pockets. That was the thing about murderers, Sebastian reflected as he studied the group—they never looked like monsters. The killers were oft-times intelligent, charming, and even loving individuals who were rarely suspected of wrongdoing by those closest to them.

Sebastian returned the photograph to Mr. Vance, who replaced it on the wall. His expression softened as he resumed his seat.

"I am sorry for the individuals who have been so cruelly used, but what happened to them has nothing to do with the Westminster. We stand by every one of our surgeons and can vouch for their integrity."

"I hope so. Thank you for your time, Mr. Vance," Sebastian said.

"Good luck to you, Inspector. I hope you find this man. For all our sakes."

It was past five o'clock when Sebastian left the hospital. By the time he returned to Scotland Yard, he thought, Ransome would have gone for the day, which was just as well. Although Joss Stevens made for a convenient suspect, Sebastian had yet to find anything to tie him to the murders. He would wait until tomorrow to update the superintendent. With any luck, he might have discovered something by then.

CHAPTER 33

Gemma felt deep sadness settle over her shoulders like a mantle once she had bid Colin goodnight and retired to her room. As she prepared for bed, her thoughts kept returning to Tamzin and Deb. Two young women, each expecting her first baby and looking forward to life as a family of three. Gemma understood the odds—either of them could have died in childbirth or delivered a stillborn—but in her mind they would have lived happily ever after had they not come to the attention of their killers.

And what of the Pruitt twins? Would they have lived happily? Perhaps not, but the boys had made it to adolescence, and, although Gemma couldn't begin to imagine the realities of their life, they must have experienced some joys and probably had hopes for the future. It galled her to think that someone had seen them as nothing more than subjects, disposable people not worthy of consideration. But were all people not disposable to some degree? Mabel had been thrown over by Jacob, and Poppy had been dismissed from her job without adequate warning. Any one of them could die at any time, and the only thing that mattered was the present, the right now.

These morbid thoughts brought Gemma back to her own predicament. She had promised Colin that she would remain in his employ until the end of August, but perhaps she had been hasty in agreeing to his request. He seemed in no hurry to find a replacement, and, although Gemma wanted to be there for Anne and help Colin in any way she could, she was also beginning to feel like a hostage. At this juncture, Colin was the only impediment to her marriage, but she couldn't go back on her word. It would be selfish and unprofessional. She had hoped that he would find a new nurse and release Gemma from her commitment, but since she had named the first of September as her wedding day, he saw no reason to rush. And there was still no guarantee he'd offer the job to Poppy.

Another six weeks until the wedding. The days stretched before her like a barren landscape, with nary a comforting rest stop in sight, only endless emptiness spread beneath a vast, stormy sky. Anything could happen in six weeks. Six weeks ago, Tamzin and Deb had been alive. Six weeks ago, Sebastian and Gemma hadn't been betrothed. Six weeks ago, Mabel had thought she might have a different future.

Gemma's chest constricted with anxiety, and she desperately wished she could share her fears with Sebastian, but she could hardly turn up at the boarding house two nights in a row. The Quinces had already pointed out that her forwardness bordered on impropriety, and she didn't want Sebastian to think the same. She would have to wait until she saw him tomorrow, possibly even until the case was closed, to discuss her frustrations. And what was the sense of rushing things when they didn't even have a home to go to? Some days it felt like they would be apart forever, going to their respective abodes—she couldn't refer to them as homes, since she and Sebastian were nothing more than lodgers—and getting into bed alone each night. At least Sebastian had Gustav. All Gemma had was a book to keep her company until she felt tired enough to fall asleep.

What joy it would be not to have to part every day, she thought as she climbed into bed, reached for her current read, then set it back on the bedside table. To be able to have supper together, to talk, and to touch without having to mind their audience. To retire together and fall asleep in each other's arms, their bodies stripped of the layers of fabric that separated them during the day. Such racy thoughts would have caused Gemma to blush in the past, but now they filled her with longing, and all she wanted was for her life to finally begin. She was always waiting, always hoping, and always so alone. Even Victor seemed to have deserted her of late. Gemma used to talk to her twin in her head, and he would offer counsel and unwavering support, but her brother had been gone for almost nine months now, and his voice was becoming fainter, his features fading from her mind. All she had to remember him by were a few photographs, and the gravestone in Highgate.

How many years until Gemma slept beneath a stone? She was twenty-eight years old. No longer a young woman and well on her way to middle age. And how many years did she have until it was too late to start the family she longed for? What if another disaster struck, and she was once again trapped in the waiting room that was her life until society permitted her to come out?

Gemma turned onto her stomach and punched the side of the pillow, then punched it again. Respectability and professionalism be damned, she thought viciously. She was tired of waiting.

CHAPTER 34

Friday, July 22

Anne's bedroom was stuffy and warm, the air sour with the miasma of prolonged illness. The street beyond the window was bathed in brilliant summer sunshine, and Gemma opened the window, but Anne became agitated and said they would run through their stockpile of coal too quickly if they had to heat the rooms. Gemma pointed out that it was July, but there was no reasoning with Anne, so she gave up and concentrated on getting her ready for the day. She scored a victory when she convinced Anne to come downstairs for breakfast and have something more substantial than toast and tea.

Anne had just started on her soft-boiled egg when there was a knock at the front door. Mabel had left for the fish market to get fresh haddock for dinner, so Gemma excused herself and went to open the door, to find Sebastian waiting on the step. Despite the early hour, he looked tired and put upon, and she thought he'd probably stayed up half the night, going over everything he'd learned in order to fit the scant bits of information into a cohesive narrative. She was just about to ask when Colin emerged from the cellar and came up behind her.

"Sebastian, how nice to see you, and so early in the morning," he quipped. "Would you care for some breakfast?" He seemed to recall that Mabel had left and amended his invitation. "Cup of tea?"

"Thank you, no," Sebastian said as he stepped into the foyer. "But I would appreciate a few minutes of your time."

"Of course, of course," Colin said. "Anything I can do to help."

The three of them adjourned to the dining room, where Anne was happily munching on a slice of toast.

"Good morning, Mrs. Ramsey," Sebastian offered politely.

"Good morning, Inspector," Anne replied. It seemed she had recognized him today.

Colin smiled at her encouragingly and sat across from her. "Sebastian has come to visit us, Mother," he said.

"It's rather early for social calls, isn't it?" she asked. "But I don't suppose you keep a gentleman's hours, do you, Inspector?"

"I'm afraid not," Sebastian said. "Duty calls."

"And it called you here?" Anne asked haughtily.

"It would appear so. But please, don't let me interrupt your breakfast."

"I'm quite finished. Gemma dear, help me to the parlor."

Gemma escorted Anne to the parlor and got her settled, then hurried back to the dining room. Sebastian wouldn't have called round so early unless he had something important to discuss, and she was eager to hear the news.

Colin had poured himself a cup of tea and was stirring in sugar. There was tea left in the pot, so Gemma poured herself a cup as well, but realized it was lukewarm and set the cup down. She turned to Sebastian.

"Has something happened?" she asked.

"I stopped by the Westminster Hospital yesterday and had a word with the head of surgery."

"Mr. Vance," Colin supplied.

"Colin, are you acquainted with Joss Stevens?"

"I've heard the name mentioned, but I have never met the man. Why do you ask?"

Sebastian was just about to reply when there was a loud knock at the door.

"And who might that be?" Colin asked irritably. "Perhaps Mabel forgot her key."

Mabel rarely locked the back door, so that wasn't very likely. Since Colin made no move to get up, it fell to Gemma to see who was at the door. She excused herself and left the dining room.

When she pulled open the door, she came face to face with Poppy's landlady. Mrs. Sloane wore a straw bonnet with slightly misshapen silk flowers, a pale blue shawl over her blue-and-beige striped cotton morning gown, and clutched a knitted reticule in her gloved hands. She looked anxious, her cheeks bright pink with either heat or exertion. Gemma hadn't realized that the woman knew where she lived and was instantly alarmed.

"Mrs. Sloane, are you quite all right?"

Colin appeared in the corridor, Sebastian behind him. They must have heard Gemma's exclamation of surprise and had come to investigate.

"Please forgive the intrusion, Mr. Ramsey," Mrs. Sloane said to Colin. She clearly knew enough about the two men to distinguish one from the other. "It's only that Poppy never came home last night. Perhaps it's silly of me, but I am terribly worried."

"Are you certain she hasn't come and gone?" Colin asked.

Mrs. Sloane nodded. "I always hear her come in, and she never goes out early, not when she doesn't get home until the wee hours. I let her sleep in and then make her breakfast once the other lodgers have gone. I usually eat with her, and she tells me all her happenings." Mrs. Sloane gripped her reticule even tighter. "I waited a while, but then I became concerned. What with that lunatic on the loose, and Poppy working so close to the asylum. I thought I'd check with Miss Tate before I sent word to Poppy's sister. Mrs. Harbor is sure to go to the police, and Poppy would hate to be a bother." Her gaze slid to Sebastian, who had remained silent until now.

"There's no need to send for Mrs. Harbor," he said. "I will go to the infirmary. Perhaps Poppy decided to stay the night." The urgency in his voice immediately put Gemma on guard. Sebastian was clearly worried and thought Poppy might be in trouble.

"I'm coming with you," Colin said.

"I'll get my things," Gemma exclaimed.

She had expected both men to try to dissuade her, but neither one suggested she remain at home, especially since Mabel just then came hurrying towards them, her basket slung over her arm.

"Go on home, Mrs. Sloane," Sebastian said. "We will find Poppy." He turned to Mabel. "Mabel, if you wouldn't mind keeping an eye on Mrs. Ramsey for a little while."

"Of course," she said, and disappeared inside.

"Thank you, sir. You're most kind," Mrs. Sloane said. "Poppy is lucky to have such devoted friends."

She seemed relieved not to have to join the search, and turned for home now that she had passed on the responsibility to someone else.

"Colin, you and Gemma go to the infirmary," Sebastian said as soon as Mrs. Sloane was out of earshot. "I will head to the Lambeth Marsh Asylum. Send word if you locate Poppy."

"And if we don't?" Gemma asked.

"Then search the streets around the infirmary. I will find you if I don't hear from you."

"What exactly do you hope to find at the asylum?" Colin asked.

"I need to know more about Algernon Stager and find out precisely what sets him off," Sebastian replied.

Gemma was about to ask how that would help Poppy if she'd encountered the lunatic, but changed her mind. Sebastian had his reasons, and Gemma wasn't sure she wanted to imagine what they might be. She was worried enough already. The three of them hurried to the cab stand, and she and Colin climbed into the first cab in the queue. Colin called out the address through the panel in the ceiling, and the hansom pulled away from the curb, Sebastian's cab directly behind them.

The traffic came to a near standstill on Blackfriars Bridge, and Gemma became more and more agitated. She supposed Poppy might have stayed the night if an extra pair of hands was needed or if she felt safer waiting until morning to travel, but even if that were the case she would have been back long ago. It was a half-hour journey when traffic was light, and even during the busiest time of day only about an hour.

It was now ten o'clock, and Poppy had been missing for nearly five hours.

CHAPTER 35

The traffic finally thinned, and the cab moved at a steady clip until they reached the infirmary. The limestone building was a bit run-down and had the forlorn air of a charitable establishment. There was no money for fresh paint or replacement shingles. The funds went to pay the doctors and nurses and to obtain the supplies necessary to treat the poor, for many of whom the infirmary was the penultimate stop on the way to the grave. A few patients, those who'd suffered minor accidents or were younger and naturally more resilient, regained their health, but most were so ill by the time they finally sought help that all the doctors and nurses could do was try to make them more comfortable in their final days. It was a grim place to work, but for Poppy, who'd witnessed wholesale slaughter in Crimea and had treated hundreds of young, broken boys who'd rarely recovered, this was a place of peace and safety, and a chance to do some good and offer someone kindness when they needed it most.

There was no reception desk, since visitors weren't permitted. A stern-faced nurse strode towards Colin and Gemma as soon as they walked through the door and found themselves in the narrow entryway.

"Sir. Madam. How can I help you?" and the nurse blocked the inner door with her back as if she were worried they would try to breach the inner sanctum.

"We're looking for Nurse Bright," Gemma said. "She is on the evening shift." The woman's disapproving expression sent a shiver of apprehension down her spine.

"Is Nurse Bright here?" Colin asked. He'd clearly noticed the nurse's rancor as well and was looking at her anxiously.

"Nurse Bright never deigned to show up for her shift yesterday. I expect she didn't think it was worth the bother, seeing as how she was let go. I suppose it's all right for some, if they can afford to forfeit their wages," the woman said spitefully.

"Poppy left for work at the usual time yesterday," Gemma cried. "Are you saying she never arrived?"

"Is everything quite all right, Nurse Dixon?"

A man in a white smock had come down the stairs and approached the small group. He was in his mid-thirties, and his eyes were a soft brown behind wire-rimmed spectacles. His chestnut hair was threaded with silver at the temples, and he wore a short beard. Gemma would have felt favorably disposed towards him if she didn't know that he had tried it on with Poppy without her consent and was the sort of man who didn't take no for an answer.

"I was just telling these people that Nurse Bright never turned up for her shift yesterday, Mr. Evans."

"I'm Gemma Tate. Poppy's friend. And this is Mr. Ramsey," Gemma said when Colin remained silent. "We're looking for Poppy."

Colin contemplated Mr. Evans as if he were trying to place the man, but he must have mistaken the doctor for someone else since Evans did not appear to recognize him. He was familiar with Gemma's name, though.

"Miss Tate, Poppy spoke of you often." He smiled warmly at Gemma. "I heard all about your exploits in Crimea."

"Did you see Poppy last night, Mr. Evans?" Colin asked.

"I already told them she never turned up," Nurse Dixon interjected.

Mr. Evans nodded his agreement. "It would seem Poppy decided not to come in yesterday," he said. "It was really quite negligent, since I rely on her help, but she was upset about losing her position and probably thought it didn't much matter at this stage."

"Poppy wouldn't do that," Gemma said firmly. "She was on her way to work when I saw her yesterday."

Mr. Evans's face creased with concern. "Are you suggesting that something untoward has befallen her?"

"There is the escaped lunatic, Mr. Evans," Nurse Dixon reminded him with obvious relish.

What a horrid woman, Gemma thought as she fixed Nurse Dixon with an angry look. Was her life so devoid of meaning that she derived pleasure from the fear and suffering of others? Sadly, she wouldn't be the first caregiver to lack compassion. With so few positions open to women, that a woman chose to become a nurse didn't always mean she had the necessary qualifications, or the kindness and sympathy, needed to look after the sick and dying.

Mr. Evans didn't appear to notice the woman's spite and considered her suggestion. "Yes, but what are the odds that Poppy would run into the escaped inmate at this stage?" he mused. "He must be miles away by now."

"If he's an imbecile, he might still be in the area, so it is possible," Nurse Dixon replied.

She clearly didn't care about Poppy's welfare, but her expression of reverent adoration when she looked at Mr. Evans explained a lot. If she harbored tender feelings for the doctor, she would resent any woman who might have caught his attention. And Poppy had mentioned that Mr. Evans had been keen. Was it any wonder? Poppy was lovely and generous of spirit, whereas this woman, though not unattractive, oozed unpleasantness and seemed unable to hide her malice towards Poppy. Colin had to be thinking much the same thing, because he looked angrier than Gemma had ever seen him and she thought he might say something he would regret later if Gemma didn't intervene.

"We must find Poppy," she said.

"Nurse Dixon, kindly hold the fort," Mr. Evans said. "I'm going to join the search party." He unbuttoned his smock, shrugged it off, and handed it to the nurse. "I'll just get my coat and hat. I'll meet you outside the front door."

CHAPTER 36

The Lambeth Marsh Asylum was a forbidding redbrick building surrounded by a tall wrought-iron fence topped with sharp spikes. It stood on its own at the center of what used to be Lambeth Marsh but was now flat, scrubby ground. The nearest residential buildings and shops were some distance away, and only one narrow road led to the gates, which were locked. No one appeared to be about. The façade was a profusion of architectural excess in the form of dozens of narrow windows, several stunted turrets, a tall tower, and a half-dozen arches that seemingly led nowhere. The windows stared outward with a hollow gaze, while an oppressive silence clung to the building like impenetrable fog.

Sebastian walked the length of the fence but saw no other way in, which meant that the escaped inmate had to have walked out the gates. This raised a number of questions, none of which he could resolve until he spoke to the director. A brass bellpull was attached to one of the brick gateposts, so Sebastian yanked on it in the hope that, somewhere inside, a corresponding bell would ring and alert someone to his presence.

All was eerily quiet until, at last, the door in the tower opened, and a white-smocked attendant set off towards the gates.

"Visits are by appointment only, sir," the man said once he'd approached the gate and peered at Sebastian. Given the violent nature of its patients, Sebastian didn't expect the asylum received many unexpected callers. "Meetings are scheduled by post," the attendant continued. "You can address your request to Mr. Treadwell."

Sebastian held up his warrant card and saw the man's eyes widen in surprise. "I will speak to Mr. Treadwell now, if you please. Unlock the gate," he demanded.

"Is this about Algernon Stager, Inspector?" the attendant asked, but made no move to let Sebastian in.

"It is."

"But we've already had the police here," the man protested. "From L Division," he added, as if that detail gave his argument more weight.

"I'm from Scotland Yard, and I need to speak to Mr. Treadwell urgently," Sebastian insisted.

He realized there was little he could do if the man refused to allow him access. The gates were firmly locked and too tall to climb, Sebastian had no authority over a privately owned institution, and he didn't know anyone at L Division who might be willing to assist him should he ask for help. Since the local station had already conducted an investigation, they might see his insistence on speaking to the director as interference and take his visit as a thinly veiled insult to their competence.

"I'm not leaving until I speak to Mr. Treadwell," Sebastian warned, but the attendant just stood there, seemingly paralyzed by indecision.

Commitment to civic duty finally won out, and he unlocked the gate and invited Sebastian to follow him. They walked in silence, the man a few steps ahead. He led Sebastian around the side of the building and through a low arch, then pulled out a keyring, selected a key, and unlocked a door. The corridor led directly to Mr. Treadwell's office. It would appear that the director did not wish visitors to pass through the main building nor come into contact with the inmates. This could be for the visitors' safety, but Sebastian strongly suspected that the detour was entirely for the director's protection, since no one could make a complaint if they didn't know how the patients were treated.

The director's office was painted dark green, the only bright spots the white ceiling, door, and window frames. The furniture was constructed of heavy dark wood, and there was a brown-and-green carpet. A muddy painting of what appeared to be the Tower of London hung above the mantel, the Tower captured in some distant past and during a raging storm. The window was hung with green velvet curtains and barred on the outside, and the air was close, the pungent odor of cigar smoke clinging to the curtains and the carpet. The oppressive interior made Sebastian feel like he was underwater, and his chest tightened with anxiety, making him wish he could return outside.

Mr. Treadwell was an imposing man in his mid- to late forties, but, despite his distinguished appearance and well-tailored suit, he bore the weary look of someone pushed past endurance. There were dark circles beneath his dark eyes, and a sheen of perspiration covered his forehead. A half-empty bottle of brandy and a nearly empty glass stood within arm's reach.

"Inspector Bell of Scotland Yard," the attendant announced. "He insisted on speaking to you right away, sir."

"Thank you, Bates." Treadwell gave the man a meaningful look, and the attendant made himself scarce. "Good morning, Inspector," the director said once Sebastian had taken the only guest chair. "Fine day," he added caustically.

When Sebastian didn't reply with the expected pleasantry, Treadwell drawled, "You asked to speak to me, so how can I help you?" His indifferent tone turned mocking. "Or do you have a mad relative you wish to hide away from the world? A wife who's becoming inconvenient?" He scoffed. "I assure you, you cannot afford this place on a policeman's salary."

"How dangerous is Algernon Stager?" Sebastian demanded.

He had no time to waste on small talk and wanted only to get what he'd come for and go to find Gemma and Colin. He hoped they had been reunited with Poppy, but his gut instinct warned him that Poppy wouldn't be so easily recovered. Something had happened to her last night, and his only hope was that it wasn't Algernon Stager.

"Did you not see the leaflets?" Treadwell asked. "I thought the message was clear."

"Are you saying that he will indiscriminately attack anyone who gets in his way?" Sebastian asked.

Treadwell sighed. He'd probably been asked this question a number of times already.

"Algernon Stager is as dangerous as they come. He's entirely devoid of a sense of right and wrong and incapable of distinguishing between those who mean him harm and those who simply cross his path. Unlike most of our patients, who don't require restraints, Stager was kept under lock and key at all times and chained to the wall for additional security."

"So, how did he manage to escape?"

From everything Sebastian had heard so far, Stager was no better than a wild beast, but he had to have had enough sense to plan his escape, unless some careless attendant had made the mistake of setting him loose. But even if that were the case, how had Stager got out of the building and past the gates? And how had he avoided capture for this long? Perhaps the man had a propensity for violence, but he was clearly capable of intelligent thought and therefore could be reasoned with.

Mr. Treadwell sighed so heavily, he appeared to physically deflate, and Sebastian saw genuine fear in his eyes. Perhaps Mr. Treadwell feared for the individuals Algernon Stager might have hurt, but Sebastian suspected the man actually only feared for himself and the future of his directorship.

"Stager did not escape," Mr. Treadwell admitted. His voice sounded like a mere exhalation of breath, and Sebastian knew it for what it was—surrender. "I and the other members of staff were led to believe that he overpowered his attendant while the door was unlocked and managed to get outside, but, as I have recently discovered, that wasn't quite the truth."

"So, what did happen?" Sebastian asked when Treadwell paused and reached for the bottle of brandy. He topped up his glass but did not offer Sebastian a drink.

"He was sold, Inspector," Treadmill admitted at last, and raised his glass, as if toasting his imminent downfall.

"Sold to whom?"

"To an individual who wished to dissect Stager's brain for the purposes of research."

"Who is this man?" Sebastian growled.

"I don't know. After I had the leaflets printed and distributed, Lloyd Pinter, Stager's long-term attendant, admitted to what he had done in order to reassure me that Stager wasn't a danger to the public and I wouldn't be responsible for the deaths of innocents. Once he confessed, he refused to say anything else."

"And where's Mr. Pinter now? Have you allowed him to leave?"

Mr. Treadwell's expression turned ugly. "I had him chained and locked in Stager's cell."

This was not what Sebastian had been expecting to hear, but he swiftly recovered from his shock. "Because you believe he's mad, because you need to appease the governors of this institution, or because you wanted retribution?"

"Because I need answers," Treadwell exclaimed. "Can you imagine what will happen if this gets out? The ethical implications..."

Sebastian didn't think Treadwell or the governors were particularly concerned with ethics. He'd visited several such institutions in the course of his duties, and the way the inmates were treated was not only abhorrent but utterly inhumane. Even facilities that catered to the more genteel and nonviolent cases kept the inmates isolated and locked up and rarely allowed them a glimpse of sun or a breath of fresh air. If the patients weren't insane when they entered the institutions, they went mad from sheer loneliness and the lack of hope.

Mr. Treadwell was concerned with the inevitable loss of funding and his own position, both of which would be forfeit if the truth got out and Mr. Pinter publicly admitted to what he had done. To fetter a patient, starve him, and beat him was perfectly acceptable, but to sell him to some butcher was another matter altogether and would bring unwelcome attention to the institution and the men who oversaw it.

"I need to speak to Pinter," Sebastian said.

"You won't get much out of him," Treadwell warned.

"I'd still like to try."

"Then I will come with you."

Treadwell was likely terrified of what Sebastian would see and hear and would attempt to minimize the repercussions by controlling the interview, but Sebastian intended to speak to the attendant alone and get answers by any means necessary.

"I'll send for you if you're needed," Sebastian replied. "Now, have someone take me to Pinter's cell. And don't even think of trying to deter me. My colleagues know where I am and will tear this place down brick by brick should I not return."

Treadwell nodded and yanked on a bellpull, but the look in his eyes warned Sebastian to beware. Desperate men did desperate things, and the director was fighting for his professional life.

CHAPTER 37

Despite the early hour, the deserted floor was in near darkness. A gas sconce at each end of the corridor did not provide nearly enough light, and there were no windows to light Sebastian's way. He followed Bates, who led him past closed doors fitted with metal grilles. Sebastian strongly suspected that the man had spent the past quarter of an hour making certain he wouldn't see anything that might lead to further police interference or a write-up in the papers, which wouldn't do Mr. Treadwell or the institution any favors.

The patients Sebastian could see were all in their rooms, listless men and women who wore identical smocks and appeared to be in various stages of mental deficiency. A few were muttering to themselves, while others stared vacantly into space, too far gone to rebel against their sad reality. The only concession to humanity was the small window in each cell, or perhaps it was another act of cruelty since the inmates could look upon a world they would never reenter. The corridor reeked of human waste and bodies that hadn't been washed properly in years, and there was the inevitable smell of boiled onions and cabbage that seemed to haunt such institutions.

The tightness in Sebastian's chest intensified when the attendant opened a door at the end of the corridor and motioned for him to follow.

"Where are we going?" he asked.

"The more dangerous inmates are kept in the cellar."

Downstairs, the doors were reinforced steel, and there were no windows. Lamps in the corridor dimly illuminated the dark cells. Sebastian could just make out hunched figures who sat on the floor dressed in nothing but shapeless sacks. The moaning and grunts that reverberated off the walls were no different than the cries of the caged animals at the zoological gardens, and he felt deeply sorry for these unfortunate souls whose lives had taken such a cruel turn.

Bates approached the last cell on the right and called out through the grille, "Someone to see you, Mr. Pinter. Mr. Treadwell expects you to behave in a manner that befits an employee of this institution."

Given the state of the man within, the request was ludicrous, but it was clear that this was a warning to keep anything that might incriminate the asylum to himself.

Bates unlocked the cell and was about to replace the keyring on his belt when Sebastian held out his hand. The man stared at him.

"Give me the keys," Sebastian said.

"I cannot do that."

"You can and you will, or I will arrest you, and then you will find yourself in a cell just like this one."

"On what charge?"

"Take your pick. Personally, I like conspiracy to commit murder."

"I didn't murder anyone," Bates cried.

Sebastian cast his gaze towards the row of steel doors. "Are you telling me that these people are not being murdered? And how long does it take Mr. Treadwell to notify the family after someone passes? I wager he takes his sweet time and continues to collect the fees, which probably find a way into his own pocket. You are party to that, Mr. Bates, so hand over the keys."

The attendant held out the keyring. "I'm just doing my job," he said sullenly.

"As am I," Sebastian replied. "So let me do it, and we'll say no more about it."

"I'll wait right here," Bates said, and positioned himself next to the door.

"Mr. Bates, unless my eyes deceive me, the man is fettered and there's a leather collar around his neck. Unless he's possessed of superhuman strength, I doubt he's going anywhere. I would like to speak to him privately. I would ask you to wait at the end of the corridor. I won't be long."

Bates nodded and moved away, but Sebastian was certain the attendant would creep towards the cell as soon as he was inside and try to hear what was said. He had to admire the man's dedication, or maybe just his sense of self-preservation. Perhaps Pinter wasn't the first employee to find himself inside one of these cells.

Sebastian stepped inside and closed the door behind him. The cell was filthy and smelled like it hadn't been cleaned in decades. A soiled mattress was pushed up against the wall, and a moth-eaten blanket was the only item of bedding. Mr. Pinter, who was hardly more than a boy, was dressed in nothing but a shirt that barely covered his hips and offered a glimpse of yellowed cotton drawers. He was barefoot, his hair was matted, and his face was covered with several days' growth of beard.

"Mr. Pinter, I'm Inspector Bell of Scotland Yard," Sebastian said. "I need you to tell me who approached you regarding Algernon Stager."

"I can't," Pinter moaned, but Sebastian could see the desperation in his eyes. The only thing that prevented the man from sharing what he knew was fear, and Sebastian didn't think it was fear for himself.

"If what Mr. Treadwell tells me is true, then Algernon Stager is already dead, and, even though he did not die by your hand, you are an accomplice to murder and can be sentenced to death by hanging. Now, I expect after spending several days in here you might think that's not such a terrible outcome, but allow me to assure you that once you've been condemned, there will be no hope of reprieve; however, if you help me, I can ensure that you are treated with lenience and get you out of here."

"And how can you do that?" Pinter croaked. His lips were cracked, and he was trembling. Sebastian handed him the blanket, but he didn't think Pinter was cold. He was frightened.

"I can inform the magistrate that there were mitigating circumstances. Were there?"

Pinter nodded, and his eyes brimmed with tears. "The men said that if I didn't do what they asked, they'd take my wife instead. She's with child," he whispered. "I had to protect my family."

"I quite understand, but there will be no one to protect your wife and child once you've been executed, or if you remain locked in this cell." Sebastian let that sink in. "Now, tell me what happened."

Pinter's fearful gaze slid to the grille, then back to Sebastian. "Do I have your word that you will help me? For all I know, you'll leave me to rot in here."

"I will help you," Sebastian promised.

"All right," Pinter said and sighed deeply. "About a fortnight ago, on my way home, I was approached by a man. He said he would pay me ten quid for Algernon Stager."

"How did this man know you had access to Stager?"

"He said he heard me talking to my mates at the pub," Pinter admitted. "I shouldn't tell anyone about the inmates, but I can't talk to my Polly about what goes on here, and I have to tell someone. It weighs heavy on me, Inspector."

The fact that the man who'd approached Pinter had been at the same pub was obviously no coincidence, but Pinter seemed to have played right into his hands.

"Did this man have a name?" Sebastian asked.

"He didn't bother to introduce himself."

"So, what exactly did he want you to do?"

"He asked who the most dangerous, deranged inmate was. And once I told him it was Algernon Stager, he said I was to give him fifty drops of laudanum on a prearranged night and wait until he passed out. Then I was to unlock the gate and the back door and leave. The man and his partner would arrive at midnight and take care of the rest. The next morning, I was to raise the alarm and say that Stager had escaped during the night."

"Is there anyone normally here at night? A watchman?"

Pinter shook his head. "Mr. Treadwell leaves at five on the dot, and the attendants leave at seven, after they've fed the inmates. No members of staff are here until seven in the morning. It wasn't difficult to remain behind. No one noticed that I hadn't left."

"So, you gave Stager laudanum, unlocked the door and the gate, then what?"

"I left at nine, and immediately after supper I went to the pub. I wanted to make sure I was seen and would have an alibi should anyone blame me for Stager's escape." Pinter paused briefly then went on. "I wanted to go home after the pub closed. I was so tired and scared of what I had done, but I was also worried that the men wouldn't show, and the laudanum would wear off. Fifty drops is a very large dose, but Stager was a big man and would begin to resurface after a few hours. If he escaped, innocent people would get hurt."

"What did you do?"

"I came back and waited inside the arch closest to the back door. I didn't want them to spot me, but I needed to see them. They came just after midnight and drove the wagon through the gates and up to the back door. They carried Stager out and laid him in the back of the wagon. Then they left. I waited a few minutes, then locked the door and the gate and ran home."

"Can you tell me anything about the man who approached you?" Sebastian asked.

"He was older, in his forties maybe. Not very tall but muscular. He had reddish hair, pale blue eyes, and pockmarked skin. He must have had smallpox."

"How was he dressed?"

"Like a working man. Collarless shirt, black waistcoat, worn coat, and a flat cap."

"Did you ever see the other man?"

Pinter nodded. "He was at the pub. Young, fair hair. His cap was pulled down low, so I didn't see the color of his eyes. I noticed he had a lisp, though."

"Did these men mention the name of the person who'd hired them to snatch Stager?"

Pinter shook his head again. "They referred to him only as 'the client.'"

"Is there anything else you can recall?" Sebastian pressed. "No detail is too small."

Pinter bowed his head as he tried to remember, then looked up, excited. "The older man said there was no time to get Stager to the livery. The client was waiting, so a bucket would have to do. I don't know what he meant."

But Sebastian did. The two men would drown Stager in a bucket of water before delivering his corpse to their client. This way, the body would remain mostly undamaged and yield whatever information the client was in search of.

Pinter had looked frightened and defeated over the course of the conversation, but his eyes suddenly flashed with anger. "I'm not sorry I gave up that monster to protect my loved ones. Stager was completely deranged. An abomination. He enjoyed inflicting pain and watching his victims suffer. His parents had him locked up when he was twelve. They were terrified of him after he'd set a schoolmate on fire. The world is a better place without him. I'm only sorry I got caught up in all this."

Sebastian knew he was meant to say that it was up to God to decide who lived and who died, but he'd leave the lies to the ministers. Men played God all the time, from officers who sent inexperienced boys into battle to magistrates who sentenced people like Glory Cates to transportation to Botany Bay for a minor offense, knowing all the while that they were sentencing her to death. Sebastian himself had taken justice into his own hands on more than one occasion, and he didn't feel an ounce of fear or remorse for the things he had done. God wouldn't punish him, because he didn't believe God existed. Not anymore, not after what had happened to Louisa.

Perhaps the world was a better place without Algernon Stager in it, but that didn't mean the men who had murdered him or the client who'd ordered said murder should walk away without consequences, especially if they had also been responsible for the deaths of Tamzin, Deb, and the Pruitt twins. Unfortunately,

Sebastian was no further along in his investigation after speaking to Pinter, since the man didn't know anything that would lead Sebastian to the killers. These men were smart and had managed to cover their tracks. There was, however, one positive thing to come out of Pinter's confession. If Algernon Stager had never been on the loose, he couldn't have hurt Poppy, so whatever had prevented her from coming home couldn't be related to the case.

"Will you help me now, Inspector?" Pinter pleaded. "I told you everything I know."

"I'll see what I can do," Sebastian replied, and walked out the door.

He handed the keyring back to Bates and asked the man to take him back to Treadwell's office.

"What have you learned?" Treadwell asked as soon as Sebastian walked in.

"Release Lloyd Pinter," Sebastian said. "The man's family was threatened. He did what he had to do."

"I can hardly allow him to get away with such malfeasance," the director countered.

"I agree, but to incarcerate Mr. Pinter carries a charge of illegal imprisonment. Your only alternative is to report him to the authorities and allow the law to take its course."

"Well, in view of the circumstances, I think we can perhaps dismiss him without wages and a character," the director said. "That would be punishment enough."

"That is up to you," Sebastian said. "But I will not allow you to keep him locked up like an animal."

Treadwell and the governors would not want to draw attention to the case, since it would tarnish the reputation of the asylum and frighten potential clients from committing their family members to its care. From a business perspective, the best course of action would be to sweep the entire unfortunate affair under the carpet. Sebastian could arrest the attendant for his part in Stager's death, but if someone had threatened Gemma he would have done anything to keep her safe, so he could sympathize with the man and acknowledge that he had been placed in an impossible situation. That didn't mean Sebastian condoned Pinter's actions, but he would leave it up to Treadwell to decide if he wanted to prosecute the man under the law. He could do that once Pinter had been released.

"Bates, bring Pinter to me," Treadwell bellowed to the attendant, who was no doubt lurking just outside the door. "And get his things."

"If you've no objection, I will escort Mr. Pinter off the premises," Sebastian said once Bates had departed.

Treadwell nodded curtly. "He's all yours."

Sebastian breathed a sigh of relief when he stepped outside. The sun shone brightly, the air smelled sweet, and at least one couple would be reunited thanks to his efforts. He walked a weakened, limping Pinter to the gates and made certain he was allowed to leave before setting off to the infirmary. He hoped that Poppy had spent the night there and was perfectly safe.

CHAPTER 38

It didn't take Sebastian long to learn that his hope had been in vain. When he presented himself at the infirmary, he was told that Poppy had never arrived for her shift and that Miss Tate, Mr. Ramsey, and Mr. Evans were out searching the streets of Lambeth. Sebastian's heart squeezed with renewed worry as he stepped outside. All he knew for certain was that Poppy had left Colin's house in time to get to the infirmary for her shift. Anything could have happened after that. It was unlikely that she had decided not to go to work. She wasn't the sort of person to let others down or cause unnecessary worry. So, if the decision to not show up for work hadn't been hers, what had happened, and where was Poppy now?

Sebastian hailed a passing hansom and instructed the cabbie to drive up and down the streets until he finally spotted Gemma and Colin. They were moving at a slow, deliberate pace, pausing to peer into every shadowed doorway and narrow alley. Even from a distance, Sebastian could see the tension etched into their faces, and felt an answering foreboding in his own soul. He called to the driver to stop and jumped down.

"Sebastian," Gemma cried, and hurried towards him. "Poppy never arrived for her shift."

"I know. I stopped by the infirmary."

"I fear she may have been attacked by the escaped inmate," Colin stated morosely. "There's no other explanation."

"The inmate was never a threat," Sebastian replied. "He was sold to an anatomist."

Colin and Gemma looked simultaneously shocked and relieved, and, although they clearly had questions about what had happened to Algernon Stager, Poppy was still their primary concern.

"So, where is Poppy?" Gemma asked. She looked to Sebastian for an explanation, but he didn't have one to offer.

"Might she have gone to her sister?" Colin mused.

"I don't see why she would. She specifically told me she was going to work," Gemma replied.

"She must have been waylaid. That's the only logical explanation. Perhaps she's already back at Mrs. Sloane's."

"She's clearly not here," Sebastian observed. He'd covered enough streets in the hansom to be certain that Poppy was not in the vicinity of the infirmary. Few people were. Frightened by the news of the inmate's escape, many of the residents of Lambeth remained behind closed doors, and the pedestrians were mostly men. The few women Sebastian had seen had walked in groups and had looked around fearfully as they hurried to and from the shops.

"Perhaps we should return home," Colin suggested.

Gemma looked set to argue but then seemed to see the sense in Colin's suggestion. Perhaps Poppy had never even crossed the bridge, and they were looking in the wrong place.

"We should let Mr. Evans know we're abandoning the search," she said, and her shoulders drooped with defeat.

"We need to locate him first." Colin looked around, but the doctor did not appear. "Let's head back to the infirmary. We can leave a message with Nurse Dixon."

"Do you believe the cases are connected?" Gemma asked Sebastian as she slipped her arm through his and they set off.

"I do, but at this stage it's impossible to tell if this is the work of one or several individuals. Perhaps there's more than one surgeon involved."

"I think it may be several," Colin volunteered.

"Why do you think that?" Gemma asked.

"Because of the variety of the victims. Perhaps one anatomist is interested in women who are expecting, while another is researching congenital birth defects."

"Deb's brain was removed," Gemma reminded him, and Sebastian felt a shudder pass through her. "And whoever took Stager would almost certainly dissect his brain."

"How on earth did they get to Stager?" Colin asked. "Surely no respectable institution would sell a patient. Or had Stager died before he was turned over?"

"From what I have learned, Stager was drugged and then drowned in a bucket of water."

"Just like the rest of them," Gemma concluded.

"There are too many similarities to doubt that these killings are connected," Colin said. "But I don't know any surgeons who are willing to ignore their Hippocratic Oath."

"We know of at least one," Sebastian replied. "Joss Stevens. He experimented on patients who came from a nearby workhouse and killed most of them as a result. He then used their bodies to conduct postmortems for his students."

Gemma looked horrified, while Colin exclaimed, "Are you certain? Surely the Royal College of Surgeons wouldn't knowingly protect him."

"The RCS chose to protect itself," Sebastian replied. "Much like the Lambeth Marsh Asylum, which has chosen to withhold the truth from the authorities and the public. The RCS expelled Stevens, but they did not file charges against him, which left him at liberty to continue his experiments. And I have it on good authority that an anatomist recently approached the warden of Millbank Prison in the hope that he might purchase fresh cadavers."

"And you think it was Joss Stevens?" Gemma asked.

"My source thought the anatomist was associated with the Westminster Hospital, but he could be mistaken, or the surgeon might have misrepresented himself in order to gain the confidence of the warden."

"Did the warden agree to sell the bodies of deceased inmates?"

"I don't know for certain, but I can't rule out the possibility. And if he did, then it's very likely that Glory Cates, who was with child and hanged herself in her cell the night before she was due to sail to Botany Bay, was one of his subjects. Her body was never returned to her husband."

"Is there any way to find out?" Colin asked.

"Not without exhuming Glory's remains and ordering a post-mortem to verify that the body buried in that grave was indeed of a pregnant woman who hanged herself." Sebastian sighed. "I won't resort to that unless I'm left with no other choice."

"That's kind of you," Gemma said.

"It's not so much kindness as practicality," Sebastian admitted ruefully. "I'm not likely to learn what I need to know, especially if the remains are not those of Glory. And her husband has suffered enough. I have no wish to cause him any more pain."

"Then you must find another way to unmask this scoundrel," Colin said. "Ah, there's Mr. Evans," he exclaimed when a man came walking briskly towards them. It wasn't lost on them that he was alone.

Mr. Evans held out his hand to Sebastian as soon as he approached. His smile seemed genuine, but the lenses of his spectacles reflected the sunlight, preventing Sebastian from seeing his eyes.

"Joseph Evans. You must be Inspector Bell. Miss Tate was hoping you would locate Miss Bright, but I see that sadly she's not among us."

Sebastian silently shook the man's hand. Mr. Evans's handshake was firm and his manner self-assured.

"I hope you will forgive me, but I must return to my duties. I have been gone too long already. If you will provide me with an address, I will send word if I hear anything."

"Thank you, Mr. Evans," Gemma said dejectedly. "We appreciate your assistance."

"I only wish I could have done more. I will pray for Miss Bright's safe return."

After Colin recited his address, Joseph Evans tipped his bowler and walked away. Sebastian watched him as he strode confidently down the street. There was something familiar about the man, but he was certain they had never met.

Sebastian turned to Gemma when she called his name. "What should we do?" she asked.

"I suggest you both return to the house. I will check with Mrs. Sloane, then, if Poppy is not back, I'll call on Mary Harbor. Perhaps Poppy is with her."

"And if she isn't?"

"Then I will return to Scotland Yard, file a missing person report, and ask Ransome for reinforcements. We will find her," he promised with more confidence than he felt. How was he to find one woman in a city of millions?

"But will we find her alive?" Colin asked, and earned himself a look of outrage from Gemma.

"Poppy is resourceful and smart," she said. "She has to be all right."

They located the cab stand, and Sebastian saw Gemma and Colin off in the first cab before setting off for Mrs. Sloane's boarding house in the second. He tried to tell himself that there was no reason to think that Poppy was hurt or, worse, dead, but his copper's instinct kicked like a deranged mule, and he knew that something awful had befallen Poppy Bright.

CHAPTER 39

Sebastian had walked up the steps to Mrs. Sloane's boarding house and was about to knock when something caught his eye. The woman was about fifty yards away, so he couldn't see her clearly, but she was obviously in distress. She was holding on to an iron railing and was bent over nearly double, as if in great pain. The brim of the woman's bonnet obscured her face, and a short cape flared over her abdomen, but Sebastian thought she might be in labor. Worried as he was about Poppy, he had to offer the woman assistance, since no one else had stopped to help.

He hurried down the street and was almost within speaking distance when the woman lifted her head. The sight of her stopped him in his tracks. Her face was swollen and covered in bloodied bruises, and her right eye was almost swollen shut. The woman's hands were smeared with dried blood, and she barely managed to remain upright as she swayed on her feet. Sebastian lunged towards her and just managed to catch her as she collapsed into his arms.

"Sebastian," the woman whispered, and it was only then that he realized he was clutching Poppy.

He swung her into his arms and held her close as he glanced at the boarding house. It was near, but Poppy was in need of medical assistance, and the best Mrs. Sloane could offer was a cool compress and hot tea. Decision made, Sebastian rushed to Colin's house. Passersby stood aside to let him through, their faces alight with curiosity as they stared at the limp woman in his arms. An empty hansom rolled past but didn't stop, the driver clearly not wishing to get involved in whatever drama was playing out in the street. One elderly woman stepped forward.

"Do you need help? I live just there," she said, and pointed at an open door. "Let's get her inside."

"Thank you," Sebastian managed to reply as he raced past. "Nearly home."

Poppy wasn't stout by any means, but to run half a mile with a grown woman in his arms was no easy feat. Sebastian's arms ached, and the muscles in his thighs protested as he bounded up the steps. He gulped several deep breaths to calm himself and managed to bang the knocker without letting go of Poppy. She moaned pitifully as she pressed her face to his chest, probably to avoid scrutiny. Sebastian was about to knock again when Mabel opened the door.

"Oh, my sweet Jesus," she exclaimed. She was about to say something more, but, having heard the knock and Mabel's exclamation of alarm, Gemma had come running down the stairs, and Colin was pounding up the cellar steps.

Colin instantly took control, issuing orders as if he were on the battlefield. "Sebastian, take her into the parlor and set her down on the settee. Mabel, vinegar, warm water, and clean cloths. Gemma, calendula, yarrow, honey, and boiled linen strips," he rattled off.

As soon as Sebastian set Poppy down, Colin untied the ribbons of her bonnet and undid the clasp on the cape, which he pulled out from beneath her and tossed across a nearby chair. Anne, who had been dozing in her chair, was startled awake and stared at Poppy, her mouth opening in incomprehension. She made to stand and nearly lost her balance, her arm flapping helplessly as she searched for something to grab onto. Sebastian caught her under the elbow and held her until she was steady on her feet, then tried to get her to leave the room, but Anne refused and sank back down, her gaze fixed on Poppy.

Mabel and Gemma came rushing back, and Colin went to work. He cleaned Poppy's face with warm water, then dabbed vinegar onto the cuts while Gemma cleaned Poppy's hands. Colin treated the cuts that still oozed blood with yarrow and applied a bit of honey to keep them from becoming infected. Once he was finished, he prepared a poultice of calendula, which he explained would reduce the swelling.

Although she remained silent, Anne's confused gaze traveled from Poppy to Gemma to the chair where Colin had thrown the bonnet and cape. It was only when he looked at the cape more closely that Sebastian realized it was Gemma's, and he wondered why Poppy had been wearing it when he'd found her. He wanted to speak to Poppy, to ask her what had happened and where she had been since yesterday afternoon, but she was in no condition to answer his questions. Now that she was safe and being ministered to by Colin, she was in a state of semi-wakefulness and seemed oblivious to what was going on around her. Colin, meanwhile, was white to the roots of his hair, his frantic gaze never leaving Poppy's face as he tended to her injuries.

"We will take good care of you," he said softly. "You needn't worry about a thing. And, of course, you will stay here with us. I'll have Mabel prepare the spare room."

"Gemma can act as chaperone," Anne suddenly said. "Propriety must be observed at all times."

"Yes, of course," Colin hurried to reassure Poppy, who was in no fit state to care about such trivialities. "Gemma will act as chaperone."

"Gemma, I would like to go to my room now, please," Anne said, her voice reedy with distress. "I don't understand what happened. Why is that woman bleeding?"

"Allow me to help you, Mrs. Ramsey," Sebastian offered.

Anne peered at him as she tried to place him, then nodded in recognition. "That's very kind. I do declare, I'm quite overcome."

Sebastian assisted Anne up the stairs and left Gemma, who'd just come upstairs, to help her into bed. Gemma returned to the parlor a few minutes later and collected Poppy's things from the chair. She held the misshapen bonnet and soiled cape away from her as she carried them to the laundry room. Sebastian followed.

"Isn't that your cape?" he asked as soon as they were alone.

"I lent it to Poppy. She was cold," Gemma said. She sounded tearful and didn't seem to know what to do with her hands once she set the cape and the filthy bonnet down on a wooden bench. "Oh, Sebastian, why would anyone do this?"

"I don't know, but I mean to find out. As soon as Poppy feels up to speaking to me, I will ask her what happened."

"She needs to rest and recover."

"How badly is Poppy hurt?" he asked. He had formed his own opinion but wanted confirmation from a medical professional.

"She doesn't appear to have any broken bones or missing teeth. The cuts will heal, and the swelling will go down. But she was badly beaten and must be in a great deal of pain."

"I'm sure Colin will give her a few drops of laudanum to help her rest."

Gemma nodded, then walked into Sebastian's arms and pressed her cheek to his chest. He gathered her to him and held her, his own cheek resting atop her head. "Poppy will be all right," he said into her hair. "She is safe now."

"I know. It's just so…" She seemed at a loss for words, so he supplied his own description.

"Barbaric," he said.

"I think they must have tried to grab her reticule, and she fought back."

"Maybe," Sebastian replied, but he wasn't convinced the attack on Poppy had been the result of a robbery. It would have taken time to administer such a beating, and it wasn't likely that someone would go to such lengths to rob a woman who clearly didn't have a lot to take. For whatever reason, Poppy had been singled out, and he meant to discover why. But until he could speak to her, they would remain in the dark.

CHAPTER 40

"The client was willing to pay ten quid for Algernon Stager?" Gemma asked once Sebastian had summarized his visit to the asylum.

"Yes, which tells me that whoever is doing this has ready means and access to individuals who're willing to comply."

"And who seem able to locate victims who fit the bill." She reached for a brush and began to clean the dirt from the velvet cape, more to release her nervous energy than because there was any urgency to salvage the garment.

Sebastian leaned against the wall and crossed his arms. "Problem is that we don't know anything for a fact. The anatomist could be one man or a group of like-minded individuals. The client or clients could be operating from one place or multiple locations. There could be only the victims we know about or a string of others whose deaths never made the papers or even mattered to anyone. But the one thing I feel certain of is that the victims are specifically chosen."

"À la carte," Gemma supplied.

"À la what?" Sebastian asked, one eyebrow lifting in incomprehension.

"It's a term Mr. Ellis used. I expect he'd picked it up while working in Paris. It means off the menu."

"If one could consider people's afflictions items on a menu, then I suppose the description fits," Sebastian replied sourly, and sighed. "I'm truly at a loss, Gemma. With nothing to connect the victims aside from their obvious conditions, it's impossible to find a common thread. We understand the motive, and even the means by which the victims were murdered, but anyone with a willingness to kill and a bucket of water and a wagon can do the deed. And there's no obvious link to the client. It's totally random."

"But it's not, is it?" Gemma set down the cape. Her attempts to get it clean were proving futile, so she would have to try vinegar and water to get the stains out, but that could wait. She was desperate to help Sebastian, but the only thing she could do was try to reason out the facts. "The men who took Henry Boyd sound like the ones who came for Algernon Stager. An older man with reddish hair and a younger lad with a lisp. And might they be the ones who threw Deb's body off the bridge? Didn't the Misses Spires say the man they saw had red hair?"

"Yes," Sebastian agreed. "But although Henry was taken to a stable in Pimlico, and Tamzin's and Deb's bodies were dumped near there as well, the Pruitt twins were snatched from and dumped in Kennington, and Algernon Stager was taken from Lambeth. And there could be unidentified victims who were taken from other parts of London. How am I to locate a redheaded man and a boy with a lisp with nothing else to identify them?" He huffed in annoyance and ran his hand through his hair, making it stand on end. "The thought of these men walking away without facing justice for what they've done makes my blood boil. If that happens, then I've failed. I've failed the victims, the people who loved them…" He swallowed hard. "And you."

Gemma fumbled for words that might soothe Sebastian's troubled soul, but nothing she said would make a jot of difference. To him, every case was personal, and every defeat had the potential to haunt him, because it reminded him of the one failure that mattered most, his inability to save Louisa.

"My dear," she began, her hand going to Sebastian's cheek, but she was interrupted by a pale-faced Colin walking into the laundry room.

"Poppy is asking for you," he told Sebastian. "She says she has something to tell you."

"I'm sorry," Sebastian said softly, and strode from the room.

Gemma knew he hadn't been apologizing for leaving. Sebastian was a proud, self-reliant man, not given to bouts of self-doubt or emotional outbursts, and he was likely embarrassed by what he would see as burdening her with his fears. She made to follow, to reassure him that she loved him and valued the trust he placed in her, but Colin laid a restraining hand on her arm.

"Poppy said she needs to speak to Sebastian in private," he said. He looked as worried and dejected as Gemma felt, and walked away before she could offer him words of comfort.

Left on her own, she picked up the brush and resumed her cleaning, her movements jerky as she vented her vexation on the filthy cape. What did Poppy have to say to Sebastian that she didn't want Gemma to hear? She would have thought Poppy would welcome her help and support at a time when she was helpless and in pain. It suddenly felt as if everyone were trying to push her away, but there had to be something she could do to help.

Her arm dropped to her side when she suddenly recalled a detail she had failed to register before. And why would she have when she hadn't understood its significance until now? Gemma set down the cape and pushed a stray lock of hair behind her ear. She needed to speak to Sebastian right away, but she could hardly burst in on his conversation with Poppy. Her revelation would have to wait.

CHAPTER 41

"Shut the door," Poppy said weakly when Sebastian entered the parlor.

He did as she asked, then brought a chair and sat as close to her as he could without crowding her. "How are you feeling?" he asked.

Poppy tried to smile, but changed her mind when the cut on her lip opened and began to ooze blood. She pressed a linen square Colin had left to her mouth and waited for the bleeding to stop. Even with her face washed clean of blood, she looked awful. The bruises were turning a nasty shade of purple, and her eye was badly swollen.

"I'm grateful to be alive," she said at last. "And I'm thankful to you for bringing me here. I don't think I would have made it."

"Of course you would have. You were nearly home."

Poppy sighed, and tears slid down her temples and into her tangled hair. "I really didn't think I could go on."

Sebastian laid a gentle hand over her wrist. "Colin said you had something to tell me."

"Don't let Gemma go." Her voice was barely more than a whisper.

He smiled down at her. "We're to be married in September. Have you forgotten?"

Poppy made a huffing noise that could have been the result of her inability to breathe properly or her frustration. "The men who took me… thought I was Gemma," she rasped.

That pronouncement landed like a punch to the gut. "How do you know?" he exclaimed, and immediately moderated his tone. "Did they say something to you?"

Poppy's hand went to her chest, and she tried to clear her throat. Sebastian handed her the glass of water Mabel had left on the occasional table by the settee. Poppy raised her head, took a long sip, then handed the glass back to him.

"Thank you," she said. Her voice sounded a little clearer. "I think they must have been watching the house. They pulled a sack over my head when I turned the corner and hit me over the head. When I came to, I was in the back of a wagon, and there was something covering me, like a horse blanket."

"Where did they take you?"

He fully expected Poppy to say that she had been taken to a stable and was surprised when she said, "An empty, ramshackle building." A sob tore from her heaving chest. "They beat me and told me to mind my own business and stop asking questions, or next time they would kill me."

"Poppy, I'm so sorry," Sebastian said, and squeezed her hand. "You were never supposed to get caught up in this."

"Just get them, Sebastian," she hissed. "Make them pay."

I need to find them first, he thought bitterly. "Did you see their faces?"

"They never took the sack off, but I heard their voices. One man sounded older. He had a deep, gravelly voice, and the other sounded young. He lisped."

Sebastian nearly growled with frustration. Poppy's description aligned with what he'd been told by Henry Boyd, Lloyd Pinter, and the Spires sisters, but he had absolutely nothing to go on aside from the fact that the two men appeared to be the only connection between the victims. He needed something more precise if he were to track down this duo.

"Poppy, I know what you endured at the hands of these men was harrowing, but please, try to remember. Did they say anything else? I need a name or a location."

She shut her eyes. She was clearly exhausted, and he felt awful pressing her for information, but she was the only person who could help him, so he had to try.

"Poppy," he called.

Startled out of her doze, she seemed embarrassed to have given in to fatigue. "Sorry," she muttered. "What did you say?"

"Did you hear anything else? I must have a way to identify these men," Sebastian reiterated.

Poppy sighed and seemed to sink even lower into the settee. "The younger man said something as they were leaving. I expect he thought I had passed out and he wasn't being careful."

"What did he say?" Sebastian leaned forward in his eagerness, but knew that whatever Poppy had heard wouldn't really help. If it had been important, she would have told him already.

"He said, 'This ain't right, Ed. I don't want this on my conscience.' And the older man said, 'Not like we have a choice, lad.' And then they left and shut the door behind them."

Sebastian nodded. What Poppy had heard confirmed that the older man's name was Ed but didn't offer any new clues to the men's identities. And just because the younger man's conscience was playing up didn't mean he was ready to confess. To admit to what they had done would mean certain death, and, if he had been involved in several murders over a period of months, clearly he wasn't that desperate for absolution.

"Did they lock you in?" Sebastian asked.

"No."

"Then why didn't you get help once they left?"

Poppy drew in a shuddering breath. "I must have passed out, and, when I came to, all was silent and dark. I had no idea where I was, and I couldn't manage to get up. So I stayed until first light, and then I crawled to the door and used the doorframe to pull myself up."

"Where were you, Poppy? Surely you must have spotted something familiar."

"The building wasn't far from the Whitefriars docks."

This wasn't terribly helpful, since Sebastian could hardly examine every building visible from the docks. He sucked in several calming breaths. He needed to keep a cool head to solve this case, but his blood frothed with fury, and he leaned on his anger to distance himself from the terror that was sure to crash over him once he fully acknowledged that this vicious beating had been meant for Gemma. Her inquiries had reached the ears of whoever was behind this, and they were willing to hurt, possibly even maim or murder, an innocent woman to shut her up. Which was hardly surprising when they were happy to kill on demand. These two took mercenary to a whole new level.

"I just remembered," Poppy suddenly said. "I heard them say something else, but I don't know what they meant. I might have even been delirious."

"What did they say?"

Her eyes fluttered with fatigue, but she fought valiantly to stay awake. "The younger man mentioned a henchman, and the older man said something about keeping the pig away from London Bridge this afternoon. I'm sorry, Sebastian. I know it's not very much to go on."

Sebastian knew he should leave Poppy to rest, but he needed to ask her a few more questions. Holding off by even a day could result in another victim or another attack on someone he loved, and he couldn't allow that to happen.

"How well do you know Mr. Evans?" he asked. Something about the man bothered him, but he wasn't sure what it was.

"Not well. Why?"

"He was very concerned about you."

Poppy's lips quirked. "I think his reasons were purely selfish. He tried it on with me when he took me home the other night."

"How long has he worked at the infirmary?"

"Since February. I think it took him a long while to find work, but I don't know why that should be. He's quite knowledgeable, and I think his abilities are wasted at the infirmary, since there's little he can do for the patients who end up there."

"Where did he work before?"

"He never said, but I got the impression it was at one of the bigger hospitals."

"Do you know why he left?"

Before Poppy could reply, a jolt of recognition struck Sebastian like a lightning bolt, and he recalled precisely where he'd seen Joseph Evans before. The doctor had grown a beard and had donned a pair of spectacles, but he was without doubt the man Sebastian had seen in the photograph Mr. Vance had shown him. Joseph Evans was Joss Stevens. And even though he now went by a different surname, he had retained his Christian name, since Joss was an abbreviation of Joseph. And Evans and Stevens sounded alike, which perhaps made it easier for the doctor to accustom himself to his new identity.

"What is it?" Poppy asked.

"Has Mr. Evans ever said or done anything you thought was immoral?"

"Immoral? Are you referring to how he treated the female staff?"

"No, I was referring to the patients. Did he ever perform procedures you thought were unnecessary? Poppy, this is really important, so please think carefully."

She became visibly alarmed by his urgency. "Why do you keep asking about Mr. Evans? What's he to do with anything?"

But Sebastian didn't reply. He had more questions of his own. "You said he took you home the other night. Do you know where he lives?"

"He directed the driver to continue on to Warwick Street, in Pimlico."

"Around the corner from the Premium Livery Stables," he muttered.

"What?"

"Nothing. I will leave you to rest now. Thank you for your help, Poppy."

"Did I help?" she asked, bemused.

"More than you know. Is there anything you need?" Sebastian asked as he returned the chair to its place.

But Poppy didn't respond. He had tired her out more than he had realized, and she had slipped into fitful slumber. Sebastian walked out of the parlor and shut the door softly behind him so as not to disturb her, then went in search of Colin. His friend was in the cellar, but he didn't appear to be working on anything. He simply stood there, his gaze fixed on the brain that floated in its jar of formaldehyde.

"Are you all right?" Sebastian asked.

"I never gave a second thought to the person that brain had come from," Colin replied.

"I always assumed it belonged to one of the individuals you'd worked on before we met."

Colin shook his head. "It was a gift, from a fellow medical student. I never asked how he'd come by it."

"Sometimes it's better not to know," Sebastian said, his mind instantly supplying the grotesque image of Deb Peck's empty skull.

"Every person deserves respect, in death as well as in life."

Clearly unable to look at the brain a moment longer, Colin reached for a linen towel and covered the jar. Sebastian thought he would get rid of the specimen at the earliest opportunity, but decided not to ask how one went about disposing of unattached body parts. Perhaps Colin would bury it.

"Gemma is not to leave the house," Sebastian mandated once he had his friend's full attention.

Colin scoffed. "You'd better tell her yourself."

"She's not very likely to listen."

"She's even less likely to listen to me," Colin countered. "Do you believe she is in danger?"

"All I know is that someone known as the 'henchman' doesn't want us anywhere near this investigation. And the man Poppy has worked with since February has a history of experimenting on patients."

"Are you suggesting—" Colin began, but Sebastian cut across him.

"Joseph Evans is Joss Stevens."

Colin stared at him in astonishment, but Sebastian didn't have time to explain.

"We'll talk later," he said, and left Colin to reevaluate the macabre souvenirs of his work. He needed to get to Scotland Yard without delay.

If Joss Stevens suspected he was in danger, he would hardly remain at the infirmary. He would leave, and quite possibly flee the city. With the number of train stations in London and the various railway lines that spread from the city in a spiderweb of diverging tracks, it was impossible to say which way the man would go, or at what time. The only clue Sebastian had to work with was the vague mention of London Bridge and the reference to a pig. He was certain the pig in question wasn't an animal but a person, and that person had to be himself.

Among other derogatory terms, policemen were frequently referred to as pigs, and were thought of as sellouts, their critics claiming that they dedicated their lives to protecting the rights of the rich and powerful. There were policemen who fit the bill; Sebastian couldn't argue with that. And the powers-that-be invariably devoted more resources to a crime committed against the upper crust, but Sebastian treated every victim equally, be they a duchess or a streetwalker. But that mattered not a jot to those who saw him as a turncoat and treated him with contempt.

In this instance, he was the only policeman on the case, so he had to assume that his name was known to whoever was responsible, and it was clear that they were aware of his connection to Gemma. Perhaps she had unknowingly poked the bear, or maybe whoever had ordered the attack had intended to use her to send him a warning. *If you don't back off, next time she won't get off with a beating.*

If Joss Stevens was behind the attack, then he already knew that the wrong woman had been targeted. If he wasn't, Sebastian might have some time until the real culprit found out, but that could mean that they had already selected the next victim. In either case, there was no time to lose.

CHAPTER 42

Sebastian's plan was derailed the moment he stepped outside. A crowd had gathered at the corner, and the excitement of the onlookers was at fever pitch—men, women, and a number of street children jostling for a better view of whatever was at the center of the throng. Sebastian had decided to head in the opposite direction when a woman cried, "For the love of God, someone fetch a constable."

"Not much a bobby can do now," a male voice responded.

"Are you going to move it?" the woman retorted. "It's right in front of my house."

"Gruesome, innit?" a boy who had finally managed to get to the front exclaimed. He seemed more gleeful than frightened.

Sebastian couldn't see through the throng of bodies but thought there might have been an accident and someone, or more likely something, had been run over. Given the breadth of the circle, he thought it might be a horse.

"It's him! It's definitely him!" a new female voice cried out.

"I told ye it were, didn't I?" someone replied.

Sebastian heard a high-pitched cry, and the crowd shifted and heaved as if someone had fallen.

"Give her some air," an authoritative male voice exclaimed. "Step back, all of you."

Impatient as he was to get on his way, Sebastian could hardly walk away. He didn't intend to stay, but he could at least assess the situation and maybe summon Colin if the victim was human and in need of medical attention. And if the individual was beyond help, which seemed to be the case, then Sebastian could send someone to the nearest station. It would either be Bridewell or the King Street station, which was operated by A Division. If the person was dead, it didn't much matter if it was the City of London or the Metropolitan Police that got called out.

"Inspector Bell. Scotland Yard," Sebastian shouted as he pushed his way through the crowd.

The onlookers parted immediately, clearing a path to the center. Their relief at his arrival was palpable, since they longed for someone to take charge and relieve them of responsibility for the victim. The woman who had fainted seemed to be coming around, but all Sebastian's attention was on the individual at the center, whose body lay sprawled on the pavement, his unseeing gaze on the heavens above. Sebastian opened his mouth, but what he really wanted to say wasn't fit for mixed company. He clenched his hands in impotent fury and knelt next to the body.

"Bloody hell," someone cried.

The voice sounded familiar, so Sebastian turned around. Constable Henry Boyd had just come up behind him. The lad was chalk white, his eyes wide with horror.

"Constable, flag down a passing wagon," Sebastian instructed. "The body needs to be moved."

"Isn't that…?" Boyd's trembling finger was pointing at the man on the ground as his gaze registered recognition.

"Yes, it is."

"Were he—"

Sebastian had no choice but to cut across him before the rest of the onlookers fixated on what Henry was looking at.

"Now, Constable, and be quick about it," Sebastian snapped.

"Yes, sir, Inspector Bell," Constable Boyd bleated.

He pushed past the individuals who had moved in to get a better look and ran into the road, waving his arms in front of an approaching dray wagon and calling for the driver to stop.

Sebastian returned his attention to the body. The dead man was Algernon Stager, and his corpse bore the scars of a recent postmortem. There was a thick seam at the top of his forehead, the incision running from ear to ear. Given what he now knew of what had been intended for Stager, Sebastian thought his head was probably lighter than it should be, his brain no longer inside his skull. A wide Y picked out in black thread decorated the man's torso beneath the thin linen of his shirt, and there were several marks on his forearms that looked like burns from a lit cigar. Stager still wore his trousers, but a dark stain that had to be blood had saturated the fabric at the groin, and Sebastian's stomach heaved with the realization that the man had probably been castrated while still alive.

Sebastian pushed to his feet and faced the crowd. "Go on home," he told the onlookers. "The show is over."

"But what happened to him?" a shrill female voice cried. "Just look at the state of him."

"It's that lunatic as escaped from the asylum," someone said. "I have the leaflet right here."

"He was butchered like a pig, and serves him right, the depraved wretch," a stout woman exclaimed.

"Loathsome degenerate," someone else cried out, and the crowd surged forward as if they meant to tear the corpse limb from limb.

Sebastian put himself between the body and the mob. "The man is dead," he cried over the din. "He will face God's judgment now. And so will you if you desecrate his corpse."

The threat of divine punishment seemed to bring people to their senses, and most drew back, looking shamefaced. The crowd began to thin, and after a few moments there was no one left but Sebastian and several boys who obviously had nowhere else to be. Constable Boyd returned with a burly, red-faced man who wore a leather waistcoat over a collarless linen shirt and a beige slouch hat that was discolored with sweat stains. He took one look at the body on the ground, then lifted his gaze to Sebastian.

"I ain't doing the polis no favors. Pay up, or I'll be on me way."

Sebastian could hardly leave the body in the middle of the street, so he took out a florin and held it out to the man.

"Ye must be joking," the driver scoffed, and shook his head in disbelief. "I ain't touching that for less than a half-crown."

Sebastian emptied his purse and handed over everything he had on him. The driver counted the coins, then pushed them into the pocket of his waistcoat. "All right, then," he said, and bent to lift the body beneath the arms.

Algernon Stager had been a large man, and in death his body was as heavy as a marble plinth. It took the three men several tries to lift the body and load it into the wagon. By the time they had finished, they were sweating and breathing heavily, and Henry, who was scrawny for his age, had his hand to his belly and was bent over in pain.

"Are you all right?" Sebastian asked the constable.

Henry nodded. "It's like lifting Moby Dick," he complained, then added when he noticed Sebastian's surprise at the reference, "I can read, you know. Taught myself."

"Well done," Sebastian said, and meant it. Given Henry's start in life, it was a miracle he'd come this far.

"Which of ye is coming wif?" the driver demanded impatiently as he looked from Sebastian to Henry and back again. "I ain't got all day."

Henry began to back away, so Sebastian thanked him for his help and let him go. This was Sebastian's case, and there was no point in involving the City of London Police. He had been on his way to speak to Ransome anyhow, so he climbed onto the bench next to the driver and said, "Scotland Yard."

"As ye say, guv'nor," the man said, clearly pleased with the amount he'd been able to extract for his services. "It's yer coin and yer lookout."

"*The best-laid schemes o' mice an' men gang aft agley, an' lea'e us nought but grief an' pain,*" Sebastian muttered as the wagon turned into Cannon Street and encountered heavy midday traffic.

It would take an hour at least to get to Scotland Yard in this traffic. Then probably just as long to unload the corpse, explain the situation to Ransome, decide what was to be done with Stager's remains, and allocate the necessary conveyance and men to remove the body either to the city mortuary or the nearest dead house. The wagon rattled over the cobblestones, the driver intent on his task as he guided the horse through traffic-thronged streets. There was nothing for Sebastian to do but pick apart the latest development and wonder at the cleverness of the man who'd ordered the body dumped mere yards from Colin's door.

Sebastian was relieved that no one from Colin's household had been aware of what had occurred, but he didn't think they had been meant to know. He was certain the body had been left there with one objective in mind—to delay him. Just as he was convinced that the *henchman* was toying with him.

CHAPTER 43

By the time Gemma emerged from the laundry room, Sebastian had gone. Whatever Poppy had told him must have been important, which meant that she must have either withheld information from the rest of them or recalled something vital that she thought might help Sebastian track down the men who'd done this to her. Gemma was just about to check on Poppy when Colin came up from the cellar. He held the brown bottle of laudanum that he kept in a locked cabinet downstairs in case Anne, who enjoyed an afternoon tipple, should mistake it for sherry.

"Mabel has prepared the spare room," he said. "If you would help me get Poppy settled, I will give her a few drops so she can rest. Sleep is the best cure in this instance," he went on to explain, in case Gemma should object to the use of laudanum.

She didn't disagree. Poppy was in obvious pain, and if left on her own for any length of time would probably relive the events of last night again and again. Both her body and her mind would benefit from sleep, and Gemma had no reason to worry about habitual use since Poppy understood the dangers of opium dependency.

Poppy was awake and stood up gingerly, leaning on Colin's arm for support as he explained that Gemma would help her to bed. Together, Gemma and Colin walked her up the stairs, and then Colin left the two women alone.

Gemma helped her undress, and Poppy breathed an audible sigh of relief when Gemma unlaced her corset. The men had punched her in the stomach, and, although the stiffened fabric and whalebone had taken the brunt of their violence, she was still swollen and bruised. Gemma pulled the pins that remained from her friend's hair, released the dark curls, then wove them into a loose braid so Poppy could rest comfortably. Once Poppy had got into bed, Gemma was ready to call Colin back in, but she couldn't resist the need to ask a few more questions first.

"Sebastian left without saying goodbye," she said as she adjusted the counterpane. It wasn't cold, but Poppy was shivering and curled into a ball, though the position had to be uncomfortable. "What did you say to him?"

"It's not important."

"Do you know where he went?"

Gemma felt awful pressing Poppy for answers when she was in such a state, but she was worried about Sebastian and feared he'd get hurt. He had been lucky thus far, but even cats ran out of lives, and there might come a day when he would not come back to her. The thought was so frightening, she had to push it away before it took hold and paralyzed her with anxiety.

"He didn't say, but I expect he went in search of the henchman," Poppy mumbled through her swollen lips.

"What henchman?"

"The men who took me mentioned him, when they thought I couldn't hear them."

"Do you know who this man is?" Gemma asked.

Poppy shook her head. "I don't know anything. I heard disjointed bits of conversation that made little sense." She gave Gemma a pleading look. "Please, no more questions. I'm weary to the bone."

"Just one," Gemma replied. "Would you like me to send word to Mary?"

"God, no," Poppy exclaimed hoarsely. "Mary will use this to pressure me to go and live with her."

"All right. Mary shall never know. But I must send a message to Mrs. Sloane. She is very worried about you."

"Yes, please let her know I'm all right. And thank you, Gemma."

"Think nothing of it," Gemma replied.

Once Colin had given Poppy the laudanum, Gemma kissed her friend on the forehead and turned to leave. Poppy's eyelids fluttered, but just as she started to drift off she whispered, "I'm so sorry about your cape. I hope it's not ruined."

"Don't worry about the cape," Gemma assured her. "It's nothing a thorough cleaning won't fix."

Gemma waited until Poppy was asleep, then went to check on her other patient. Anne's graying hair was spread out on the pillow, and she looked pale and very small in the large bed. She was as fractious as a child, and complained bitterly about the draft from the open window and the ceaseless noise from the outside.

"There was a crowd," Anne said. "And your inspector told everyone to disperse."

"It was just a bad dream, Mrs. Ramsey," Gemma replied soothingly.

"No, it wasn't," Anne insisted. "I heard his voice clear as a bell."

"It's quiet now, so you can rest. Can I get you anything? Tea or a glass of warm milk?" Gemma had hoped to distract Anne, and the ruse worked.

"Yes, a dish of tea," Anne replied imperiously. "Is there any cake?"

"I don't think so, but I can bring you a few digestives or toast with butter and jam."

Anne glanced at the window, seemingly gauging the time by the position of the sun. "The bakery is still open. I would like a slice of cake."

Gemma couldn't deny Anne this small request. There were so few pleasures in her life these days, and, if a slice of Victoria sponge and a cup of tea would make her happy, then that was the least Gemma could do for her. She wasn't paid only to see to Anne's physical needs but also to support her emotionally, and the older woman needed every last bit of joy she could derive from the long, monotonous days during which she alternated between hours of impenetrable confusion and moments of clarity that, in the end, left her even more disoriented. And, Gemma decided as she shut the window before Anne complained about the price of coal again, she would benefit from a walk. She needed time to think, but she couldn't seem to gather her thoughts in a house full of emotional, fretful people who leaned on her for support.

"Let's get you dressed, and Colin will get you settled downstairs," she suggested. "You can have your tea in the parlor once I come back with the cake."

"No," Anne suddenly cried. She grabbed the edge of the counterpane and held it to her heaving bosom, her eyes wild with panic. "I'm frightened. That woman is there. Until Colin took off her bonnet, I was sure she was you. Gemma, I thought you were dead."

"Poppy had a fall, that is all," Gemma replied, and laid a hand on Anne's wrist to soothe her. "You know Poppy, don't you? She comes to see you, and you and I have gone to visit her as well. Do you remember Rabbit?" Anne loved the ceramic dog that lived on Mrs. Sloane's mantelpiece. She said it reminded her of the little dog she'd had when she was a girl. The puppy had been inexplicably called Rabbit.

Anne looked dubious at first but allowed herself to be calmed. "Poppy will be all right?"

"She just needs a few days' rest, and then she will be right as rain. She will stay with us until she's better."

"And you will chaperone?" Anne asked, her eyes narrowing in suspicion.

"Of course."

"Can't have the likes of her around my darling George," Anne muttered as she slid lower against the pillows. "George loves me. He told me so. He even wrote me a poem. It was quite silly, really, but I thought it terribly romantic."

Anne's moment of lucidity had passed as quickly as it had come, and she was once again in the past, memories of her own courtship intruding on the present. Gemma didn't correct her. Anne was happier when she thought she was still a girl, young and beautiful, and admired by a handsome man who wrote her silly poetry.

"I'll be back soon," Gemma promised, but Anne didn't answer. A coy smile played about her lips as she patted her hair into place and pinched her cheeks to bring color into her face. She was getting ready to receive George.

CHAPTER 44

"I'm sorry, but I'm afraid you can't leave," Colin said when Gemma came downstairs, already wearing her spare cape and bonnet and carrying her reticule.

"I beg your pardon?"

"Sebastian's orders." He smiled apologetically.

"Orders?"

"Gemma, please, this is no time to be obstinate. Someone is butchering people for their own wicked ends, and Sebastian thinks it might be Mr. Evans."

"Mr. Evans?" Gemma exclaimed.

That was the last name she had expected to hear. Despite his unwelcome advances to Poppy, Mr. Evans had impressed her as a decent man. He had seemed genuinely worried about her, and Gemma thought he was sincerely interested in Poppy.

"How does Mr. Evans fit into all this?"

Colin sighed, and she thought that perhaps he regretted sharing the information with her. "Sebastian recognized him," he admitted. "Joseph Evans is Joss Stevens, and he could be anywhere by now if he thinks Sebastian is on to him. Surely it's not urgent that you go out this very minute."

"You mother would like a slice of cake with her tea."

"I will go to the bakery myself if you promise not to leave the house."

Colin looked so anxious that Gemma didn't have the heart to argue with him. It didn't matter who got the cake, and, if it made the men in her life feel better that she remain indoors, then indoors she would stay. Both Anne and Poppy were safe in their rooms, so Gemma removed her cape and bonnet, set down her reticule on the console table, and walked into the parlor, where she sank into an armchair. She needed a moment to process what she had learned and see if she could make the pieces fit.

The first bit of news Gemma had to examine was Mr. Evans's true identity. If Sebastian was correct and he really was Joss Stevens, then it was quite possible that he was behind the killings, but what reason would he have to hurt Poppy? She wasn't interested in him romantically, but she had always spoken highly of him as a doctor. If Mr. Evans worked the night shift with Poppy, then he wasn't at his secret surgery, working on the bodies at night. And if he worked on his victims' remains during the day, why were the bodies dumped first thing in the morning, unless he had instructed his assistants to dispose of the remains at a time when he was accounted for?

She didn't know what Poppy had told Sebastian, and Gemma wasn't the sort of person to listen at keyholes, but if his decree was any indication then Poppy had said something that had really frightened him. Her friend may have unwittingly confirmed his suspicions about Mr. Evans, but Gemma thought that Sebastian had realized something else, and she could guess what it was. Poppy had nothing worth stealing, and any items of value she did have, such as her tiny earbobs and the silver ring that had belonged to her mother, had still been on her person when Sebastian had found her. And if the men who'd attacked her had been after her money, they could have easily taken the reticule off her without taking the time to kidnap her and administer a prolonged beating. All they would have had to do was push her to the ground, grab the reticule, and run.

The fact that Poppy had walked out of Colin's house and had been wearing Gemma's cape had to be the reason she'd been attacked. And then it dawned on her why Sebastian was so worried and had ordered her to remain inside. Whoever had been watching the house had clearly mistaken Poppy for Gemma. And that could mean only one thing—Gemma had come uncomfortably close to the truth and needed to be warned off. The question was, what had she discovered that had marked her as a threat? She hadn't heard Joss Stevens' name until that morning, and when she'd met Mr. Evans he hadn't appeared surprised or angry to see her. He had been the soul of courtesy and had treated her with the utmost respect. Although of course, a man living under an assumed name had to be skilled in the art of deception.

Yesterday, Gemma had spoken to Alice, who had told her about Glory Cates and Deb Peck. Both women had been with child and were now dead, Glory by suicide and Deb by the hand of whoever had taken her. Deb Peck and Tamzin Norris had both lived in Pimlico, had known each other, and their bodies had been left within walking distance of their homes. Glory Cates had died in Pimlico as well, but she had not been murdered, nor had her body been tampered with as far as Sebastian was aware, so perhaps her death wasn't relevant to the case.

The latest victim to be taken was Algernon Stager, whose life and presumed death had been paid for by an unknown malefactor—an anatomist who played God with the lives of his victims without any apparent remorse. Gemma supposed Joss Stevens could have handpicked Stager, just as he might have selected the Pruitt twins and the Wolf Boy, and directed his men to the Lambeth Marsh Asylum, which was near the infirmary where he worked. But Stevens wasn't interested in birth defects, was he? At least not so far as they were aware. But there was a renowned surgeon who would have a vested interest in conjoined twins, a boy covered in hair, a pregnant dwarf, and someone who had been afflicted with madness since childhood. Spencer Ellis worked within walking distance of Pimlico, had met Gemma in person, and had returned to England shortly before the murders began. He'd even used the term à la carte, and that was precisely what the killer was doing. Choosing victims from a menu of disabilities.

Ellis claimed to limit his research to subjects who'd died naturally, but how many stillborn children and infants with birth defects did he have access to? Women delivered their babies at home, with the aid of a midwife. Ladies of quality sometimes had their physicians or respected accoucheurs attend them during the birth, but those men would hardly summon Mr. Ellis to their patient's bedside, especially if the child was stillborn or had been born with a noticeable defect that would leave its parents heartbroken and, at times, ashamed.

To compile the information needed to make a case for an in-depth study would take years, if not decades, and Mr. Ellis had not struck Gemma as a patient man. He was sharing his theories and trying to influence a new generation of surgeons who might be willing to lend their skills to autopsying and studying individuals who'd been afflicted with unique conditions. Perhaps medical men of the future would praise Mr. Ellis for his groundbreaking research, but, as with Burke and Hare, the measures taken to gather the evidence were nothing more than acts of murder. And murderers had to be brought to justice.

Sebastian might eventually come to the same conclusions and question Spencer Ellis about the recent deaths, but as long as he didn't have any proof of the surgeon's involvement Ellis was free to go about his work. If no new cases were reported, Scotland Yard would lose interest and focus on new investigations. And innocent people would continue to die until Ellis had the data he needed to publish his findings. Sebastian hadn't come across any evidence that linked Ellis to the murders, but she might, Gemma realized. Spencer Ellis taught and practiced medicine at the Westminster Hospital. Unlike the doctors, who viewed the nurses who assisted them as nothing more than tools, the nurses knew all there was to know about the men they reported to and could not only describe their temperaments but recall precisely when they had been on duty and what had occurred.

And if she needed insider information on the happenings at the Westminster Hospital, Gemma knew just who to ask. A friend from Crimea worked there, and, if Gemma recalled anything about Veronica Saxe, it was that she was an incorrigible gossip and an unapologetic flirt. Even if Veronica did not work closely with Spencer Ellis, she was bound to know a lot about him.

Gemma's gaze slid to the carriage clock on the mantel. It was nearly two in the afternoon—she'd be in plenty of time to catch Veronica if she worked the day shift, but she had to leave right away. If she waited until Colin returned from the bakery, he would be sure to prevent her from leaving the house, and she would be trapped for the rest of the day, helplessly waiting for news.

Her decision made, Gemma hastily put on her bonnet and cape. She thought she should tell Mabel where she was going, but Mabel must have gone out, since she wasn't in the kitchen preparing dinner, as she normally would be at this time. Gemma grabbed her reticule and slipped out the door. Thankfully, Colin was nowhere in sight, but if there had been no line at the bakery he could turn the corner at any moment. Gemma quickened her stride until she was half-running, reached the cab stand in mere minutes and climbed into the first cab in the queue.

"The Westminster Hospital, please," she called to the driver.

"Yes, miss," the man replied, and shut the roof panel.

Breathing a sigh of relief, Gemma settled against the leather seat. It was only now she was safely on her way that she realized how frightened she had been of being followed and accosted by the men who'd taken Poppy. Just to be safe, she bowed her head, her gaze on her beaded reticule. The brim of her bonnet was wide enough to hide her face in case someone made a point of peering inside the passing carriage—as far as anyone was concerned, she was a random woman on her way to an unknown destination. As the hansom approached the hospital, Gemma began to relax, knowing her plan had gone off without a hitch, but her efforts would be wasted if Veronica Saxe wasn't there when she arrived.

CHAPTER 45

Gemma got to the hospital without incident and found her way to the surgical floor, but that was where she met with resistance. She refused to be intimidated by Matron's withering gaze when she made her request to see Veronica. Matron inhaled sharply, her nostrils flaring and her lips pressing together as she bristled with annoyance. Gemma could understand her vexation. Nurses were kept busy every minute of their shifts, and were allowed to take a few minutes only to eat and to see to their personal needs. To receive visitors during work hours was strongly discouraged, and in some institutions strictly prohibited.

"This is not the time to pay social calls, miss," Matron reproved her. "Miss Saxe is currently on shift."

Gemma refused to back down. "This is not a social call, Matron. I need to consult Miss Saxe on a matter of great urgency."

"What could be so urgent that it can't wait until Miss Saxe is finished for the day?"

"The preservation of life," Gemma announced.

Matron squinted at her as though Gemma had taken leave of her senses, but could hardly refuse. "If you would wait in the foyer, Nurse Saxe will find you as soon as she can be spared."

"Thank you," Gemma replied, and took this for the victory that it was. She might have to wait ten minutes or an hour, but she was certain Veronica would be able to help once Gemma explained the situation.

It took nearly twenty minutes, but Veronica Saxe finally glided into the foyer, her gaze anxious as she searched for Gemma among the knot of waiting patients and visitors. At first glance, Gemma didn't think Veronica had changed significantly since the last time they'd met, but on closer inspection she noted that, although still beautiful, Veronica resembled a flower that was beginning to wilt. Her complexion was sallow, faint worry lines striped her forehead, and the corners of her mouth were turned down just enough to reflect her disappointment. The women who had been in their early twenties when they answered Florence Nightingale's call were now nearing thirty, and the stresses of a life in which they had no one to rely on had left their mark.

"Gemma, what on earth has happened?" Veronica cried as she approached. "Has someone died?"

"In a manner of speaking," Gemma said, and took hold of Veronica's elbow. "Let's talk outside."

"Matron will have my spleen for a bonnet ribbon if I'm not back in a few minutes."

"Then we'll talk quickly."

Gemma drew Veronica outside and away from the ornate portico, where a passing doctor might overhear them. It wouldn't do to compromise Veronica's position and leave her open to reprimand or, worse yet, dismissal. For an unmarried woman, the loss of employment could be the difference between life and death, as Poppy had so recently reminded Gemma.

"Veronica, what can you tell me about Spencer Ellis?" Gemma asked after she'd presented Veronica with an abbreviated version of events in which she'd shared that she was assisting the police but did not explain why or how she had come to be involved. She also didn't tell her that Poppy had been set upon or that Gemma was engaged to marry a police inspector. The news might cause Veronica to clam up, since she wouldn't want her name mentioned in conjunction with an official investigation.

"Spencer Ellis?" Veronica asked, her surprise evident. "Why, nothing. He's a perfectly lovely man, quite married to his work."

"But is he..." Gemma paused, wondering how to phrase the question in a way that wouldn't shock Veronica.

"Is he what?"

Gemma took a deep breath and plunged in. *In for a penny, in for a pound*, she thought. "Is he capable of ordering the deaths of people who might further his research?"

Veronica gaped at her. "I really don't think so," she said at last. "But what do I know? Men I thought honorable and decent sent thousands of young men—boys—into battles they knew they couldn't win and wrote off their deaths as inconsequential. They never gave those boys or their grieving parents another thought once the war was over. They are still bragging about their exploits while their victims rot in mass graves, their bones far away from home."

Veronica's brothers had both died in Crimea, and clearly the loss was still as fresh and raw as it had been at the time of their passing.

"Perhaps they mourned them in private," Gemma suggested. She wasn't an officer, nor had she sent men into battle, but she knew she still grieved for the patients they'd lost and saw their faces every time she dreamed of Scutari.

Veronica shook her head, her tone brittle and bitter as she said, "I very much doubt it. I see the officers' names in the social columns all the time. They're happy and gay, dancing at balls, joining their cronies for shooting parties and hunts, and enjoying holidays abroad. When, in the course of the social whirlwinds that are their lives, do you think they have time to reflect on the adolescents who will never grow old, or the parents who will die alone because their children perished decades before their time?"

Or the bereaved sisters who were left alone, forced to fend for themselves in a society that doesn't give a toss about working women? The question seemed to hang in the air between them.

"I think of all the men we lost too," Gemma admitted, "but they were casualties of war, not innocent civilians who had been chosen for their value to one man. And you and I both know that some men's ambitions know no bounds."

Veronica sighed resignedly. "I'm sorry, Gemma, but I can't confirm something I don't know for certain, not when an innocent man might find himself facing the gallows because of something I said."

"Is Mr. Ellis inside?"

"He did not come in today, but surely you don't mean to confront him on your own," Veronica exclaimed.

Gemma was about to reply when she was struck by a thought that most definitely warranted closer examination. Was it at all possible that the man who had been referred to as the henchman wasn't a henchman at all? What if what Poppy had heard was "Frenchman"? There was a Frenchman who'd arrived in London at the same time as Spencer Ellis and worked at the Westminster Hospital. And Allard had mentioned that he would be getting married at a church in Pimlico, which might mean that his lodgings or the home of his bride-to-be were nearby.

"Veronica, what about Mr. Allard?" Gemma asked.

"The Frog?" Veronica replied with obvious distaste. "He's handsome and charming, I'll give him that, but the man is as slippery as an eel. I heard it said that he was barred from the hospital he worked at in Paris."

"On what grounds?" Gemma could barely breathe as she waited for her friend to reply.

"Unseemly behavior. Perhaps he made free with the nurses."

They both knew a respected surgeon would not be sacked for making advances to the female staff. It was practically expected, and the doctors saw the hospitals as their personal fiefdoms. If a nurse lodged a complaint against a doctor, she would be sacked, while the man in question would walk away unscathed and no doubt transfer his attention to another woman. Young, pretty nurses were ten a penny, since there were always so many women seeking respectable employment.

"Or maybe Allard made free with the patients," Gemma mused.

"Gemma, you are jumping to unfounded conclusions based on hearsay," Veronica rebuked her.

"Is Mr. Allard here?" Gemma asked. Perhaps she could speak to him and discover the real reason for his banishment.

"No, Mr. Allard has resigned his position," Veronica said with a tired shake of her head.

"Resigned? When?"

"This morning. He's decided to return to France."

"What of his fiancée? I thought he had come to England to be with her."

Veronica shrugged. "I expect she will join him in Paris once she's able. Or perhaps they've ended their engagement. Who knows? I have my own life to worry about. And I must safeguard my position here at the hospital until things finally change and I no longer have to support myself."

"And is such a change imminent?" Gemma asked, her curiosity piqued by her friend's cryptic reply, but Veronica's gaze slid to the door, and Gemma knew the conversation was effectively over.

"I must get back. I wish you luck with your investigation, Gemma, but I really think you should worry less about some madman and focus on your own prospects. You're not getting any younger and, unless you find a man who wants to take you to wife, you will spend the rest of your life scrambling to make a living and moving from one mean boarding house to the next until you either die prematurely or grow old in some squalid hovel."

Gemma felt the sting of tears as she looked at her friend. The vivacious woman she had known had gone, replaced by a lonely, frightened spinster. Veronica may have been choosy in her younger years, but now she was ready to accept any man who'd have her. At twenty-eight, Gemma was one of the lucky ones. She needn't settle for some bloated widower who wanted a mother for his children. For once, life had been kind, and not only had she been blessed with the love of a gorgeous, intelligent, capable man, but she had also found purpose that went beyond earning a wage. There was tremendous satisfaction to be found in solving an intricate puzzle and bringing a killer to justice. And if her hunch proved correct, she just might make headway in this confounding case.

"Perhaps we can meet for a cup of tea once the case is closed," Gemma offered.

"I doubt we will see each other again," Veronica said.

"Why?" Gemma asked, taken aback by Veronica's pronouncement. Was she so offended by Gemma's association with the police that she would refuse to speak to her ever again?

"I'm to be married," Veronica admitted with obvious reluctance.

"Congratulations. Who is the lucky fellow?"

"Mr. Vance. He's head of surgery here at the Westminster. He's a good man, Gemma. I'm very lucky."

Gemma thought Veronica was attempting to convince herself of her good fortune but didn't quite succeed. There was sadness in her gaze, an admission of defeat that was difficult to hide from someone who'd known her before she'd become so disillusioned.

"I'm happy for you," Gemma managed, and hoped she sounded convincing. "I expect you will stop working?"

"Yes, of course, but until I'm married I will not give up my job. It's too great a risk."

"Do you think Mr. Vance is having second thoughts?"

Veronica winced at the suggestion. "No, I don't believe he is, but his children are vehemently opposed to the marriage."

"Are they very young and missing their mother?" Gemma asked, and realized once again that she had said the wrong thing.

"Mr. Vance's adult sons think their father has been seduced by a heartless gold digger. My fiancé is very well off, you see, and they're terrified that they will have to share their inheritance with any future children we might have."

"I'm sorry they're not being more welcoming, but it's not an uncommon concern," Gemma replied.

"No, which is why Mr. Vance has finally set a wedding date. Once we're married, their objections won't matter as much. But until I'm his wife, I'm still the orphaned, penniless Miss Saxe, and I will not risk my future security for some madcap inquiry."

Veronica turned on her heel and disappeared through the door, leaving Gemma feeling deeply unsettled.

CHAPTER 46

As expected, it took Sebastian considerable time to get to Scotland Yard, explain the situation to Ransome, convince him to take possession of Stager's body, and send a pair of constables to bring in Joseph Evans. He would have liked Ransome to station a constable outside Colin's door to protect Gemma, but he had no proof that Poppy had been mistaken for Gemma, especially not when she had worked closely with a man who had a reputation for questionable practices. It wasn't too difficult to imagine that Evans had taken his research to the next level and branched out into new areas of interest, but Ransome wasn't prepared to arrest him just yet.

To the obvious dismay of Constable Forrest, Sebastian asked Constable Burrows to accompany him to London Bridge. He wasn't sure what he expected to find once he got there, but at this rate, he thought it wiser to arrive with backup. Constable Burrows was new to Scotland Yard, having been referred to Ransome by Sebastian only a few months ago, but he was observant and helpful and knew how to follow orders, unlike Forrest, who was usually more hindrance than help and needed everything to be explained multiple times. Sebastian instructed Constable Burrows to bring the police wagon, and, once the horses were hitched, they set off.

Sebastian was as jittery as a child. He had no idea what he was up against, nor what or whom he would encounter at London Bridge. Whatever the culprits had been planning could have occurred hours ago or might not be meant to take place until later, and he might see nothing at the bridge but steady traffic moving across the river. He now had a suspect, which was a step forward in the investigation, but he was loath to admit that all he had against Evans was circumstantial evidence that would not stand up in a court of law.

Evans, né Stevens, had experimented on patients he'd thought no one would miss. He had worked with Poppy, who'd been kidnapped and beaten, and may have been the intended victim all along. Evans had also spent his time in areas associated with the kidnappings. In Pimlico, he lived within walking distance of the Rose and Thorn, Millbank Prison, the livery stable, and the residences of both Tamzin Norris and Deb Peck. And in Lambeth, he was close to the Kennington fairground—the last place the Pruitt twins had been seen alive, the spot where Henry Boyd had been taken, and the Lambeth Marsh Asylum.

Stager may have been a dangerous man, but the state of his corpse had filled Sebastian with simmering rage. Stager had clearly suffered before he'd died, either abused by his kidnappers or tortured by the anatomist who'd wished to study his brain, and possibly his reproductive organs. The burns on his arms looked recent, so probably not the work of Lloyd Pinter. Had his abductors tried to provoke him for a reason, or had it been just a bit of fun for them, like bear baiting?

Stevens had been exiled and disgraced, but his downfall hadn't been made public. If he was the first to publish his findings pertaining to congenital birth defects, he could stage a triumphant comeback that would enable him to worm his way back into the Royal College of Surgeons and probably acquire a wealthy sponsor who might wish to fund further research. Stevens had means, motive, and opportunity, but Sebastian still needed tangible evidence to link him to the case.

And then there was Spencer Ellis. The man had worked with a renowned scientist known for his study of congenital birth defects while in France. Unlike Stevens, who didn't know Gemma and had probably only heard about her from Poppy, Ellis had met Gemma and knew of her association with Colin. He could have easily obtained Colin's address from the RCS and sent his men to lie in wait. Spencer Ellis had returned from France just before the killings had started, and unlike Stevens, who had worked on patients he'd had access to, the person responsible for the murders focused on specimens with very specific afflictions. By not having to wait to examine such individuals, the anatomist could make leaps and bounds in his research and be the first to attain fame and fortune as a result of his discoveries.

Stevens and Ellis might be working together, working separately, or not working on the same area of study at all. The lack of evidence made it impossible to embrace any one theory, and, unless Sebastian managed to track down Ed and his lisping partner, he was pissing in the wind. His only hope was to catch someone red-handed, but, now that the corpse of Algernon Stager had been dumped, it was entirely possible that whatever had been meant to happen at London Bridge was no longer on the cards.

CHAPTER 47

After Veronica left, Gemma remained by the hospital entrance, where she was relatively safe, and took a few moments to consider her options. She could return home and try to mollify Colin with some creative excuse for sneaking out of the house, or she could follow through on her suspicions. There had to be a reason François Allard had suddenly resigned and decided to return to France. Perhaps Veronica was correct, and his defection was the result of domestic discord or romantic disappointment, or maybe, given recent events, he'd come to realize that he was sailing precariously close to the wind.

The same could be said of Spencer Ellis, who had not come to work the day after Poppy had been abducted. Was it possible that he had become aware of the mistake and feared that Poppy could identify her assailants? It was a stretch to imagine that Poppy could lead Sebastian to Ellis, but perhaps the surgeon had thought it wise to lie low for a spell. Or maybe he was working on a new victim, one they had yet to hear about, or wouldn't if Ellis intended to be more careful about disposing of the corpse.

Until a few days ago, no one had been looking into the deaths of the Pruitt twins, Glory Cates, or Deb Peck, but Tamzin's murder had changed all that. It was a sad reflection on society that no one had bothered to investigate the murders of people they considered disposable, but, whatever the shortcomings of the police, or the press that had failed to report the murders, Sebastian was now on the case, and he wouldn't stop until he got to the bottom of this conspiracy. He had been able to uncover a connection between the victims, and a list of possible perpetrators was beginning to emerge. Gemma had yet to share her reservations about François Allard, but Sebastian already suspected Joss Stevens and was aware of Spencer Ellis's research and his connection to the hospital, and possibly the prison. Could the three men be working together? The medical community was tight-knit enough for the surgeons to have learned of each other's interests, but for now the three men had to be treated as separate entities. And the one Gemma was interested in at the moment was François Allard.

He could hardly cause her harm if she approached him in a public space, and she had some questions to put to him before he was forever beyond her reach. She looked around, her gaze sweeping her surroundings. If Allard intended to travel to France, the most direct way would be via a South Eastern Railway train to either Folkestone or Dover. From there, he could board a steamer that would take him across the Channel. Gemma had no idea how often the ships sailed or if the train schedule aligned with the sailing. Most likely, Allard wouldn't have set off on his journey last night, not unless he'd planned to overnight near the port. And if he had been the one to order the attack on Gemma, he might wish to remain in London long enough to ensure it had been carried out and pay the men once the job had been done. He'd also need to dispose of Algernon Stager's corpse if he had still been in possession of the man's remains. It wouldn't do to leave the body anywhere near his lodgings for fear of being accused of the crime, especially if he intended to come back to London in the future.

That was a lot of ifs, and there was absolutely no guarantee that Gemma would manage to track the man down, but if she did, and if she could find proof of his guilt and convince a local bobby to detain him, then Sebastian would be one step closer to solving the case. It would prove more difficult once Allard crossed the Channel, but not impossible. England and France did not collaborate on police investigations, and barely trusted each other enough to let down their guard, but if Allard managed to escape, the French police weren't likely to ignore a tip from an English detective if it provided irrefutable evidence of multiple crimes.

As she climbed into a hansom and directed the driver to London Bridge station, Gemma acknowledged that Allard might already be halfway to France and that, even if he were still in London, he might leave from Ludgate Hill station this afternoon, this evening, or at any time over the next few days. Going after him was a long shot at best, utter folly at worst, but, even if she failed to locate the man, she could ask after him at the ticket booths. How many Frenchmen could have purchased a ticket since yesterday? Given the odds, it wasn't the worst use of her time, so she decided to continue on to London Bridge station, since it was the most convenient starting point for a trip abroad.

CHAPTER 48

As the police wagon drew closer to the bridge and pulled into Tooley Street, the traffic became almost impassable, the area before the station bustling with waiting omnibuses, carriages, and delivery wagons. The London Bridge train station wasn't the grandest by any means, but it was the oldest terminus in London and served two railways, the London, Brighton and South Coast lines, and the South Eastern Railway. The redbrick and timber station, which comprised several buildings, wasn't elegant, nor was it particularly functional. Each line had its own platforms, facilities, and booking offices, and, since the areas weren't clearly marked, the terminal was usually a mob of confused passengers and frustrated porters.

Sebastian was about to ask Constable Burrows to drive over the bridge when a new theory presented itself. Perhaps the men who'd taken Poppy had been speaking of the station and not the bridge, and that could only mean that their client was bent on escape. And that he was most likely headed for one of the port cities. It was a bit late in the day, since, as far as Sebastian knew, there were only three sailings. The steamer from Folkestone left in the morning and early afternoon, and the one from Dover sailed only once a day, in the late afternoon. The trains scheduled for the ferry ports were timed with the sailings, but crossings were added as needed, and it was possible that the steamers operated more frequently during the summer months, when more people tended to travel abroad. He would check the station and send Constable Burrows to the bridge.

No sooner had Sebastian come to this decision than he spotted a familiar silhouette. He squinted into the crowd, certain that his eyes were deceiving him, but no, there she was, hurrying to the entrance, the wings of her old, outmoded cape fluttering in the breeze. *Bloody, bloody hell!* What in blazes was Gemma doing here? He railed at the fact that his instructions had been so thoroughly ignored and Colin had allowed her to leave the house, but the more likely explanation was that Colin had been outfoxed and outmaneuvered by Sebastian's sharp-witted bride-to-be. And cunning she was, he had to admit, his chest swelling with pride despite his mounting chagrin. Gemma had clearly deduced where the culprit would be, and, if Poppy had shared with her what she'd heard, Gemma had realized that London Bridge meant the station and not the bridge itself. Clever girl!

"Find a place to leave the wagon," Sebastian called to the constable, and jumped off the bench as soon as the wagon finally came to a stop.

He charged after Gemma, but she had several minutes' start on him, and he couldn't see her in the crowd. The terminal was like an anthill, with hundreds of passengers disembarking or waiting to board, perspiring porters wheeling loaded trolleys, and the waiting areas filled to capacity. Due to a shortage of approach tracks, the trains were frequently delayed, which created a backlog that only began to ease as night set in, and the trains weren't running as frequently. The terminus was equipped with both open-air and partially covered platforms, and the canopies of the covered platforms cast the multitudes beneath in deep shadow. The air was filled with soot and smoke, and the din was like a solid wall of noise that left one feeling aggravated and disoriented.

Sebastian paused to get his bearings, then sprinted towards the South Eastern side of the terminal. All he cared about was getting between Gemma and the man who'd killed countless people to fuel his ambition. He turned, searching for some sign that would direct him to the correct stairway, but couldn't seem to find any markings. He ran to the nearest set of stairs, but his path was obstructed by an industrious porter, whose trolley was stacked with so many trunks and cases they looked about to topple. He groaned with frustration, pushed past the cart, ignoring the outraged cries of the porter, then squeezed between two slow-walking couples who blocked his way, and raced up the stairs and onto the walkway that led to the platforms below. He slowed his step and scanned each platform, searching for Gemma, but all he saw was a sea of bonnets and crinolines, bowlers, and top hats. He would have liked to consult the train schedule, but there was no time, and, given the number of people in the station, the trains clearly weren't running on time anyhow.

A huge black locomotive chugged into the station, the hissing engine shrouding the platforms on either side in clouds of smoke. As soon as the train came to a complete stop, the porters sprang into action, positioning themselves near the doors. The packed cars disgorged dozens of people, and the racket intensified as the passengers claimed their cases and pushed towards the exits. Sebastian paused and attempted to take stock. How was he to find anyone in the melee? The upside was that, even if the surgeon was there, Gemma wasn't likely to locate him either, but the downside was that, unlike him, she might have figured out exactly which train the man planned to board. The next train was already on its approach, so Sebastian hurried to the stairs that led to the platform between the two most recent arrivals. They had to be the next ones to depart, so that was where Gemma was most likely to go.

Except that as soon as he got to the platform, Sebastian realized Gemma wasn't there.

CHAPTER 49

The acrid smoke from the engines made Gemma's eyes tear, and she nearly slipped on a smear of engine grease as she hurried down the passage and peered at the blur of faces around her. She hated to admit it, but this had been an ill-considered and rash undertaking, and the only thing she was likely to accomplish was to get soot in her hair and grease on her boots. What had she been thinking, that François Allard would turn up at the precise moment she arrived at the station? That was as unlikely as it was terrifying. And he would hardly admit to any wrongdoing when he was so close to freedom.

She really should have known better, Gemma berated herself as she turned on her heel. Colin was right; she was addicted to danger, and she would do well to rethink her actions. She was to be a wife soon, and hopefully a mother, so her priorities would have to shift. Of course, she wasn't going to simply walk away from everything she had accomplished and twiddle her thumbs as she waited for Sebastian to come home to her—she fully intended to continue her studies and practice medicine—but she'd have to be more judicious. If she carried on like she was invincible, she would end up like Poppy, terrified and barely recognizable after an encounter with men who'd suddenly realized she was a threat. It was a sobering thought, and Gemma knew it was time she left the hunt for the perpetrator to the professionals, at least this time. It was time to go home.

She was making her way to the main exit when she suddenly realized she was in desperate need of the toilet. She wasn't familiar with the layout of the station and was in no mood to wander the warren of passages, so she stopped a passing porter. The young man nodded, then leaned uncomfortably close and yelled in Gemma's ear in order to be heard over the cacophony.

"The retiring room for ladies is that way, madam," he said, and pointed to a crowded corridor that led deeper into the station. "There's a narrow passageway between the dining room and the general office. It's somewhat difficult to locate, but you can ask at the office if you can't find it."

"Thank you," Gemma yelled back.

The porter tipped his cap and rushed off.

It probably took no more than five minutes, but it seemed like an eternity as Gemma fought her way through the oncoming crowd, then made a wrong turn before finally locating the general office and the narrow corridor that led to the retiring room. There were, in fact, two rooms—one for first class passengers and the other for the rest. She supposed the first-class facility had flushing toilets, but since she didn't have a ticket to show the attendant she had no choice but to use the second room, which had a washbasin and three partitioned stalls, all of which were occupied by members of the same family, who kept calling out to each other. The grouchy female attendant instructed her to wait, and she thought she might burst by the time a harassed mother of three girls under the age of ten shepherded her tired, cranky flock out the door and the attendant emptied the chamber pots into a bucket. Gemma finally nipped into the stall and was back out again in no time. She washed her hands at the basin, tipped the attendant a penny, and was all set to leave the station and find her way home.

She had just stepped out of the passage and was passing the crowded dining room when she spotted a familiar face. The man had just paid his bill and was heading to the door. He wore a three-piece sack suit of brown tweed and a brown bowler, and clutched a handsome leather portmanteau. She froze, unsure what to do. As soon as Allard saw her, she would have to either explain her presence or flee.

Gemma was about to step behind a wide iron support until her decision was made when the choice was made for her and Allard turned, his eyes widening in surprise at what had to be the horrified expression on her face. He raised his hand as if to tip his hat, then must have realized this couldn't be a coincidence and yanked his hand away. Striding the way Gemma had come in search of the facilities, he turned into the passage that led to the South Eastern Railway platforms and vanished from view.

Before her mind had even acknowledged what she was doing, Gemma was on the move. Her reticule clutched in one hand, she lifted her skirts with the other to keep them above the filthy floor as she hastened down the passage. She craned her neck in an effort to spot the brown bowler above the stream of humanity, but a number of men wore similar hats and it was difficult to tell if she was following the right person. But there were only three platforms on the South Eastern side of the terminal, and François Allard had to be heading to one of them.

The train at Platform A was leaving, and the cars slid past very slowly until the train picked up speed once clear of the terminus. The train at Platform B was boarding, and a dark green locomotive just visible in the distance was on the approach, presumably bound for Platform C. Gemma looked this way and that, trying to locate Allard among the passengers. Once the crowd had thinned and most of the passengers had settled into their compartments, she finally spotted him near the end of the Platform B. He walked rapidly but did not board the train. He would probably jump on if he had no other choice, but this clearly wasn't the train he had been waiting for.

Gemma hurried down the steps and walked down the platform. The green locomotive was growing nearer, the reek of smoke and hot engine oil filling her nostrils as she hurried towards the Frenchman. He had seen her, she was sure of it, but he kept his back to her, his portmanteau firmly gripped in his right hand. Gemma didn't know what she would say to the man once she reached him, but she couldn't allow him to leave without questioning him. This went against everything she had concluded earlier, and she knew she should admit defeat and walk away, but it was as if her feet were moving of their own accord and propelling her towards the inevitable confrontation.

Just when she thought she had a few more moments to compose her speech, Allard came to a sudden stop and spun about. His expression was difficult to read, since it was something between disbelief, annoyance, incredulity, and possibly even amusement.

"What do you think you're doing, Miss Tate?" he demanded as soon as Gemma was within earshot.

"I know what you did," Gemma proclaimed. "It was you who had all those people murdered and autopsied."

"Yes, and?" Allard asked, and cocked his brow in a most insolent manner.

"And you can't get away with killing innocent people."

"Why not?" The corner of his mouth quirked. "Incompetent English surgeons kill more people each year than any war or disease, and no one accuses them of murder."

"They're doing everything they can to save lives," Gemma retorted.

"So am I," Allard barked. "It's impossible to prevent hideous birth defects without understanding the science behind them."

"You mean you can't bake a cake without breaking a few eggs?"

"Something like that."

"You murdered expectant mothers and their babies. Don't you have a heart?" Gemma's voice cracked with emotion, but Allard just laughed.

"The heart is a muscle, Miss Tate, nothing more, nothing less, and, until we know how to keep it pumping while we operate on it, countless more people will die of heart disease. But we won't figure it out without trial and error. Just as we'll never understand what makes one child perfectly normal and another child a dwarf, or a parasitic twin. Or a raving lunatic. Brutality is the price of progress."

"Is that really what you tell yourself?" she cried.

Allard shrugged. "You know as well as I do that those mothers and babies could have just as easily died during childbirth. Just as you know that conjoined twins rarely grow into adulthood, or that a lunatic will spend whatever is left of his pitiful life in an asylum, chained to a wall. I did those people a favor. At least their deaths meant something and will benefit humanity."

"You mean benefit you."

"And me," he allowed. "My name will be forever synonymous with great scientific discoveries."

"You're mad," Gemma concluded. "Absolutely barking mad."

It infuriated her that all he could think about was his own legacy and had no thought to spare for the people he'd murdered or the broken families he'd left behind.

"All great men are accused of madness," Allard said with a shrug. "Some were put to death for proposing theories that are now accepted as fact but were thought blasphemous and downright insane in their day. It's becoming dangerous for me to remain here, so I will go back to France and continue my work in a new city. Marseille, perhaps," he mused. "Lots of sailors and whores, and other scum no one will miss. You cannot stop me, Miss Tate, so I suggest you go home and stop meddling in things that don't concern you. Oh, and please apologize to your friend. I never meant to hurt her."

"So, you admit that beating was meant for me?"

He nodded. "An honest mistake. The lady was wearing your cape."

"And you decided to hurt me because I got too close?" Gemma asked.

Allard smirked. "Don't flatter yourself, dear lady. I needed a way to distract your very persistent inspector until I was finished with Stager. He was still breathing when those bungling idiots brought him to me, so I kept him alive a bit longer," he admitted. "He made for an interesting study." The Frenchman sighed with exaggerated regret. "Unfortunately, in the end things didn't go as planned, so I was forced to improvise."

"What did you do?" Gemma demanded, her extremities growing cold with foreboding. If Allard could target her, he could just as easily go after Sebastian and have him beaten within an inch of his life. Or even killed. Allard clearly didn't place great value on human life.

As if reading her mind, he replied, "Don't worry. Inspector Bell is alive and well, but otherwise engaged at present."

"Engaged in what?"

"Instead of dumping Algernon Stager on London Bridge as I had intended, I instructed my men to throw him in Inspector Bell's path. That way, he would be kept gainfully occupied and well away from the station until I made my escape. But now you have shown up." Allard threw up his hands in incomprehension. "I suppose I should have known you'd get here first." He chuckled. "Women are much smarter than men give them credit for, and I can assure you, my dear Miss Tate, the female brain is no different than that of their male counterparts. But until science can prove that women are as intelligent and capable as men, they will remain at the mercy of the patriarchy and be treated no better than handmaidens."

"So, you're doing us all a favor."

"Precisely. I'm working hard to improve your lot," Allard replied with a grin.

"Inspector Bell will track you down in Paris," Gemma hurled at him.

"And do what? I didn't kill those people. I simply performed postmortem examinations on individuals who were already dead. That's not a crime. Your employer does it all the time, and I have a sneaking suspicion you are not far away when he sets about his work. You really are too clever for your own good, and, in women, unchecked ambition leads to nothing but trouble."

Gemma ignored that, even though it shocked her just how much Allard knew about her personal life. Had he investigated her after meeting her at the lecture, or was he simply a very perceptive man who noticed things others didn't and based his opinions on those impressions?

"It's a crime to order a person's death," she countered. "You have done that."

Allard shrugged. "You can say you want me dead, but unless you kill me you're still innocent in the eyes of the law."

"But not the men who followed your orders. They are not innocent."

"I didn't make anyone do anything," the Frenchman replied. "The men I hired were seduced by the promise of easy money. We're all driven by something, Miss Tate, and Edward Polk was driven by his need to protect the woman he loves and keep his bastard son out of debtor's prison."

"What woman?" Gemma exclaimed.

She'd attempt to make the connections later, once she'd had more time to slot everything into place, but for now she just wanted to keep Allard talking, so that she could learn as much as possible before he escaped.

"The woman whose feckless husband lost every penny he possessed to Hume Macklemore before he died and whose wife has to work at his tavern and service the old goat every night until the debt is paid. I have to admit that meeting Barry Garrett at the livery stables proved rather fortuitous. The boy really does talk too much for his own good."

Gemma's mouth opened in shock. "Was that why you chose Tamzin Norris, because of her father?"

"I didn't choose her," Allard said dismissively. "That was Polk's doing. He murdered Tamzin to punish Macklemore for defiling his woman and threatening his son, but I can't say I minded overmuch. Macklemore refused to rent me a room in his tavern because he didn't trust me to pay. He said, let me see, what was it exactly?" Allard said, even though he probably recalled the insult word for word. "Ah, yes, 'You Frogs wouldn't know honor if it slapped you with a glove.' But, you see, I'm an honorable man, Miss Tate. I put considerable effort into sewing up Tamzin Norris, and instructed Polk to return Macklemore's daughter's body so that he could bury Tamzin and mourn her and her child properly. I could have had her corpse tossed off a bridge, like that midget, and Macklemore would never have known what had happened to his precious girl."

Gemma was incandescent with fury, her heart hammering in her breast as she faced down the remorseless fiend. To speak of these women and their babies as if they were nothing more than worthless rubbish was almost as bad as using them for postmortem experiments. Tamzin and her baby had been innocent of any wrongdoing but had paid with their lives for the meanness and prejudice of her father. And Archie Peck hadn't even been afforded the kindness of being able to bury his wife. To someone like Allard, Archie didn't count because he was a dwarf and therefore not worthy of compassion. But what could she expect from a man who paid others to murder innocents, and from the soulless monsters who'd been happy to do his bidding?

It was something of a surprise that Allard's henchmen were Tessa Garrett's lover and their son. She must have been carrying on with Ed Polk for years before her husband had passed and found herself inheriting his debt to Hume Macklemore, but this? Did Tessa know what her menfolk were up to, or did she think Tamzin was a random victim, like Deb Peck? Gemma wasn't sure she wanted to know the answer. To think that another woman, a mother, could sanction such cruelty was beyond her comprehension, but at least she had something to bring to Sebastian. She couldn't do anything to stop François Allard from getting away, but she could name the killers.

She had just opened her mouth to express her anger and disgust when the incoming train finally reached the terminus. As the steam-sputtering locomotive drew abreast of François Allard, he reached inside his coat, and she saw the pistol tucked into the waistband of his trousers. It was only then that she understood what he meant to do and why he had been so forthcoming with her. She hadn't been clever at all, getting all this information from him; he'd meant to keep her talking until the steam from the engine concealed them from prying eyes and the clanging of the incoming train masked the sound of the shot. As if on cue, the departing train at Platform B began to move, and more steam billowed onto the platform between the two moving trains. Allard pointed the gun at Gemma's chest and pulled the trigger.

CHAPTER 50

The shot was barely audible, but it had done the job. Gemma felt the hot sting of the bullet and the brutal tearing of her flesh. And then she was falling. Her heart hammered against her ribs, her breath catching as her vision was blurred by both the pain and the nearly impenetrable steam. Her nostrils filled with the metallic tang of blood mixed with the greasy, sulfuric exhalation of the coal-fired engines. Her cheek scraped against the rough surface of the platform, but, although weak and in pain, she thanked God the wound wasn't fatal. Allard's bullet had hit her, but he'd missed the mark. Gemma was alive because a man had flung himself at Allard and knocked him sideways. Her savior had been on the departing train, and the door of the compartment he'd occupied hung open as the train chugged out of the station.

Allard's exclamation of shock and pain was swallowed by the din of the two engines, but Gemma saw the terror in his eyes as he staggered towards the edge of the platform. He windmilled his arms in an effort to right himself, but he was precariously close to the passing train. The edge of a swaying carriage caught him on the shoulder, and the impact pushed him past the point of no return. Allard screamed in terror as he listed to one side, then fell between two moving cars, his head knocking between the carriages as his body was yanked downward. Gemma cried out when a spray of blood splattered the platform near her feet. Allard's body had been torn apart by the huge metal wheels that continued to turn as if the man they'd just dismembered were nothing more than a rodent on the tracks.

The man who'd saved her emerged out of the smoke like some avenging angel, and a sob tore from Gemma's heaving bosom when she recognized his beloved face. She didn't know how Sebastian had come to be there; all she cared about was that he was unharmed. If he had miscalculated, he might have gone the way of the Frenchman, and his body would even now lie on the tracks, crushed by the wheels of the train that had finally come to a stop.

"Gemma, are you hurt?" Sebastian exclaimed as he knelt next to her and gathered her into his arms.

Suddenly freezing, she tried to snuggle deeper into the folds of her cape, but her teeth were chattering, and she could barely feel her left arm.

"It's just a scratch," she muttered, but her words were drowned out by screams of horror and the pounding of booted feet as several uniformed men sprinted towards the newly arrived train. She was surprised to note that Constable Burrows was among them. He fell to his knees next to Sebastian and Gemma.

"Is the lady wounded, sir?" Burrows exclaimed. "Shall I see if there's a doctor among the passengers?"

"I want to go home," Gemma whispered through the convulsions. "Please."

"Constable, take charge of the situation," Sebastian said as he pushed to his feet.

"Yes, sir," Burrows replied, and hastened towards the porters who were attempting to pull Allard's remains off the tracks.

Sebastian swept Gemma into his arms and carried her down the platform and away from the mayhem of the terminus. He barely seemed to notice the stares of the passersby or acknowledge the effort it took to carry a grown woman down several crowded passages and outside until he located the cab stand. Sebastian settled Gemma in a hansom, climbed in next to her, and gave the cabbie Colin's address.

"How did you know?" Gemma whispered as the conveyance pulled away from the railway station and she slumped against Sebastian's side. She felt a little warmer now, and the shaking began to subside. "How did you ever manage to find me?"

"I knew from Poppy that something was meant to happen at London Bridge, but I didn't know what or at what time. I couldn't believe my eyes when I saw you enter the station. And then you disappeared, and I didn't see you again until I was on the overpass."

"How did you get from the overpass to the train?"

Sebastian hadn't met François Allard and probably hadn't even suspected him, but when he had seen him with Gemma he must have realized she was in danger, because he had sprung into action. By the time Allard had pulled the gun, Sebastian had already been on the train.

He confirmed her musings when he said, "I didn't think the man would allow you to walk away. There was something in his face, that single-minded determination you sometimes see." He pulled her closer, as if he could keep her safe by melding her to him. "I wouldn't have got to you in time even if I ran, so I jumped onto the roof of the train and climbed into the closest compartment just as it began to move."

"Sebastian, you could have died," she admonished him.

"I have nine lives," he quipped.

"I know who murdered all those people," Gemma began, but he wasn't listening. He'd just noticed the blood that had trickled down her arm and soaked into the cape and stained the cuff of her gown.

"Sweetheart," he exclaimed. "You're bleeding. Are you shot?"

Gemma tried to respond, but she suddenly felt lightheaded, and her tongue was like a flannel rag. Her vision dimmed at the edges as she tried to focus, and she knew she was experiencing delayed shock. She clung to Sebastian as darkness enfolded her, and then she went limp, his arms the only thing tethering her to reality.

CHAPTER 51

Gemma barely registered Mabel fussing or heard Colin's torrent of rebukes as Sebastian carried her through the door and settled her on the same settee where Colin had tended to Poppy only a few hours before.

"I cannot believe you confronted that man alone," Colin was saying, but Gemma shut her eyes and allowed him to minister to her as Sebastian looked on and made Colin swear that she would be all right.

"Is it deep?" Sebastian demanded. "Will she recover?"

"She'll be fine," Colin grumbled. He sounded like an irate parent. "The bullet gashed her upper arm. I don't think the wound needs to be stitched. A thick bandage will do." He huffed with self-righteousness. "I should give you stitches just to teach you to not go chasing after madmen, but even without stitches you'll have a scar to remind you of your daft behavior."

"Go easy on her, Colin. I think she's suffered enough," Sebastian said, but he looked no less incensed than his friend and would probably rip into Gemma once she felt better.

"I need a word with Sebastian," she said once Colin had cleaned the area and affixed the bandage, which was uncomfortably tight.

"You need to rest."

"And I will once I've spoken to Sebastian," she insisted.

"I guess that's my cue to leave," Colin muttered under his breath, and left the room. He made sure to leave the door wide open in case Gemma and Sebastian took this highly inopportune moment to engage in improper behavior.

"Gemma—" Sebastian began, but she held up her hand.

"Just listen. You can chastise me later."

"I'm afraid I must chastise you now. What were you thinking? You could have been killed."

Gemma sighed with impatience. "Need I remind you that none of Allard's victims had gone looking for a killer? They went about their daily lives, never suspecting that someone was watching them and making plans to have them murdered. And Poppy had nothing to do with any of this, but she was badly beaten because she was mistaken for me."

"What's your point?" Sebastian grumbled.

"My point is that anything can happen to anyone at any time. I am sure François Allard never imagined he was walking towards his death when he set off on that platform, and Algernon Stager was supposedly safe in his cell. Life will happen. All we can do is live it and hope we have time. And if we don't, we have to be satisfied with the way we have lived and the things we have accomplished."

"A pretty speech," Sebastian said, and his mouth quirked at the corners. "But if you think you can talk circles around me, think again."

"I will, but for now, please hear me out. Time is of the essence."

She told him everything she had learned from François Allard. The man was dead and couldn't be held to account for his actions, but Edward Polk and Barry Garrett were still at liberty. As long as they weren't aware that they had been betrayed, Sebastian would know where to find them. If they got wind of Allard's death, they'd likely go to ground and vanish into one of London's many slums, or leave the city altogether and make a new life elsewhere. Gemma couldn't help but wonder why they hadn't done that to begin with rather than give in to Macklemore's threats, allow Tessa to be used for sexual slavery, and resort to murder.

Now that she thought back on it, she remembered Tessa's son from the day she had visited the tavern, and the man with him had to have been Edward Polk. The man did have reddish hair. The killers had walked right past her, two ordinary, seemingly helpful individuals who'd just murdered the daughter of the man they despised and destroyed an innocent young family. Why was it that murder was so easy for some people? Was it because they focused on their own goals and were able to excuse anything they had done in the pursuit of those goals, or because they simply didn't value anyone's lives but their own?

Gemma supposed some people were only held back by fear of the consequences rather than their own conscience. That was why London was plagued by murder, and, as long as there were those willing to kill, there would be men like Sebastian, who would risk their own lives to stop them.

"Go get them, my love," Gemma said, and brought her hand to his face. "I will be here when you return."

Sebastian covered her hand with his own, then turned his head and pressed a kiss to her palm.

"I love you," he said. "You are no doubt the bravest, most selfless woman I have ever met. And that terrifies me."

"You're not exactly the sort of man to sit by the fire with a hearthrug over your knees and a pipe in your hand."

"I'd die of boredom," Sebastian said, and stood to leave.

"So would I. Better to go out in a blaze of glory."

It was only when she'd said that that she realized she hadn't asked Allard about Glory Cates. She didn't suppose it really mattered now, but it would be nice for her husband to know where her remains were dumped so he could pay his respects to the young woman and child he'd lost. At least Glory had died by her own hand and hadn't been murdered for her body, Gemma thought as the door closed softly behind Sebastian.

Or had she?

CHAPTER 52

As soon as Sebastian walked out into the street and saw the bloodstained pavement where Algernon Stager's body had been left, he resolved to focus on finding Ed Polk and Barry Garrett. He had multiple thoughts and feelings to wade through once he took the time to reflect on the day's events, but at the moment he couldn't afford to get distracted, or he'd come apart at the seams. Poppy was on the mend, Gemma would be all right, and Colin would minister to them both until Sebastian was able to get back to Blackfriars.

Once he arrived at Scotland Yard and requested backup, it didn't take long to round up the two men. In fact, it was surprisingly easy. They were drinking at the Rose and Thorn, laughing merrily at something Tessa had said with seemingly nary a care in the world when Sebastian walked through the door. Ed Polk tried to fight his way out, but Constable Burrows laid him out flat before cuffing him. Barry just held out his hands, what remained of his conscience clearly getting the better of any instinct for self-preservation.

Back at Scotland Yard, Sebastian decided to start with Barry, and called in Ransome to sit in on the interview. He wouldn't have minded if Ransome had taken over so he could get back to Gemma, but this was Sebastian's case; he'd asked for it, so he had to see it through.

Barry looked almost relieved when Constable Hammond brought him in and cuffed him to the ring in the table. Sebastian didn't think Barry would try to escape. He seemed resigned to his fate and ready to take his punishment.

"When did you start working for François Allard?" Sebastian asked.

"In April. He'd just come from Paris and wanted to borrow a horse from the livery." Barry's lisp was quite pronounced and confirmed that he was one of the men who'd attacked Poppy. "We got to talking. Macklemore had just turned him away from lodgings, it felt good to complain about the man. I was upset and shared that I was in debt and didn't make nearly enough at the livery to pay off my late father's debts. Mr. Allard said he knew a way I could make money, but I would need a partner, so I asked Ed."

"Did you know Edward Polk was your natural father?" Ransome asked.

Barry shook his head. "Not then."

"And you were happy to kill innocent people to pay off your debts?" Sebastian inquired. It was hard to believe this unassuming boy was responsible for the deaths of so many.

Barry shook his head. "I was horrified when Mr. Allard told us what he wanted. And I refused, but over the next few days Ed talked me into it. He told me things about my mum." He faltered, and Sebastian realized that he probably hadn't realized his mother had to do considerably more than work behind the bar. "Ed said I'd go to debtor's prison if I didn't pay what Garrett had owed and that my mum would have to sell herself on the street."

"How much did Allard pay you for each job?" Ransome asked.

"A crown each," Barry said. "I'd never seen so much money in my whole life."

"Made it easier to kill, eh?" Sebastian asked.

"It wasn't easy. After each job, I swore I'd never do it again. I prayed and prayed for forgiveness, but I needed the money, and I had to help my mum. She had to go to Macklemore every night after her shift. He made her do things."

Ransome nodded. "No son needs to hear that about his mother."

"Ed eventually told me he was my real father, and he tried to make it better," Barry said.

"Better how?"

"He said people like the Pruitt twins were an abomination and weren't meant to live. And he said Deb Peck would probably die in childbirth anyway since her body wasn't made for motherhood." Barry began to cry softly. "But Tamzin... That near killed me. And that nice nurse lady..."

"Yet you went on to do another job," Sebastian reminded him.

Barry nodded through the tears. "Stager was a lunatic. He was dim, and violent, and he would have spent the rest of his days chained to a wall."

"He was tortured before he was killed."

"I didn't know Allard would hurt him. I thought he'd be like the others—we'd drown him, and he'd work on him then—but Stager proved more difficult to kill. He came to when we brought him to Allard and he... Allard sliced Stager's bollocks off while he was still alive. He said he needed to study them to see if his seed was different from other men and would condemn Stager's children to madness."

"I'm not even going to ask how Allard got his other samples," Ransome said with a sigh of disgust.

Barry cringed with embarrassment, then looked down at his hands.

"Did you kill Glory Cates?" Sebastian asked.

"Who?"

"The woman who was found hanged in her cell at Millbank Prison."

The young man shook his head. "We didn't kill her, but we were sent to collect her body once she was cut down. The warden sold her to Allard because she was with child."

"What happened to her remains?" Sebastian asked.

"We threw her body in the river, once Allard was done with her. The warden didn't want her found."

Ransome slammed his hand on the table, and Barry looked up, startled. "Tell me true, son," Ransome demanded. "Did you do the killing?"

Barry shook his head again. "I couldn't. I refused."

"So, what was your part in this?" Sebastian asked.

"I helped Ed take them, but he was the one to finish them off."

"Just as I thought," Ransome said softly.

"Will I hang?" Barry whimpered.

"Probably," Ransome replied, his tone devoid of pity, "but if you can convince the judge you didn't take any lives, he might sentence you to deportation to Botany Bay instead. Not that it's much better, mind. Sometimes a quick death is its own reward."

Barry was trembling, and tears ran down his cheeks. "I know I deserve it, but I'm scared."

"Doubtless your victims were scared too," Ransome replied. "Or did you not think it mattered?"

"I'm sorry," Barry wailed. "Please, can I see my mother?"

"Did she know what you were up to?" Sebastian asked. If she did, Sebastian would bang Tessa Garrett up next to her men.

Barry sniffled. "Mum had no idea. She thought we got a job guarding a warehouse to make extra cash."

"Do you swear to me?"

"Mum hated Hume, but she liked Tamzin. And Deb. She would never…"

"Can you write?" Ransome asked.

"I can read, but I'm not so good at writing," Barry admitted.

"You can dictate your confession, and once you sign it I will decide if I want to charge you with murder or if accessory to murder will do. Up to you, lad.

"Take him away," Ransome told Constable Hammond with disgust. "And take down his statement."

Sebastian heard Barry sniffling and his cuffs clanking as he was led away. "Just when I think I've seen the worst men can do, someone goes and shows me the error of my ways," he said.

"There's no end to human depravity," Ransome replied, and pushed away from the table. "That's why you and I are here, and why one of the first things settlers always build is a lock-up. Times may change, but human nature remains disappointingly the same." He patted Sebastian on the shoulder. "Well done, Bell. And give my compliments to a certain lady who shall not be named in these halls."

"I will." Sebastian was suddenly exhausted, but there was one more matter to discuss. "What about Joss Stevens?"

"What about him?" Ransome asked as he approached the door.

"Have you interviewed him?"

"I have," Ransome replied.

"And will you charge him with murder?"

"At this stage, we can't prove he murdered anyone, and there's no one to file a complaint on behalf of the deceased. He's been punished, so let's leave that there for now."

Sebastian nodded. He was too tired to speak.

"Go home, old chap," Ransome said, his tone gentle. "You've earned your rest."

CHAPTER 53

Night was falling by the time Sebastian returned to Blackfriars, the summer sky strewn with stars. The air was cool and brisk, the fresh breeze sweeping away the pungent smells that plagued Londoners during the day. Although still weary, Sebastian was buoyed by the promise of spending some time with Gemma. They had much to discuss, and he wanted to consult her regarding the house they had meant to visit. He thought the prospect of looking for their future home might raise her spirits after this harrowing day and allow them to focus on happier times.

Colin was in the parlor on his own, his expression pensive as he stared into the empty hearth, an empty glass in his hand. The decanter on the sideboard was empty, so there was no chance of a drink.

"What's on your mind?" Sebastian asked as he came to stand next to his friend.

Colin smiled wryly and chuckled. "Women."

"Did something happen after I left?" Sebastian didn't think Colin was pondering all women, just the ones under his roof, and, given his bemused expression, he had much to think about.

Colin nodded but didn't bother to explain, so Sebastian went in search of Gemma. He found her in her room, sitting in a chair by the window, her expression dreamy as she gazed at the dusky sky. She had changed out of her bloodied dress and wore a simple muslin gown. Her hair was loose, the chestnut waves cascading over her shoulders. She looked young and vulnerable, and strangely calm after the day she'd had.

"May I come in?" Sebastian asked from the doorway.

She smiled and nodded. "Shut the door."

"Colin will flap about like a hen in a fox's shadow if he sees the door closed," he replied, and smiled wistfully when he recalled that this was something his father used to say.

"Not after this afternoon, he won't," Gemma said cryptically.

Sebastian didn't shut the door—as long as she lived under Colin's roof, the rules had to be observed—but he advanced into the room and lowered himself onto a stool before her chair. "What happened after I left?"

Gemma's grin transformed her tired face. "First, Mabel gave a month's notice."

"What? Why?"

"She's to marry Jacob."

"I thought he was avoiding her and stepping out with the new parlormaid from across the road."

"It would seem the parlormaid is his cousin, and has been coaching him on how to declare himself to Mabel. He chose rather an unfortunate day to do it, but Mabel has been flying so high all evening, her feet barely touched the ground. She will, of course, work out her notice and make sure Colin has a new maidservant before she leaves."

"And was there something else?" Sebastian asked. He was genuinely happy for Mabel and hoped that dolt Jacob would make her happy, but he could see how Colin would be upset. Mabel had been with the Ramseys since she was an adolescent girl, newly arrived from the country.

Gemma nodded. "Poppy informed Colin that she wants my job once I'm gone. And Colin agreed. I'm not sure what that means for them as a potential couple, but today, I mean to think only of myself."

"Which means what, exactly?" Sebastian asked, his heart fluttering in his chest.

"It means that I'm through with waiting." The look Gemma gave him put an end to the fluttering and made his blood simmer.

"We can marry?" he asked cautiously. He would hate to have misunderstood her intentions.

"As soon as you wish."

"Really?" He was surprised she was willing to break her promise to Colin, but, now that Poppy would be there to look after Mrs. Ramsey, he supposed there was no longer a valid reason to delay.

"Really. But I would like a few days to heal. And I suppose we need to find a house of our own, too."

"A house of our own," Sebastian repeated softly. The words filled him with delight. "I'm sure the one in Pimlico is still on the market."

Gemma wrinkled her nose with distaste. "I don't think I could live there now, not after everything."

He completely understood. "I will purchase the papers tomorrow and begin a search. Once I narrow down a few options, you can choose."

More than anything, he wanted to pull Gemma into his arms and kiss her until her knees buckled, but he could wait; it wouldn't be long now until they were finally in their own home. As if reading his thoughts, she stood and walked into his arms. She settled in his lap and wrapped her arms about his neck, kissing him with abandon as her silky hair caressed his skin. Sebastian pulled her closer and prayed that Colin wouldn't come upstairs at that moment. They'd earned this, and he meant to enjoy his future wife's ardor, if only until he mastered himself and wished her a good night before he did something he might later regret.

Gemma must have been thinking the same thing, because she reluctantly pulled away. Her eyes shone with passion, and her heart beat in time with his as she rested her head on his shoulder.

"A few more days," she whispered, and the breath caught in Sebastian's throat.

It seemed the future had finally arrived.

EPILOGUE

Tuesday, August 2, 1859

The room was pleasantly cool and still dim, sunrise at least an hour away. A steady rain beat against the roof and the shutters, and raindrops slid down the windowpanes like falling tears, but this morning they were tears of joy. Gemma burrowed deeper under the covers and pressed herself to Sebastian's side. His skin was warm, and his breath was soft as he slept on. She smiled a secret smile, glad she had a few moments to herself to examine her feelings. She was no longer a sad, lonely spinster, still a maid at twenty-eight. She was a wife, a woman who was loved and who had taken the first tentative steps towards learning how to love her husband in return. And she couldn't wait to touch him again, and have him kiss and caress her the way he had last night.

The memory warmed her cheeks, but she knew she never had to feel shame with Sebastian. If he'd wanted a cold fish who feared all the things that made a person's heart race, he could have found one long ago. But he wanted her, and he was willing to let her be entirely herself, even if that meant breaking society's rules and inviting some people's scorn. They were two of a kind, and now they were joined for eternity.

The wedding had been lovely, as had the intimate reception hosted by Colin. He had encouraged Gemma to invite the friends she'd made at Scutari, but after some consideration, she had decided not to. Except for Poppy, those friendships were in the past, and she was looking to the future. Sebastian had invited his brother, but Simian and Hannah had been unable to attend at such short notice, so it had been decided that Sebastian and Gemma would visit them in the near future. So, it had been just her and Sebastian, Colin and Poppy, Mabel, and Jacob—who'd looked a bit uncomfortable but had tried his best to be sociable—and Anne. Ransome had come to the church and had given them a wedding gift, but had declined the invitation to the celebration, citing a prior commitment. The Quinces had also made an appearance but had left after the ceremony. They had a business to run, and they weren't exactly friends.

Sebastian and Gemma had enjoyed the lovely meal Mabel had prepared in their honor and had drunk the champagne Colin had insisted on providing, but all they'd really wanted was to make their excuses and leave. They'd finally said their goodbyes at eight o'clock and practically ran to their new home, which was just a few streets over. Gemma had thought it would be nice to live nearby, since she could see Poppy and Anne, continue her lessons with Colin, and hopefully keep up with Mabel.

The rest of the night had been spent in dreamlike bliss, the candles casting a golden halo of light onto their marriage bed, Sebastian and Gemma utterly lost in each other. Even Gustav hadn't dared to interrupt, but he slinked into the room now and jumped onto the bed, fitting himself to Gemma's side.

"Good morning, you little rascal," she whispered as she stroked him between the ears.

"Good morning," a deep voice replied, and Sebastian's arm snaked around Gemma's waist and pulled her closer, making her giggle as he nuzzled her neck.

A fortnight from now, he would have to return to work, she would go back to her studies, and perhaps there would be a new case for them to solve. But until then, they were free to do what they pleased and enjoy their wedding trip to the Lake District, their first outing as a married couple.

The Bells, Gemma thought, and her heart pealed with happiness.

A LETTER FROM THE AUTHOR

Huge thanks for reading *The Carnival Murders*. I hope you were hooked on Sebastian and Gemma's latest case. Their adventures will continue. If you want to join other readers in hearing all about my new releases and bonus content, you can sign up for my newsletter.

www.stormpublishing.co/irina-shapiro

If you enjoyed this book and could spare a few moments to leave a review, that would be hugely appreciated. Even a short review can make all the difference in encouraging a reader to discover my books for the first time. Thank you so much.

Thanks again for being part of this amazing journey with me and I hope you'll stay in touch—I have so many more stories and ideas to entertain you with.

Irina

irinashapiroauthor.com

instagram.com/irina_shapiro_author

facebook.com/IrinaShapiro2

x.com/IrinaShapiro2